job slut

BY
ASHLEY BROWN

Copyright © Ashley Brown, 2017
All rights reserved.

No part of this publication may be
reproduced, distributed, or transmitted in any form
or by any means, including photocopying, recording,
or other electronic or mechanical methods without the
prior written permission of the author.

ISBN 978-1-9998099-0-4
Printed in the United States of America

Edited by Jill Saginario.
Thank you for your hard work and patience; you are a diamond.

A big thank you to all those that allowed me
to interview them for research purposes.

Cover design by Carol Chu
Photography by Tomas Skaringa

For my friends, family, and the curious

"Not all those who wander are lost."

–J.R.R. Tolkien

FOREWORD

Ambition: it can be a slippery little fucker. It can take us up, down, around in circles, and make a darn right mockery of the best of us. Ambition and ego are like life petrol—all well and good when you are on the right track. Otherwise, before you know it, you're racing down the wrong road to a destination you never wanted to end up in.

We are not built with fancy satellite navigation systems with our journeys mapped out for us. We don't just tap in like a pilot on a flight path. We are the pilots of our lives. We can pull up the hand brake, change direction, speed up, or slow down. One path is not the only path.

If there is a secret formula for staying on a single-career track no one told me about it. Somewhere along the course of my many path changes, I had a long hard look in the mirror and realized, out loud:

"You, Miss, are a total jobslut."

TABLE OF CONTENTS

Chapter 1 – JOBSLUT _____ 3
Chapter 2 – HUMBLE BEGINNINGS _____ 4
Chapter 3 – LEGALLY BLONDE _____ 20
Chapter 4 – ENTERING THE JUNGLE _____ 30
Chapter 5 – TO TEMP OR NOT TO TEMP _____ 50
Chapter 6 – A JOB IS A HOME _____ 53
Chapter 7 – TAKING ON HOLLYWOOD _____ 67
Chapter 8 – BACK WHERE WE STARTED _____ 82
Chapter 9 – PREPARING THE DEAD _____ 89
Chapter 10 – IF YOU CAN'T DO, TEACH, THEY SAID _____ 102
Chapter 11 – UNDERCOVER ANGEL _____ 107
Chapter 12 – HOLY SHIT ITS NEARLY CHRISTMAS _____ 134
Chapter 13 – FREE TO TRIAL WHATEVER I PLEASE _____ 152
Chapter 14 – THE DATE _____ 160
Chapter 15 – JUST GIVE ME THE PEN _____ 180
Chapter 16 – STAR-DATING _____ 191
Chapter 17 – THE A-Z GUIDE TO CAREERS _____ 207

Chapter 1
JOBSLUT

It's not that I started out wanting to be such a floozy in my professional life. I never asked to be this hopeless romantic, drifting through occupations in search of "the one." I was staring at myself in the mirror while brushing my teeth the exact moment it dawned on me. I was somewhere between job nine or ten when I couldn't hide from it anymore. I had become a jobslut.

"So, what is a jobslut?" I hear you asking. Well, I was surprised to discover it does actually have a definition, albeit in urban diction. I am slutty with jobs. I am sure everyone has the odd day where they feel like giving up on their job and jumping on-board something else. I kind of just … do it. I have given up many promising roles that could have delivered me a stable and financially rewarding career, but I always seem to find myself an exit strategy. Cameron Diaz once said, "I don't know if anyone is really naturally monogamous." (If I'd said it was Oscar Wilde who said it, would you have given it more credit?) Whoever said it, they have a point. And I have applied this theory to my working life. I have an odd fascination in where and how other people have ended up in their jobs. Do they really like them? Are things as hunky-dory as those eyebags suggest?

My friends told me to see an occupational coach. That didn't really work out. After I convinced myself I might want to become one, it was clear the occupational coaching only highlighted my problem.

My name is Anna, by the way. I know, nice and normal, isn't it? I don't feel I deserve such a normal name. How my mum came up with it is beyond me as she's totally bonkers. I am sure I narrowly missed something a lot weirder, as when my youngest brother was born we had to stage an intervention to ensure he was not named Dirty Bertie. He is now a happy, healthy "Henry," you will be pleased to know. But it was thanks to a strong group effort.

Well, I hope you're sitting comfortably. Let's delve in, shall we?

Chapter 2
HUMBLE BEGINNINGS

Who hasn't been a waitress at some point? I got to ticking this one off the list at age thirteen. There is no better foundation for a sturdy character in life than waiting tables and embracing all the fun, blisters, arseholes, and tips that come with it. I had French fries thrown in my face, fell on my bottom in front of footballers, and did so much washing up I developed a true love for the Marigold glove. (The only way to sustain soft hands in a world that wants to harden them.) I shuffled burgers, spuds, and full English breakfasts back and forth, and I scrubbed plates clean and dry. But my true moment of glory came when I was promoted to checkout girl. Oh, how the other waitresses eyed that role with envy! As they had to carry on with the mundane tasks of washing dishes and taking orders I stood by the till greeting customers with a smile, telling them they must try the flapjacks and engaging in light banter as I hoped to be giving them the right change. Though deep down I dreaded that role. I felt so in the spotlight. So exposed.

Up until the age of about eighteen I had a bad case of blushing. Even in the most unjustified of situations. It was a self-imposed and awkward sort of torture. Especially when Mike came in. Ridiculously good-looking and definite boyfriend material, in he would come with his mates and there I was, apron on display, feeling like a rabbit in headlights. The placing of the order felt like it went on forever. Extra sausage for Jack and scrambled eggs for James (who, I later found out, helped himself to handfuls of ketchup sachets which saved him from buying sauce himself. He had a massive glass vase in his kitchen full of various sachets of sauces, pots of spreads, even salt and pepper.) As they fished around for payment my face would reveal my inner suffering. When I felt an intense burn on my cheeks I knew I had peaked to a tomato red and looked like a total twat.

"Mate, have you been squeezing those sauces on her face?" Mike's predictable joke evoked an explosion of laughter from the rest of the chaps. Torture.

Sarah, my then-partner-in-crime and quite frankly, the funniest girl I know, knew my pain. She would lurk by the wall which separated the till from the "headquarters" (basically the sink) and scoop in with a witty one-liner to take the attention away from me. Once she purposely slid on a banana skin and fell straight on her arse for me—now that's a true friend.

The waitressing days were an essential part of life training and a place where a very important device was established—the head-to-knee. When one laughs so much that the head falls to the knee. We tended to fill our days with these on a regular basis. Marigolds, sprinkles of head-to-knees, free food, and a whole lot of nonsense ensured survival during the waitressing years. I have found that, as a general observation, the more nonsense that is occurring the more likely I am to stick to something. Some people love structure and conformity, but for some reason that makes me feel tense. I gravitate towards the less ordinary. Nonsense is liberating. Everyone who I develop friendships, work relationships, or even keep in touch with, it is likely I have identified something nonsensical about them. Or just something damn right weird. When I first met Sarah, she waved a tomato in my face by way of introduction.

She then started to button up my blouse as she said, "Pervert Perry always comes in on a Saturday," and made me a name tag labelling me the "Anniemeister." We hit it off. A friendship full of shenanigans that could span pages. Alas, I better move on; we already have so much to cover.

There are certain dangers that waitresses are vulnerable to, depending on the venue in which you are allocating your services. Mine was a local cafe of a friend of my mum's where we dished up all the best of English grub. It was not quite fast food, (as the sign at the front insisted in big, bold, in-your-face letters "WE DO NOT SERVE FAST FOOD, WE SERVE GOOD FOOD AS FAST AS WE CAN,") but we did make bacon sandwiches, fry-ups, and pie and mash—the kind of stuff which left you with greasy hair and smelling generally like fried food at the end of the day. Nothing a few sprays of good old CK one couldn't sort out, mind you, if you were dashing from work to a date, or, as often was the case with Sarah and I, vodka-and-lime fuelled dancing. Besides, our philosophy at that carefree time in our lives was if anyone had a problem with the smell of our hard work they could bugger off. We were more interested in having a wiggle on the dance floor (and in our next drink) than in anything else. Alas, hangovers can make a long day feel a lot longer. Especially on a till day. By golly, you did not want to be subject to that much exposure when feeling there is still a mini DJ sitting in your head.

We have already covered the problem of boys you like popping in. Unexpectedly. It is especially not nice on such occasions when you fall over and drop your tray of food in front of a cafe full of customers. To be clear, you will feel like a total moron. Hey ho, it happens. Embrace your inner moron. It will help you get through life.

And please do not be fooled that waiting tables will land you in the next Hollywood blockbuster just because it happened to Brad Pitt. The closest I ever got to meeting a director in my waitressing days was the coordinator of the local drama club. He did offer me the role of the donkey in the Christmas nativity play.

So, to sum up a few things:

1) Do not tell boys you fancy where you work so they can't come and embarrass you.

2) Invest in a good pair of Marigolds.

3) Make sure you work with funny people—you want to try and avoid angry chefs.

4) You will stink so make sure you have your CK one to hand, and you'll be ready to rock.

I would suggest giving yourself a set time for waitressing. One lady I worked with should have hung up her Marigolds long before I joined the team. There was a dullness about her that screamed, "Get me out of here!" She smelt like an egg sandwich and seemed to have lost all hope that there were other jobs out there to try. A lifer. She is probably still at that cafe now. Chained to the sink envying the till girls. Oh well, at least she gets free flapjacks.

So you see, we were up to a pretty good, pretty normal, start. It was an average job for a teenager doing their GCSEs and looking for a way to fuel all those illegal nights out at nightclubs. How I passed for twenty-one at just fourteen I will never know. Perhaps it was the cigarettes and confident glow of alcohol that convinced the fierce bouncers to usher us through. Perhaps it was a sympathy pass for being willing to freeze our scantily-dressed bottoms off in the depths of cold Kentish winters. Anyhow, I like to look at those years as the reason why cigarettes make me sick, so it was time well spent.

We all need our fair share of sticky clubs. I embraced them in good jest.

Speaking of cold Kentish winters, that is where I am from. I was born in a small seaside village. The sort of place where a missing cat made the news, milk was delivered each morning via a milk float, and a new face in the local pub on a Friday caused weekly gossip. My school was a short drive from home. The classmates and I were all still in that exciting flurry of youth and optimism where we were deciding in which direction we were going to shoot our arrows of life. Well, one arrow was taken out of my hands.

I will never forget the day I was told by a short, bearded teacher— mentioning no names—that it may be advisable I choose to take up my A levels elsewhere. Funny that. I was never particularly rebellious or naughty or mischievous … well, maybe I did lean a little towards these traits, however there were those who behaved far worse than I did and they still made it through the net. The pot smokers, the bullies, jeez, one guy reduced my mathematics teacher to tears by telling her she smelt like dusty curtains—and he was welcome to stay! But for me it was goodbye friends. Goodbye familiarity, nice knowing you, it's been fun. The security blankets we weave ourselves all get snatched from beneath our noses when we least expect it. Or perhaps I just look for security in the wrong places. And I have found being busy is a great way to stop insecurities coming to the surface. I try to be my own therapist turning to friends and family for more superficial advice than the stuff I should probably really be talking about. It is amazing how everyone believes you're perfectly fine. How what you present on the outside covers all the inside layers, when that one glossy front cover can mask a multitude of problems. In honestly it suited me for the time being, having my glossy cover protected me from any painful self-analysis.

My cousin advised I give up learning all together. I mulled it over. I have a dangerous ability to convince myself of anything. If I threw all my hope into flipping burgers in Arizona, I could remain in happy oblivion that anything could be better. Oh, the perils of being an optimist. Mum suffers from this too. Maybe it's genetic, running headfirst into terrible ideas. She went into business, buying a café aptly named The Gossip Shop with the women from hell. Seriously, they were awful. When I came home and found her in my kitchen in layers of beige and undeserved air of authority mustered up from years of bossing her fragile husband around I would recede straight to my bedroom. I would even forgo my post-school cheese string Mum always had stocked up in the fridge. Two years of stress, argument and one actual punch in the face later, the business was dissolved. Meaning Mum lost a big investment. Not just financial, she was physically and mentally drained from being adult-bullied by lady muck for the duration of the partnership. Mum walked away in the end, after which the customers stopped going and the dragon was put out of business.

Back to my latest life dilemma: I was rejected from school, the place that had felt like my second home since I was twelve. It was a bit of a kick in the teeth, it gave me a sinking feeling in my stomach for a few nights as I relished in disastrous outcomes that could follow. I, of course, I laughed it off over milkshakes with Sarah at the café.

This was also the time one of my most significant friendships to date became severed. I had a very close friend throughout secondary school. A fabulous Libra—naturally, we had a blast together. We were united in a need to live every moment to the fullest, far before the YOLO memes started to pop up all over social media. With bank balances that limited us to our humble postcodes, we made the most of it.

The friendship hit a crossroads when we received our GCSE results. As she delighted over GCSEs that did not reflect our lack of study, I suffered a mini breakdown over, in fairness, well-deserved Cs, Ds, and even a G. There was also something to do with a boy. She stole the first boyfriend my fickle hormones told me I loved. Granted, our relationship had consisted of less than a single day of real time together and a whole load of text messages. Still, it was a big kick in the teeth. (To think I nearly invited the swine to my Aunt Sally's annual BBQ. He missed out on that, at least.)

Poor Libra. It wasn't really her fault. She'd had one too many shots and regretted her actions as much as one regrets losing your brand-new leather jacket at the local nightclub—which is a lot—and which I had also done that night, darn it, and in hindsight that was far worse than losing him.

At sixteen, one is simply not equipped to deal with the whole, "your best mate getting better grades than you, nabbing your boyfriend, and getting kicked out of school," thing. One cries into one's pillow that their life is over and ponders giving up education all together. One envisages serving bacon sandwiches and smelling like eggs for eternity. One feels like saying to all those friends, who you were only going to disappoint, to go on without you. Go forth and become pilots, lawyers, the Prime Minister if you wish, I will be by the sink with my Marigolds serving exquisite fast food should you ever be in the area.

Hoorah. The universe sent me a silver lining. I was blessed with pretty decent A-Level grades. Maybe my ex-teacher had known what was best for me all along. He had showed me that I hadn't needed school in order to finish my A levels. In his years of assessing the varied individuals in the school circus he could see the ones who would be better off in another arena. I underrated his wisdom.

Still, he could have had better timing. Around the time I left school and my friendship was crumbling, my parents broke up for the final time. They were pretty cool about it, packing up the family home like it was the end of a holiday. As you can imagine, life had become a little chaotic, so I pulled myself out of it and I started to live in the future. Everything I was doing became a temporary step to where I wanted to be, though I had no idea what or where that was. The future became a place that promised all the things that I didn't have in the here and now. I retreated from people during this time as I found it difficult to relate to the feelings my friends had. I didn't feel excited about the same things they did. It was tricky to deal with at times.

Fortunately, being an Aquarius I did make time for some fun. Being social is an essential feature of our astrological make up. I also needed a lot of time to myself to think up dreams and plans. My place of stability became my imagination. Ironically that was a constantly changing preview of the future.

I remember telling my dad when I first watched Cinderella, "One day I am going to live in a castle." He laughed at me saying, "Life isn't a fairytale, my darling. Life stinks." He proceeded to force my sister and me to watch the movie *Life Stinks* starring Mel Brooks as a man living penniless on the streets of Los Angeles. He made us watch it many times, in fact, and it became one of the most memorable features of time spent with him. *Life Stinks* and Kinder Eggs became a weekly ritual. The guys in the sweet shop gave us funny looks as we chose pick-and-mix, Dad picked up his cider, and we pulled at his sleeve and jumped excitedly, asking, "Are we watching *Life Stinks*?" There was some parenting technique in there somewhere which helped me put realistic edges to the type of fairytale I dreamed about. Nonetheless, I continued to dream.

During the mental shift I endured between leaving school and starting college, I remember one particular dinner at a college friend's parents' house. As I sat around her large family dinner table I had a sense I was perched on the edge of normality. I could see it, hear it, even feel it. It's just that I wasn't a part of it. As they spoke about their days everything seemed so safe and ordinary. Even the way her dad sprinkled salt on his potatoes, with three precise shakes then placing the shaker back down right next to the pepper. The way everything in her house was always in exactly the same place. Even that cat that made my nose itch despite never touching her. It was like being normal was a game everyone was playing. I was always waiting for the moment when everyone broke into laughter and said, "Only joking! This is what we are really like." They didn't though, they sat there and exchanged polite conversation passing the condiments and chewing their food. I could pretend for a while, and when it all got too much I would drift off somewhere else.

My daydreaming didn't go unnoticed. I would get comments like, "Anna, it sometimes seems like you're not really here." Nope. I wasn't. I was somewhere in the future. A place where anything was possible, a place I would find my own normality.

So now was the time for the next step, University. I struggled here. Normal life decisions like choosing a university and subject to study dulled the life out of me. The malarkey of application forms was painful. They were so generic, the same questions evoked the same responses. "Why do you want to study law?" Typing away into the empty blank space, filling it with sentences that no doubt they had read on countless other applications, being forced to tell them what they wanted to hear—because, really, who is going to admit someone who says, "Well, I am not really sure other than I am an avid fan of *Ally McBeal*." No. Better to pop a bit of bullshit in there, like, "the thought of regulation and structure really turns me on."

I guess I can't blame *Ally* entirely. I also had a dream that by studying law I would have all my shit together come twenty-five. By shit together, I mean I would have bagged myself a training contract based on glowing qualifications and an interview that blew someone's legal socks off. In a firm that was edgy, fun, and awesome. The *Vogue* of the legal world, I imagined high-fiving my team as we all went out-and-about doing legal stuff, winning cases. Life was going to be a professional rollercoaster, as I whooshed up the career ladder. If you had told my twenty-five-year-old self I would, in fact, be living with roommates I thought of as the Tweedles, caught in a confusing conundrum and, in fact, not even sure which ladder to climb, I would have laughed. Then probably would have wanted more info as to what the Tweedles would be like.

Suffice it to say, they are two of the loveliest girls I know. We like to high-five, when the occasion arises, though it's normally more for their successes than mine. Unless you count stuff like the day I found Tweedle Dee's passport an hour before she had to be at the airport. Between us, I had accidentally picked it up and popped it in my drawer of useful things, having mistaken it for mine. "Look what I found down the side of the sofa!" I announced to the panic-stricken Tweedle who was so grateful she had no time to think about how it may have gotten there.

"I love you!" she cried, and showered me with high fives and cuddles. She even promised to take me out upon her return. To be honest, I thought about hiding stuff and finding it for people more often.

From time to time I questioned whether I was hiding behind my peers' more grown-up successes, such as engagements and promotions, to cover up for the lack of mine. If someone else had something to celebrate, I went above and beyond what was appropriate, for sure. I celebrated so much for my successful friends I hardly had time to notice that the only truly significant one of my own was my birthday. Still, that was always a blast. When plans don't go your way, time and time again, when things don't turn out the way you mentally forecast them, what can you do? Keep calm and carry on, of course.

I remember being en route to meet a recruitment consultant about a possible position at a dental surgery (all my friends had private dentists and I thought this may be a good way to get discount on my own.) The clinic was on Harley Street, which was one of the most iconic roads in London.

"Hey Dad, I am on my way to a really important meeting. Thought I would give you a call to wish me luck."

"Oh. Well, good luck." Silence.

"Okay, thanks. Any further words of wisdom you have for me? I feel a bit confused at the moment."

"My darling, life is relentless unless you commit suicide."

"Oh, okay, thanks Dad. Speak soon."

"Goodbye."

Honestly, I do not know what I was expecting. Calling my dad was always a bit like phone call roulette. Cheerful, miserable, abrupt, or drunk? That is, if he answered the phone at all. And on that particular morning I wished he hadn't. In fact, after that phone call I decided, as confusing as it may be, to try and listen to my own inner guide. Later that day I had a good old chat with the mirror.

"Anna, where do you see yourself in five years' time?"

"I see myself full to the brim with self-belief, settled in the career of my dreams with the man of my dreams and a little dog. In a beautiful apartment on—

"Anna, are you done in there?" I was just getting into it when I was rudely interrupted by a fellow house member with an urgent need to pee. "I am about to wet myself."

Back to before I met the Tweedles, I was still very unsure if had made the best choice regarding university. I always liked the idea of becoming someone else; drama school would have been a good option. Mum and I had a coffee one afternoon, a very, very rare occurrence.

"So are you definitely going to stick with law? I would have made a great lawyer, I think."

"Yes, I guess so. I just sent off the applications. I was accepted by all three."

"Good. Why didn't you tell me you were applying? I could have helped."

"Just thought I might as well get on with it. You are always busy."

"Oh. You just get on with it, then. You don't have to be so secretive all the time."

"I am not being secretive. I don't want to argue. I'd rather save that for law school."

"Make a joke as usual, Anna. This is important, it's your future."

I thought this was a bad time to tell her I would have preferred to go to drama school. Alas, with acting being a no-go for now, I let Ally McBeal lure me into the wrong profession. I do not hold it against her. She was one of the first on-screen characters I admired, before meeting more contemporary favourites such as Bridget Jones. The crux of my mistake was Ally was not a lawyer, she was a fictional character. (Though, bravo, Miss Flockhart. Convincing work.) I have come across quite a few female lawyers who fell through the same trap door. Once fully embarked on their legal journeys they realized that Ally was the creation of a screenwriter's imagination. She did not actually suffer the misery of a two-year training contract. She was married to a Hollywood star and living the actual high life that wooed many a dreamer into the legal world.

My realization came after I had enrolled and paid my tuition fees, so off to a London university I went to study law with high hopes and some splendid notepads and pens. Yes, I was of an era where Apple laptops and iPads hadn't quite taken over the world. My education was absorbed via fast scribbles, desperate not to miss any nugget of wisdom. These scribbles would later be compared with my friends as we completed coursework. We trod a fine line between consulting textbooks and plagiarism. Copying notes from each other seemed the safer option.

I made a quick alliance with two girls and a guy who had enough life experience under their belts to make them interesting. We were all a bit aloof. Stephanie ended up moving to Dubai after three months, her dad was a high-flying QC and she was fed up with the London weather. I often wonder what happened to her. My guess is she married a sheikh. She was strikingly beautiful and far more ambitious in her shopping sprees than legal pursuits. Jess was also from a wealthy family who had fallen on harder times. She had picked herself back up and fought her way into university. She was a bit older than the rest of us and her life experience was something we all appreciated. Todd was fresh out of public school and spoke as if he had a big fat plum in his mouth. All had a justified base for their superiority I have no idea where mine came from.

My parents certainly had no airs and graces about them. The one time my mum actually suggested saying some sort of grace at the dinner table it resulted in a massive lemon pie fight. Whilst Mum sat with her eyes closed about to bless the dessert, Dad made the most of the opportunity scooping up the pie and—to our delight and shock—pushed it straight into her face. We all held our breath in anticipation of whether or not she would go mental. But she couldn't help herself, she burst into laughter and with that we all started to flick pie at each other, too. It was one of the happiest family dinners I can remember, despite the terrible waste of pie.

 I am digressing, aren't I? Where were we? Oh, being aloof. Yes, so no idea where that came from. I have come to accept this as a defining part of my character, although my loud and terribly crimped hair dictated otherwise. As did my fluffy boots, denim skirt, and pink jumper ensemble. Coco Chanel would have turned in her grave. And while other students were hanging out at the student bars, house parties, and pizza joints, my crew were quaffing G and T's in private member bars (having just joined the conservative party,) attending political dinners, smoking cigars, and commenting on current political rhetoric. For us, slumming it was a three-course lunch at our local Italian and a bottle of rosé in between lectures. I worked hard to fund these extravagances by working sales jobs and a generous helping hand from my step-dad.

 Many freshman relished in the newfound freedom and blew student loans on beer, pizza, and general wild times. This typical student lifestyle did not appeal to me. I had been able to pretty much do as I pleased since I was around thirteen. Having parents who were too busy breaking up and getting back together allowed me to escape any intense surveillance. There simply wasn't time. Having a free reign didn't seem to do much harm. I stayed over in the student dorm one night and never again. Around midnight, a horrific noise erupted in the kitchen, in the morning after a terrible night's sleep I went to the communal eating zone to find smelly takeaway boxes and half-finished bottles of stinky cheap alcohol and cigarette stubs. My feet stuck to the floor as I made my way to the kettle. I never stayed again.

Although I stayed local through my university years I did have a new home. I had moved in with my wonderful Nan. My grandpa had passed away and we both needed each other at this time to heal the empty space he left. It made me so sad to think of all the things they done together from having breakfast to grocery shopping. There is no way I could allow her to do them on her own. She was the best housemate I could ever wish for; we had always been close and spending those years living with her gave me some much-needed stability. She was caring and nurturing in a non- intrusive way, always there if I needed to talk. She never, ever judged. Whether I wanted to spend hours studying by myself or coming home after far too many gin and tonics in the early hours and making toast. Our moods always seemed to match. We could sit four hours and not say anything in a comfortable silence. We were both Aquarians, of course.

I carved out my own experience of student life, and can't complain. It was fun. I can't say I ever feel I missed out, having not lived in the dorms pretending I liked drinking beer and noisy dorm mates. Being aloof has its benefits. And so, I made it through my three years and emerged with a 2:1, some great memories, and eager to see what life had in store for me next.

University flew by.

So, what next? I hopped from university to selling family portraits. I applied to a local photographer's to be the sales girl to sell photo shoot packages. Which was pretty fun and flexible. I had a bit of talent for encouraging people to indulge themselves, apparently. Alas, only lasted a short time before

I went on to sell insurance. Now that was dull and I lasted even less. Still, it paid well and the employment helped to fund my social life, terrible wardrobe, and gin habit. I ignored my mum's advice to take a job at the Waitrose convenience store that was opening at our local petrol station. If there was ever a woman that would argue blue is black, it was my mum.

"I don't see the prospect of Waitrose being as attractive as moving away and using my degree," I reasoned.

"You could be manager within six months and it's so close by."

"Yes, and I would be bored to death by swiping groceries and the smell of petrol. Mum, I am leaving the village." She got over it eventually, and moved on to telling my brother to set up a chicken yard.

And I was off. Funny, my university clique dispersed despite our drunken promises of sticking together till we made it to the top. Contact faded from phone calls to the occasional text to a thought from time to time. If someone had told me then that these people would only reappear significantly in my life via a Facebook request in a year or two I would have laughed in the face of their stupidity. Then one day there I am and they add me. I'm browsing over their pictures, we have the occasional chat over messenger filled with exciting suggestions of reunions. Alas, they never seem to materialize. Still, I continue to like their pictures and post comments that somehow make it feel we're still close.

Despite my Mum's protests, I had decided to move to London—yes, the most expensive city in the UK—with no job. You may be wondering where salary features in my choice process. Does it drive my ambition in a certain direction? Nah, not really. I am more result-orientated in terms of praise and job enjoyment than the dollar bills. Saying that, the more substantive jobs I ended up in came with decent paychecks. Perhaps it was all down to astrology. I was an Aquarius and they do tend to gravitate towards the finer things in life, and one needs good paychecks to afford them.

So, a lack of financial security and a desire to do lots of expensive things meant I had to make money.

Fortunately, living at home had proved a good decision and I had dribs and drabs of accumulated savings, and generous family donations which were supposed to be for educational purposes. Well, isn't life the best education one can give herself? I knew you would agree, which is why I used a big chunk of what I had as a six-month down payment to move in with the Tweedles. How did I find these two? A few Gumtree searches for "clean flatmates in London" and up popped an ad for "Two young professional, fun girls looking for nice girl—no cats or parties." They sounded perfect. I spoke to them over the phone which went well enough for them to allow me to move in. *Six months will give me time to get earning*, I justified to myself as I pressed transfer after having found my new flatmates. My upfront payment removed the worry they had that I had no references and was currently jobless. I assured them I would get a job in no time. And you know me, true to form, it wasn't long before I did just that.

Chapter 3
LEGALLY BLONDE

My status post-law degree was the same as many other qualified undergrads. Oh you thought it was get a law degree and you are instantly Ally McBeal? Me too. The reality is after your law degree you are either jobless, in a job completely unrelated to law, or considering whether to press on the never-ending journey to becoming a qualified lawyer/jacking it in all together. Tempting as this was, I was getting bored of sales roles. I wanted to provide a service. Take a hairdresser, for example. A genius with scissors does not have to call people and convince them to come to a salon. (Jeez, I was lucky to get the appointment I wanted half the time.) I wanted to be a genius. Be it hair or legal, I wasn't fussy.

In the end, I decided to pursue my LPC. What is that? The Legal Practice Course is the way into the shiny law firms. If you were really lucky, and had a good degree, and some work experience, the firm might even pay for your course and offer you a job. Oh yes, many a keen undergrad will hustle away for a firm for free to gain work experience—that is CV gold dust. Sensible idea, but unfortunately I was too busy selling anything from doughnuts to insurance to bother with that. Ho hum, at least I saved a little. Every little helps.

There was no getting around the expensive and time-consuming qualifying process, Erin Brockovich, being the only exception. Truth is, I wasn't sure I even wanted to do the

LPC like so many of my peers. I just wanted to be a genius. I was torn between throwing in the legal towel and going to drama school. And though I am told you shouldn't really blame people for your decisions, in this case, I blame Martin. He was the guy I started dating during my last year of university. We had met one night over far too many G&Ts at a political event during my second year at university. He, too, was a keen member of the conservative party. He was easy on the eyes and was a skilled public speaker. For some reason that turned me on. Beyond a love of gin and mild interest in politics, we had little in common. Martin certainly did not jump on board with my flexible approach to choosing a profession. He also had to battle through some strong childhood beliefs I had about men and our poor love just wasn't strong enough for that. It all came to a head when I was finally forced to meet his parents.

I had accepted an invite to have dinner at his parents' house after having used all of my socially acceptable excuses to get out of it. It was a stunning, ginormous house in one of the more exclusive postcodes of our area. His parents were partial to all the traditions I wasn't. My coat was taken on arrival and shoes placed on the shoe rack. Most guests at our house were lucky to find a chair to throw their jacket on and as for a shoe rack? Oh, behave!

Within five minutes I was placed in my worst nightmare having a pre-dinner cocktail with his parents sitting directly opposite us. I felt stifled and a bit dizzy from the strong gin his mother had forced me to accept. Framed photos of his family life were displayed on the perfectly polished dark wooden drawers beside us. One was of Martin and his sister smiling, aged four and eighteen, in His and Hers outfits. One of a rather goofy, smiling Martin, holding his degree, proud as punch. I smiled inwardly as I pictured mine, my hat blowing off, my mum bent over to try and save it whilst my Dad looked on in a beer-induced haze of amusement.

"So, Amy, Martin says he had to talk you out of becoming an actress?" his dad asked as he crossed one knee over the other and peered over his cocktail glass at me for a response.

"Well, I will drink to that," his mother chirped in a tone as bitter as the gin. I wonder what her dream career would have been.

"Why? Have you had experience with acting?" I enquired, as she seemed so certain that my being saved from it deserved a toast.

"No, I was realistic enough to know I was never going to be Angelina Jolie." This caused a flurry of fake chuckles, an especially loud one from Martin. As I drained my glass I hoped no one could hear my inner monologue screaming *What a toss pot!*

"I doubt Angie would be where she is had she said the same thing about Marilyn Monroe."

My attempt at a joke was one they clearly didn't get, adding to the awkwardness of the atmosphere. It felt icky and stifling. I wanted to literally get up and run out of that house. The lure of a perfectly-cooked beef Wellington followed by whatever other delights their cook had conjured up for us would be happily exchanged for beans on toast with the Tweedles on my non-judgemental sofa. I made a promise to myself that night to never become like Martin's parents. The house, regardless of its lavish finishes, felt as cold as their relationship, masked by expensive gin and fancy cocktail glasses, a regimented weekly routine his mother had gone through. Twice. Oh, they had a great life externally, I just wondered what it was like on the inside. That was a place I didn't want to go.

You'll be proud to know, I got through the evening without

insulting anyone or embarrassing myself apart from having to ask if the caviar was a decoration or an actual food. The gin helped with both the swallowing of the fish eggs and the evening in general. Martin didn't. Come dessert my shoulders still felt tense.

"It's been ... delightful to meet you, Amy." His mother had said everything in the pause between 'been' and 'delightful'.

"It's Anna, and you too."

On the journey home, Martin was surprised by my request to be dropped home.

"I had wanted to ask you something tonight." He looked at me with eyes that threatened something meaningful. I sensed the question would be terribly dramatic—moving in, a romantic holiday or, worst case, engagement.

"No, please take me home. Let's talk tomorrow." I lied, knowing there would be no us tomorrow. Or again, he needed to find a girl who simply wasn't me.

Still, I stuck with my decision to finish the LPC. Part-time, naturally, so I could continue to explore other options. So many jobs, so little time. A need for adventure and desperation to escape Martin led me to the big smoke and for that I was glad.

Having grown up in a village I was one of those that took to city life like a duck to water. I find city life a little like Marmite: you either love it or hate it. I loved it. The joy of city life is liberating. I traded one bakery, three Chinese takeaways, and a local grocery store for more shops, bars, and restaurants that—even after seven years—I haven't covered half of. I traded everyone knowing your business for discretion at its finest. For example, in village life women went to the same pub as their gynecologist and his wife. He would give them a nice little wave as they ordered vodka tonics pointing to their vaginas and signaled thumbs up, for a cloak of anonymity. In my new city life, in order to see someone, you knew a time, a venue, and a date was actively picked and subject to a high chance of being rearranged or cancelled.

London is a gem. Seven years and we are still going strong. I tried to leave a couple of times but always come back with my tail between my legs, full of gratitude and relief that this insanely perfect city exists. My home, my inspiration, my favourite place in the world: I love you London. If any place has my heart, it is the very city my life truly began. As the old adage goes, "Life is not measured by the number of breaths we take, but by the moments that take our breath away," and the place where I found an abundance of those is in the Big Smoke.

A new course to throw myself on felt full of possibility. My new venue of study was in a part of town I do not venture back to too often now that my studious obligations have been fulfilled: Bloomsbury. It's strange how you can grow so connected to somewhere and years later that connection has evaporated without you even noticing. My morning commute during those days was me huddled on a tube shuffling down the Northern Line to Goodge Street come rain, wind, or snow. Often reading someone's copy of the *Metro* over a squashed shoulder to pass the time. Then, bam. Before you know it, it's all just another memory in the photo album of life.

I approached the LPC the same way as my law degree, with moderate expectations. I whole-heartedly accepted my position in the education chain. I was not destined for the top. I would have felt too much pressure had I got a first-class degree, like I had some moral obligation to the world to put it to actual use. Don't get me wrong I love learning. I have always used learning as an alternative place to lose myself. Learning was more like a hobby.

Though I did find comfort in that, despite my questionable state of mind and future, I was at least making some form of progress. I am of the line of thinking that any new skill is a bonus. A friend of mine recently started painting chairs…and I immediately wondered if I should learn, too.

The LPC taught me two things. 1) I still wasn't sure if I wanted to be a lawyer. 2) I wasn't sure what I wanted to be at all. What was I doing, then? Trying to become a lawyer. I'm thinking the key to a long happy career is choosing one that requires the skills that make you who you are. So, it allows you to be yourself. It's like with a relationship, you can't date someone too different to you or it just ain't gonna work. Like me trying to date someone who likes cats. No offence cat lovers, they just make my throat itch and one once whipped me round the face with its tail, which has left with me with a deeply-embedded fear of the crafty little things. Oh yeah, and you can just get a dog, which is way better, no? You can at least take them for a walk and paws are safer than claws.

The main problem with me tackling the challenge to become a layer was simple. It was forcing me to do something which required staying power. I can barely sit still for a manicure, for goodness sake. The first real hurdle is the two-year training contract. That was one jump I was never going to make. Come to the same office every day for two whole years. From nine to seventeen hundred? No way. From eight to twenty-two hundred? Shoot me now. I hid my concerns from my fellow students. I had a chat with one of the girls on my course on our last day, she rolled off the top five firms she was aiming for.

"I know I will get one of those, and I want be on the family law side. My Uncle runs McArthur Jones, so I will definitely get a training contract there if worse case which is my number four."

Her confidence and certainty about her future intimidated me, not that I let on.

"Where are you going to apply, Anna?"

"Oh, I am not sure yet. I want to spend some time researching."

"You mean you haven't already?" The concern in her face made me feel slightly nostalgic, and not in a good way.

I popped to the college toilets after our conversation for a chat with the non-judgmental mirror.

My hands on the sink, I asked myself, "Anna, you are going to at least give this a go? what's the worst that can happen? What are you so scared of?" The mirror gave me no answer. Nor did the girl who appeared out of the middle cubicle and stared at me like I was crazy.

So, did I try? Of course I did. I will try anything once just for the thrill of it. Even jumping out of a plane. Which I would much rather do again than a training contract. I lasted one month. We will get to that shortly. Don't worry, enough nonsense went down to make it worth your precious investment of literary time. A month in the life of a jobslut is many things though it is never boring. Come on, you must be getting to know me by now.

I invested seven years and around £20,000 for this month so attention must be paid. Technically speaking, it wasn't even the qualifications that got my rather large foot in the door. However, it did involve a lot of vodka. I had finished the LPC and was naturally celebrating with the only friend I had made on the course. A part-time stripper named Mary; I know what are the chances? A girl called Mary becoming a stripper? Whatever next! The night was coming to an end and we were in a fancy joint in Covent Garden. Mary knew the doorman. I was doing my usual, chatting nonsense in the bathroom fishing around for who would be up for late-night Maroush. (Any Londoner must agree this is the best place for a post-midnight chicken kebab in SW1.)

It was in this very bathroom that I met Susan. She was around forty-five with mousy brown hair that she hadn't updated since the sixties, bless her. She had a mousy cuteness that made you just want to hug her, especially in her current state—an intoxicated blubbering mess. We quickly got chatting and I insisted on buying her a large martini for the road (which was the only solution I could offer for her current dilemma.) Her husband of ten years had run off with the nanny. I've got to admire her spirit, though. When asking her where her friends were, she replied, "The last thing I wanted to do was go out with those judgmental sons of bitches."

Susan was a feisty one, clearly, and was totally up for a bite. (Mary did not eat a lot—the only downside about being friends with a stripper.) Over our late-night chicken dinner we exchanged vodka-fuelled accounts of where we were in our lives—you know, the British thing, having a good old rant. Susan was also, by chance, a partner of a top international law firm and by the sounds of it, bored to death. She was delighted to hear I had just finished my LPC and looked at me as though she had just found her new favourite toy.

"Fuck it," she exclaimed.

She had just informed me she had joined a new club in London called Fuck It therapy and it was clearly working. The group met once a week on a Monday and aired their problems then chanted "fuck it" for a while. Clearly it was doing wonders. I must say I really admired her coping strategies. Fuck It and vodka. She insisted I would come to her office Monday to temp for a month, and if it worked out, she could potentially fast track me on to one of only fifteen training contracts.

"You would be on average wage if you can suck that up. This could be the making of you." Susan didn't need to entice me any further. In my head, I was already the real-life Ally McBeal. Now I knew how Charlie felt when he found one of Willy Wonka's golden tickets. They say luck is preparation meets opportunity, be it on a sweet shelf or in a nightclub bathroom. After air kisses and goodbyes, Susan and I wobbled off in separate directions to hail cabs. I bagged myself a new job and a new friend: not bad for a Thursday night.

My friends had sobering thoughts on my fortunate night with Susan. My friends were also my flatmates, the Tweedles. They were great flatmates and what I refer to as sensibly social. I felt very lucky to have found them. Our flat was a small three-bedroom within walking distance to Finchley station and within wobbling distance of two great pubs. I always recommend to people who think they might be a tad nuts to try and have a few sensible people in your life. Trust me, it helps.

One was a media executive and the other an events manager. They had lived together a lot longer before I moved in and although clearly BFFs, Tweedle Dee and Tweedle Dum (as I called them) never made me feel like I was intruding on their friendship. Far from being the third wheel, I was more like the whacky wheel. Whatever—it worked. I know I made them feel substantially more successful in the career world. They had long-term roles and good salaries.

As we gulped coffee and devoured toast the following morning, they shook their heads at my apparently boozy enthusiasm. I lacked a certain trait so many of my mates in the city oozed: an urban pessimism that attaches itself and is the ultimate weapon against bullshit. I can relate more to the bullshit givers. They are only trying to help people out, even if they don't have a chance in hell of following though. Their hearts are in the right place. The way I see it, it's better to have your hopes raised and dashed than never raised at all. Speaking of which, I was speeding ahead with what every normal girl in my situation would be doing—googling Susan and her firm and feeling quite pleased to confirm everything she told me was true.

"Still, doesn't mean she will call you. She was drunk and emotional and bought you a kebab, so what. Let's move on. Who is up for a pub lunch later?" With Tweedle Dee you could always count on the glass being half full.

Staring at the two gloomy, hung-over faces I decided to leave Susan and my pending job opportunity on the back burner for the rest of the day and enjoy my Sunday. Maybe even try to cheer up Tweedle Dee and Tweedle Dum. We had ventured out to our local coffee joint. As I went inside to order a round, the diva in line in front of me, when asked by the polite Polish barista if she would like chocolate on her cappuccino, looked at him in despise and announced proudly, as if it was common knowledge, that she was on a diet. Some people. That memory sticks as it was at this point I received a text from my new pal Susan.

"Hung over as hell. Meet me at my office Monday morning. Wear a suit."

In a rush of smug excitement, I bought Tweedle Dee and Tweedle Dum a brownie and sashayed back outside to deliver my news. And asked a favour. Did either of them have a suit I could borrow?

Chapter 4
ENTERING THE JUNGLE

Tweedle Dee delivered. Okay, it was a size too big, and her being a redhead and me being a blonde meant that that particular shade of green suited her more than me, but... actually, it looked equally as bad on her, if I had to be honest.

How did I feel? This was a glorious moment for me. I was going to be inside one of the Top Fifty best law firms. I was going to be paid to be there. I was going to learn stuff and become a legal genius. I hadn't told the family yet, and for the same reason I didn't tell them I was doing my driving test—I could do without the pressure. (It made failing three times far easier to deal with.)

Trembling with excitement and a little bit nervous in the oversized green suit I promised myself I would not be late. That is one thing I can definitely list as a strength. I would like to be okay with being late sometimes. Being late is rather chic, isn't it? And it would make my life far easier as most people in it run late. My OCD about timekeeping stems from childhood. My mother was late for everything. Being one in a family of five meant getting out the door was no easy task. I remember standing by the door looking at our big, bossy brown clock telling me I was ten minutes late for assembly and feeling genuinely upset and angry. I did not stand a chance in hell—listening to all the noise in the house—of being on my way anytime soon. Ten minutes late and not even out the door?

Oh, and then there was the usual being left at friends' houses or at school trips. I once walked two hours in the dark as my dad had fallen asleep and Mum was getting drunk with an old friend. In fairness, she did give me the day off and took me shopping the next day to make up for it, but you get my point. I was forced to sacrifice punctuality for many years. Which is why I oddly relish being able to grab my bag and go wherever and whenever I like. I can be early for everything, if I please. The only thing that will, if ever, compromise this freedom is if I ever have a child. Though one thing's for sure I am never having three of them.

By eight, I was perched in a Caffé Nero near Holborn station. I was already weighing things up on route. It wasn't too bad. The Northern Line to Tottenham Court did smell a little smoky. And the Central Line was a bit squishy to Holborn. Other than that, I couldn't complain. I do love the fun in discovering a new routine. It's like trying on a new pair of shoes. The most important thing being, how comfortable is it? And of course, no day should start without a shot of caffeine or three. The sun was out, too, making London look as glorious as ever. London could get away with any weather, a little like Kate Moss could still look divine in a bin bag.

I felt so alive that morning, like an essential part of the blend in diverse crowd. United only by our desire to avoid crashing into each other we scurried along to our destinations. I was in awe at the sense of urgency. The air smelt sweet. I was horribly aware I looked nowhere near as chic as the stylish women flying by me in tailored dresses and elegant colours. I doubt I blended in as well as I hoped in my borrowed and oversized ghastly suit. Still, I wouldn't let it get me down. I exhaled all my apprehension.

So, jeez, security in fancy law firms is pretty tight. The

formality was a bit of a smack in the face. I hated the F word. It made me so uncomfortable. So intimidating. You have those who relish in it. Take Rebecca, for example. The receptionist I was now going to have to pass by every day with her bright red lipstick, dramatic eyebrows, and air brushed face. Yep, I knew from the very first slow eye roll I received I had a class-A bitch on my hands. A total snob. *Pipe down, you're only a receptionist*, I thought. A ridiculously pretty and immaculately dressed one, I'll give you that, though a receptionist nonetheless. I stood proudly in my suit and informed her I was here to see Susan Matthews.

"You cannot enter this building without a security pass." The voice matched her bitchy face. It was superficially high. She was going to annoy me.

"In that case, I will have one of those," I replied as sarcastically as possible. My inner monologue called her a moron.

I made my way through the security and soon found myself sitting in a stylish office on a plush orange chair waiting for Susan to brief me on the day ahead. I decided not to mention my opinion of Bitchface just yet. Early days.

"Made it past Rebecca, then," Susan greeted me with a familiar tone that suggested it was a phrase she used a lot.

I didn't respond right away, as I was too busy observing my new surroundings. Outside our office there were many heads bobbing up and down on computers, busy bodies rushing back and forth with paperwork. By Jove, it was not even nine. It felt a little bit like the insurance office I worked in, though a million times more professional. The décor screamed importance and forced you to be doing something—maybe that's why everyone was so busy. I could see why Susan liked this office as a hide out from the chaos.

"Morning." I beamed my best attempt at a smile that covered my nervous excitement. Excited was my default mood for most new jobs. I was like a bubbly glass of champagne, overflowing with gushing glee despite the secretary being a total bitch. She would remain under said name tag until she did something worthy to revoke the title, you know, like, smile.

Susan was as delightful as I remembered. It seemed her soon-to-be ex-husband's shenanigans had turned her into a force to be reckoned with. Any concern I had of Suze being a bit of a bore at work was dissolved with her natural sarcasm and wit. Cinderella needed a dress and glass slippers, Susan just need to stop giving a fuck. So maybe there are fairy godmothers. They may not appear in a puff of smoke, they may come along as women ten years younger than you with tight tits and take your diabolical excuse of a husband off your hands.

"Well, today is Monday. Welcome on board. I will give you a jungle tour in a mo'. I got Sarah to print you out a breakdown of the day as you won't be with me for the whole of it. I am seeing counsel for two hours this afternoon, but you can come and take notes. Other than that, she will keep you busy. We can go to Scott's for a late lunch after."

It sounded fabulous. In came Sarah. She moved like a squirrel, scurrying from one point to the other She pushed her glasses back up her nose and simultaneously smiled and squinted. No, seriously. As she smiled her eyes nearly closed. I wondered if that's how she slept with a big Cheshire cat smile on her face. She held out her slithery little hand and ever so sweetly introduced herself.

"I am Susan's secretary," she told me proudly.

Her voice threw me off guard. It was more of a squeak. As she continued I realized this wasn't a one-off squeak. She was a full-blown squeaker. I swallowed hard, as this was not a good time to laugh.

She handed Susan a pile of documents. Susan looked pleased and dismissed Sarah as if she had just delivered a pizza and was no longer of use. She flung them on her desk and I followed her as instructed for my jungle tour.

I was intrigued as to why Susan referred to a fair share of her colleagues as caged animals. Some barely looked up, as I was fed a string of names and titles I had no chance of remembering. Susan, Bitchface, and Squeaky would do for now. I had that same feeling in my stomach I had on my first day of school. I was no longer twelve and my apprehension in new situations should have developed into something far more mature by now. Yet there they were, the same old butterflies. And just as on my first day of school I was dressed like an idiot. Some things, even when put in my control will remain hopeless.

I was beginning to feel a little stifled by the seriousness of this place. It made me a little suffocated. A horrible thought hit me: was Susan planning to make me as busy as they looked? I felt out of my depth already. I wasn't good enough to be here, with my oversized suit and inner weirdo telling me to run away. A couple looked up from their desks as Susan showed me round. I knew I would and could never be one of them. Then, right at that second, Bruce arrived. Thank the Lord.

Introducing himself by a cute little knee bend and whack on the backside with his messily filed docs he asked Susan, "Is this her?"

Susan smiled. "Yes, Bruce."

Okay, so my track record for guessing sexuality was terribly shit but even I could tell that Bruce would never look twice at Miss World. I loved him from the first.

"Welcome to the jungle, doll face," he said.

His head didn't seem to stop moving as he spoke. He kept flashing from an infectious smile to a do-not-mess-with-me-face. Bruce hailed from NYC. He maintained a sweetness that many New Yorkers lose after years of battling the concrete jungle. Looks like he had made it to London in time and I was glad he did.

"Girls. Clients call. The bastards need me. Let's do lunch. We need to discuss your swine of an ex—" he said to Susan, "—and your terrible suit," he said to me.

As he walked away he looked back and, making sure no one else heard, he cupped his hand over his mouth, did another little knee bend and dramatically whispered, "and Pedro!" Roll on lunch, I thought.

Not much to report on the rest of the morning. I got shoved into the office with Squeaky and, sweet as she may be, she was rather dull. She gave me a load of documents to read about the philosophy of the company, and brochures covered with smiling young people shaking hands and sitting around tables, about the life of a trainee. I googled a few important things while I could. Starting with the salary of legal secretaries. Wow, £45,000 starting. No wonder Squeaky was busy. Then I pretended I was a secret reporter working undercover to reveal the secrets of London's top law firm—which got me to thinking that that would be a pretty fun.

By the afternoon, which came around not so quickly, Susan sashayed into the office, phone in hand, threw her handbag down, and signaled me to follow her. I didn't need telling twice, as I was fucking starving and thoroughly bored. I grabbed my coat and shuffled after her out of the building past Bitchface and back outside. There's nothing like the temporary restriction of freedom to make you appreciate the simple things like daylight and oxygen.

The rain had made its way through the morning sunshine so Susan, Bruce (who had been waiting on a bench by Bitchface in reception,) and I hailed a cab. Well, to be precise Bruce did—years of living in Manhattan had clearly made him a pro. What better place to drink in my surroundings than from the back of the iconic London cab. The toy-like black cars were one of my favorite hallmarks.

We arrived at our destination, a new trendy French place. A Tweedle had been taken on a date recently and I had heard great things about the sea bass, though I was so hungry I just hoped they were generous enough to offer a good bread basket. Bruce was not happy about the minute walk we had to endure. Us London folk will walk miles, though when we order a cab by Christ it better drop us no less than a metre from our destination or we will be enraged. Especially when it's raining.

The reasons why I loved Susan just kept growing. Once in and seated, thanks to her no-nonsense approach to faffing staff she had ordered a great bottle of rosé and we could crack on with what Bruce was bursting out his stylish balls for: a good old gossip. It sounds so patronizing to say, "I love gays," like they are a breed of cute dog, but Bruce was the exact character that elicited such commentary. His fingers held on to the edge of the table like he was playing a really long piano note then spontaneously flew into the air every time he got excited. Whilst anyone else talked they returned to this default position as he desperately waited for his next burst. Clearly awkward silences posed no threat while Brucey was around. Despite not being a big rosé drinker this was a bloody good drop and I was totally in awe of my company. Susan and Bruce: this was brilliant.

"How you getting on in the jungle, then?" Susan directed at me once she had let Bruce vent enough about Pedro.

"Yeah, been reading through, all through the ... you know ... documents." I could not be slurring already, I had only had one glass—still I made a hand dive for the bread just in case.

Bruce laughed. "Oh, all that marketing rubbish."

"Bruce, don't put her off before she's even started."

"Don't worry about that, it's something I can do all by myself." I offered freely, though held back from giving a full-blown jobslut confession. Don't think the good old truth would go down well now with Suze. *Oh, you know, I don't take jobs seriously and never stay longer than a few months at best. Just get bored, find something better, it all gets too much so I have to run away—you know, that kind of thing. Oh yes, my credentials? Law degree then LPC made you think I wanted to be a lawyer? Yes, I can see how you came to that conclusion though I failed to mention I was also massively inspired by Ally McBeal and as a matter of fact it's an actress I wanted to be. My bad.* No, I'd save that old chestnut for a bit later down the line and just hope Suze would understand my confusion. For now, though, I was all in.

"I love the jungle. Sarah is nice." *Do not say Squeaky, do not say Squeaky, do not say Squeaky.* My inner dialogue was working hard to help me not insult anyone.

"That girl is a god-send," Susan took a long sip of wine as a little toast to Squeaky. Since Nigel left I have realised how much I rely on her. She's even helped with Eva. I honestly don't know how I would have gotten past the last few weeks without her."

I had sensed this dependability about Squeaky, she was everything I would never be: reliable, organised, efficient. Admirable traits that secretly terrified me. I would happily whack them onto a job application or throw them around in an interview if I thought it would get me in, though.

So, Susan needed Squeaky. What else did I learn over lunch? Nigel was a five-star prick. Susan had come home early one evening to find him shagging the nanny. This is precisely why I encourage people to go the bar after work before going home. 1) Less chance of shocking discoveries. 2) You're in a way better mood if there are any. 3) They serve wine. Poor Susan. Though hoorah for Susan; even as I flicked though her Blackberry, I saw photos of a very different woman to the one sitting before me now. Her face glowed with a fresh joy for life.

So, we hated Nigel. Susan hated men. Bruce and Susan had worked together since he joined the London office two years ago. He was still having a whale of a time in London, thrilled with its anonymity that allowed him to ping-pong from Pedro to Pedro without so much as a reputation. There was a casual energy to their friendship that was nice to be around. It was the kind of friendship where you can say whatever the fuck you wanted. They are life's gold dust. Susan had been a partner for two years at the firm since she qualified as a trainee. She had done time in a few other offices before landing in the jungle. Now she was there with Squeaky and everything was ticking along fine. Thinking she was happily married. Then Nige has started shagging the nanny and she was now fully aware he is a first-class nob.

"Well, we best get back. We have the meeting with counsel late afternoon.

I looked at my watch. Sod it. This is the annoying thing about working—after two bottles of rosé and a nice lunch—having to go back to it. It's an awful shame to not carry on drinking, like starting a race then calling quits halfway in. Missing the finish line of being totally pissed. Though such is working life. Bruce, Susan, and I were forced to swing our tipsy way back to the jungle.

We proceeded to meet the barrister. He talked in a terribly posh voice. Lots of long ambiguous words came out of his Oxford-educated mouth. I suppose ambiguity is a part of the legal tool kit. Susan was a planning lawyer and this was a big application to turn a now well-known shopping complex in London from commercial to residential. Loads of locals were opposing and the developers were putting a lot of pressure on as they had already pumped a lot of money in to their vision. I had got myself up to speed by flicking through a few of the many files. By many, I mean around fifty boxes packed full of correspondence, legal documents, etc. Fifty boxes of bloody etcetera.

The meeting was exhaustingly boring. Though they did provide some rather nice ginger biscuits. They were the highlight of the afternoon. And fair's fair, the offices were rather snazzy. I tried my best to take notes as instructed. On the cab ride back to the office, a feeling of panic arose in me. I should have had case notes, all I had was a selection of very average doodles and a rising feeling of anxiety in my chest. I had been in this job barely a day and I was already overwhelmed with the pressure. If I couldn't cope with this, how on earth could I manage rising up the ranks? And what stage was I even at? An added extra to Susan's team? A most-likely surplus, as she was going to discover sooner or later I was pretty useless at handling responsibility. What if I missed a crucial point? What if my preoccupation with ginger biscuits and fancy windows caused this whole case to collapse? My thoughts occupied me the whole journey back home. I felt desperate for a chat with the mirror. There were few things I found more soothing than talking to my reflection.

The next week continued with much of the same. Note-taking and reading up on files as per Squeaky's orders, then lunching with Susan—which was always the best part of the day. And if I am honest with myself, those lunches were probably the only reason I stuck it out a month. The excitement of the jungle, the busy location, and being part of a law firm wore off by the middle of week two. It just wasn't quite spurring me on in the mornings like it had for the first week. Even an extra shot of caffeine wasn't really boosting my perspective on things like the norm. By the end of week two, I knew what was happening: this job and I were going to have to break up. I just had to determine how was best to go about it. This is how quickly these things happen. One minute I am in the fresh flushes of a new role, meeting fantastic people like Bruce, and settling into a new environment. I had grown quite fond of

Squeaky. Susan treated me so well, most people couldn't believe my luck to be handed this position on a plate. I mean, I hadn't even had an interview. It was all wonderfully bizarre. None of it changed the fact that it was not for me, that this path on which I was wandering down was not the one that would lead to my happy ending.

The exact moment when I had decided to finish things came when I was faced with the boxes. Susan had given Squeaky her usual to-do list which now included telling me what to do. Up to this particular windy Wednesday morning it hadn't been too bad. Plenty of time to indulge in daydreaming, checking out any talent in the jungle, that kind of thing. (Though there was not anything to report back in that department.) Boredom was raising its ugly head, as was my anxiety about never being good or strong enough to make it in the competitive environment that everyone else seemed to relish.

So, Squeaky had chirpily delivered the news as we sipped on coffee and gazed at the fifty or so boxes located just outside the office to the left. The news being I was to go through each of the fifty boxes—which has been numbered in chronological order, literally the only silver lining—and make a record of each document. Yes, that's it. Each document, in each of the fifty boxes. My head said, *No fucking way.* My mouth said, "Okay, sure, no problem." Why do we do this to ourselves? Say yes when we really mean hell no. Why on earth would I want to go through fifty boxes of paperwork I really couldn't care less about? My decision was made. Now it was just a question of how and when. Freedom was calling me. Though, right now, so was Susan—with an invitation to Fuck It club. Sounded just the tonic. I had to find the right moment to tell her about my plans to leave and hope she would not find it an incredible insult to her generosity. Maybe I would leave it till the end of the week, give her the weekend to recover. I certainly didn't want to lose Sus as a friend. I had become incredibly fond of her in a short space of time. She filled some sort of hole in my circle of friends I hadn't even known existed. Like a London Mum without the maternal dynamics that get in the way of what, in many cases, could be a perfectly good relationship.

I had liked the sound of Fuck It therapy, though considering it was pretty much how I think anyway, it never really occurred to me to join a club. Though here I found myself on a Wednesday night, vodka tonic in hand, surrounded by lots of middle-aged men and women, and a few twenty-somethings, who found it highly therapeutic getting together once a week to say "fuck it" to all their problems.

The location was in St Martin's Lane hotel, in the basement of a retro little wine bar. The room was dark with tones of red and dark oak wooden tables and chairs. Two big bendy lamps created a little spotlight for whoever dare take it. Right now, a bald guy called Simon was having his moment. Just in case you think you thought you were unlucky in life, listen to Simon's: He has been married three times and lost his first to his brother, his second wife to his best friend, and his third wife to his dad. I left the session thoroughly glad I was single and I could see why Susan went. Let's face it, smug as it may be, sometimes hearing about other people's problems makes you feel better about your own. I mean, if you can't celebrate the presence of good things in your life at least be grateful of the absence of the total shit going on in others'.

I heard a lot of things I would rather not that night, including several cases of career burn out. One lady called Sonia had lost her hair at age thirty-two due to the stress of working at a top investment bank. Jeez, no salary is worth losing your hair for—even if it was six figures.

I couldn't say I would be back, despite the infectious enthusiasm of Debbie and Dave, the founders of the group who must be laughing all the way to the bank and back at the fact they are now raking it in from charging a bunch of people to get together once a week just to say "fuck it." Capitalizing on other people's stress might not land them in the best relationship with Karma somewhere down the line. They were the type of couple you could imagine going to swinger's parties together. Dave looked like the poster boy for a macaroni and cheese advert—a bit tubby with cheddar-yellow hair that covered his very round head. Debbie had duck lips pumped with filler and big hair. She dressed in Vivienne Westwood. That alternative fashion either worked or didn't on people. In this case, it didn't. Funnily enough one good thing that came from my attendance was it made me like, and therefore use, the word "fuck" less. You know what they say about too much of good thing. Mum would be proud.

Susan and I paused our "fuck it" buttons and pressed play on the "let's drink to our full capacity" ones. I woke up with Tweedle Dee in bed with me. My initial panic was, "Shit, I have tried to turn my flatmate into a lesbian." My memory of coming home was very vague. Turns out it was my bed and her bed had broken in the night and she didn't want to wake Tweedle Dum—as apparently, her sleep is more important than mine. Fair enough, probably put to better use. Over breakfast I had cracked the old "must be because you have put on a few pounds," joke regarding the unfortunate collapse of her bed. As we both acknowledged the truth in my joke we were forced to hang out in a really long awkward silence. I try not to speak in these situations to avoid digging a deeper hole. Tweedle Dum broke it for me with a great question.

"Who ate my baked beans?"

Me, obviously, as a drunken snack. I decided now was a good time to disperse my latest dilemma. "I think I want to quit my job," I blurted out, instead of a confession of my bean theft. I really didn't mind that my commitment issues amused them.

I always used the word "think" until any final decision had been made. I also tried not to burn my bridges when I left any job because, well, you never know when you might need it back. There you go, some tricks of the trade of being a jobslut for you.

"I am just finding it all too much. The jungle is so boring it needs more lions or unusual animals. It's more like a farm full of sheep and chickens. I like sheep and chickens, they just aren't rhinos or parrots. Are you with me?"

Their blank looks and pursed lips sealing their criticism reflected their total lack of understanding. It would have made quite a sweet picture.

"Last night was fun, though. Susan and I went to Fuck It club," I added as I left, just to really baffle them. And off I went to the jungle (or farm) spending my entire journey contemplating the best way to quit. Even the commute was getting on my nerves now. How I convinced myself the smelly trip on the tube at rush hour was a good idea is a reflection of my relentless optimism. I am not too stubborn, however, to admit when my enthusiasm runs out. Like a steam engine's steam is drained after one too many journeys, that's how I felt after trekking to the jungle every day for the past nearly three weeks. I was racking my brain for inspiration on exit strategies. I had not found the right moment to tell Sus the truth yet. Besides, I liked her. She had experienced enough dishonesty by her wretched rat of ex-hubby to be. Note to self: must throw her a fabulous divorce party. Today I must tell her.

A good thing about Squeaky is she hated leaving the office unless she had too. I know. It is kind of creepy how much she actually loved shuffling around in there. Whereas I took every opportunity to pick-up office lunches, or coffees, as a way of mitigating my claustrophobia. Mini escapes into the world outside the windows. I have a tendency to get into a state of panic at the thought of missing out on fun stuff if I spend too much time in an office. So, I was all was good with the, "Could you just pop out and…" Yes. No problem. I will pop off anywhere and do whatever so long as it means reminding myself of life beyond these walls.

This particular Thursday the pop out request was a little above my level of competence. Squeaky knew it. I could see the hesitant doubt in her bubbly little eyes as she asked me. She was caught in a real-life catch-twenty-two between her laziness and her loyalty to Susan. Her laziness trumped it. The request in hand was to visit the National Archives in Kew and retrieve a map. I couldn't believe my luck to get to go all the way to Kew. It was a gorgeous day and as a smoker was lured by the opportunity for cigarettes and coffee in the sunshine. Squeaky provided me with the essentials—directions to the building and exact instructions for finding the map. I was just planning to take the easy route and plead stupidity, get someone to help me live up to my hair colour and all that. I even promised Squeaky I would stop and pick us up some Frappuccinos on the way back. This calmed her lazy nerves. She was hopeful I would return with the map and the Frappuccino; I was confident I could return with the latter. One thing I was good at was getting people's specific orders; you want a triple shot, extra swizzle of caramel, I got it. How annoying to request something like a certain flavor, and the person returns with the wrong one. Salt and vinegar and you get cheese and onion? Being one of many children, autonomy of personal choice from haircuts to sandwich fillings was not something I was blessed with until later on in life. Economies of scale made it easier we all had the same. I remember the first time I was able to choose my own outfit for a school party was quite a moment.

Kew is beautiful. I never understand people that mistake London for just a load of buildings. Hampstead Heath is breath taking, Hyde Park and the serpentine go on for miles. Kew Gardens is another one of London's gems.

A sentiment clearly shared by a positively perky gentleman wandering the grounds who announced to me with a smile, "And this is why we pay our taxes." He looked like he might pull out a chimney sweep and bust into a Dick Van Dyke-style dance. Anything's possible when you get caught up in the magic of such a place.

I stopped for a compulsory coffee and cigarette on the lake outside the building and took in how sensational it looked. Six smooth swans glided past me in the sunshine. The building is worth suffering the trip to the end of the District Line in itself. Just go see it. Or Google it. Sometimes the best way to give something justice is vision. So, I was having a fabulous morning until I entered the archives building. It's one thing coming as a tourist to gaze at all the old books and soak in the archaic atmosphere leisurely, your only commitment being eating your cheese sandwiches in the sunshine while talking about how beautiful it is. It is very much another when you have something serious to do in there.

I finally ending up in the right map room after landing in the wrong room twice. Third time lucky and all that. The place is full of all different sections, and stores years and years and years and years of documents that reflect property transactions, transitions, changes in law, planning, everything. I had not exactly struck it lucky with the guy who managed the map department though. He looked mean. I think some people feel the need to live up to their look, I mean look at Anthony Hopkins: he looks totally creepy so he played Hannibal and made a fortune. Good for him. (Despite his creepy aura, I met him and can confirm he is actually quite nice.) Though Ken, general manager of the map department, was not destined for Hollywood or very nice. He was in fact a total jerk. Mono face.

"Hi, I was wondering if you could help me." I was pissed off at wasting an hour going to the wrong sections. Perfectly good cigarette and coffee time was wasted. Though relieved I had found the map section, it smelt a bit dusty like an old library. I guess if I had to spend all day every day in here I would get a bit grumpy like Ken. No way would I do it, though. Half a day would be enough here.

"How can I help?" Ken asked with a nice dose of sarcasm.

"I need to retrieve this map," I pointed to Squeaky's instructions. They referenced the exact location of the map. Ken took me into a old room full of tables and rows of old maps and left me to have a general meltdown. I had never seen so many maps. To cut a shit story short I left after twenty minutes with the wrong map. I just kind of gave up. I really did not give a monkey's ass at this point. I realised I could spend another hour looking for the right map and still end up with the wrong one so for that reason I was not wasting my time. Besides, I strategized if I get the wrong one maybe Susan would politely sack me so it was a win-win.

Squeaky's dismay at the realization I had failed map duty was not something I had prepared myself for. She was too nice to tell me I was an idiot. She simply informed me of my mistake and I have never seen her move so fast. She was off to the Archives herself to retrieve the right map before Susan's meeting this afternoon—where said map was a crucial instrument apparently to building the case.

She grabbed her Frappuccino as she flung her big floppy black handbag over her shoulder and left with a, "Please take any important messages."

I made a decision there and then to be the one to not only admit my epic fail to Susan, but more importantly to blow

Squeaky's trumpet. She really was gold. She really cared and would go the distance for Susan. Even the care she took to organise her messy desk each evening before she left and pin a to-do list Post-it on her computer for the morning. I felt a tad guilty for not having worked hard enough to be in the office. Perhaps the nature and ease of its acquisition was what prevented me giving it the appreciation it deserved. Working hard for something was more satisfying. What had I actually done to be here? Simply waltzed in and—other than accompanying Susan to various events—had not done a lot. Josh was another young wannabe here on an internship. He and I had met at the coffee machine and had a brief chat. He already looked the part. Everything about him was so appropriate from his clothes, posture, tone, and rate of speaking. Just looking at him made me feel more of a mess. He was a dedicated, certain young man. His arrow of ambition was aimed directly at law and he had that fierce determination about him that made you know he would make it. He was still a little soft around the edges, though I am confident today he is probably partner somewhere. Maybe Susan's firm. I would Google, though don't think I would have much luck with Josh.

"Where's Sarah?" Susan asked, assuming her trusted little helper was simply taking a toilet break, fetching coffees, or completing one of her loyal duties. Big breath. A moment to contemplate whether I really wanted to turn down my first big shot at a top law firm. I had spent the last five years training for just the hope of making it into a Top Fifty. Was I about to walk away from my success? Yes. Success to me was getting my ass out the glossy doors and back into the comfort of the unknown.

"She is at the National Archives Museum trying to remedy my uselessness. I didn't get the map you need for your meeting later. Susan, Sarah really is a superstar." Here it was coming, I could feel it rising so far up the only way out was through my mouth. The truth.

"In fact, seeing her work ethic and drive and professionalism has just made me realize that I am not cut out for this. I really appreciate what you have tried to do, though not as much as someone who really deserves the opportunity and who is willing to put in the work and the dedication—like Josh." I noticed I was pointing vaguely towards his work area. Susan looked like she wanted more, tapping her chin looking a little confused.

"I met a girl in Selfridges last week, she had finished her training at Lovell's, a top law firm, only to decide she hated it and is now happier than ever working at a make-up counter." This was a bit of a cop out, using someone else to justify my decision to bail. Why did I find comfort in these stories? Relief, even? I am not the only person who is messy. People change their minds. Aren't we all secretly confused? Even if took me years to get on the right path that is surely better than staying on the wrong one forever.

Susan finally smiled.

"Okay, Anna. I can't say I didn't predict this may happen."

"Really?" I relaxed my shoulders.

"Even Bruce said he only gave you two weeks, and he has an excellent prediction rate of someone's durability." Susan sounded incredibly sincere about this and who was I to argue. Probably from his experience with his multiple lovers I thought—fortunately, not out loud. "Finish up next week and that way I can pay you a month's work, is that what you want?

"As long as you're sure you don't need me for any longer." I felt suddenly depleted at the fact I was so easily disposable. It was disappointing and yet a complete relief.

"I understand this may not be the right career for you. Though, why don't you believe in yourself more? Why do you think Josh can make it and you can't?" Susan's question forced me to go somewhere I wasn't ready to. I had no idea how to answer. "I don't want you to waste your potential because you certainly have a lot of that."

"Thanks, Sus. that means a lot coming from you."

"I am here if you ever need to talk about any of this stuff. Finding the right career isn't easy, and when you do you have to be prepared for a few bumps and hard work. When you're ready." She spoke softly. Her words were tough nonetheless, and the truth in them resonated with me.

On my commute back all I could think about was how Susan knew I didn't believe in myself, it made me feel uncomfortably exposed. Like I had been walking around with no bra. Didn't I give off the impression I believed in myself? Why was I so scared of admitting I didn't? And how was I ever going to unless I did? I hated admitting any of my insecurities to anyone, like if I didn't speak about them, I could pretend they were not really there.

When I got home a made a promise to myself. *You will start believing in yourself more.* My reflection looked confused, though relatively accepting of the challenge. It wasn't as easy as going out and buying it in bottles. *Good morning, Sir. I will take two bottles of self-belief; oh, and a paper, please.* Ha, if only. It would come though surely. And with that hope in mind and fresh enthusiasm, it was back to the career drawing board to change the colour and paint a new scene.

Susan and I had formed a strong friendship based on wine, drunken honesty, and a shared intolerance for not staying put when something didn't serve us. It was never a work relationship and our friendship has long since continued. She has maintained a genuine interest in my adventures as a jobslut and I have remained a consistent outlet for the slagging of Nigel and the nanny. Which we still do to this day, by the way, Nige, in case you're reading. Logically, if you can't do full-time commitment, the answer must be temping.

Chapter 5
TO TEMP OR NOT TO TEMP

Temping is that place artists, actors, and models go while they wait for their big break. Or jobsluts, of course. I don't get the interview process. It's all a bit serious for a bunch of people that are just looking for part-time work that they are just pissing around with till they can crack on with what they *really* want to do.

So, after some brief pissing around I found myself at the Gucci concession in Selfridges. I have to say I have always liked Selfridges, especially Gucci. I loved having a good old browse at the handbags, belts, and jewellery and the way the staff elegantly presented everything to you with their "dare you to buy it" smiles. I, as a serial jobslut, had at times envied their jobs and am sure I had mentally popped it on the bucket list. You know what they say about visualization. Well, lo and behold, here I was, behind the counter.

If you want to avoid more attitude than Mariah Carey without sleep, avoid a job at Gucci. On one particular occasion during my time as a Gucci sales doll I stepped in to help a sweet bloke (who had probably spent the last few months saving up to buy his girlfriend a bag for her birthday) from being publicly humiliated by an irritating wannabe model called Felicity. For an excruciating five minutes he was tortured by her assumption that since he had entered the Gucci section that he could actually afford all the things in the shop. She was overlooking the first rule of sales: "Know thy customer." Noticing his suffering, I stepped in and got down to business: he left with a small purse—once we established handbags were a little out his price range—and a relieved smile. From that day on my life was hell. Literally none of the girls would talk to me. I was cast to the end of the counter.

I tried to explain to Felicity, "I am not going to stand there and watch you make someone feel uncomfortable." If she is going to make anyone feel so, it might as well be me. The glare in her pretty, scary eyes told me she was going to try her best.

With the attitudes these girls were wearing it was clear which side of that counter they would remain. The Gucci counter was a little like bar work, much better to be on the other side. To give credit where it was due, the girls could gift wrap a pretty awesome box with ribbon whereas I turned into a hot sticky mess at the thought of it. I would try to conveniently pass the task on to someone else after making a sale. It was bloody awful. So was being on your feet for eight hours a day (in heels) and broken up by two pointless fifteen-minute breaks and an hour lunch. By the time you made it through the check in and check out procedure of Selfridges you barely had time to scarf a sandwich. Two weeks and I was over it. My resignation instigated a quick and easy divorce.

Ironically, despite my flippant nature I lasted such a short time temping. The thing is, when I did finally embark on a career I wanted to throw myself in, get involved, feel challenged and inspired by the people around me. The more I tried to get to know myself the more I concluded I made no sense. Temping promised all the traits you would think would appeal to a jobslut. No commitment, moving around so you never really have to get to know anyone, no long-term promises. But it left lacking so much more. Despite being a jobslut I didn't just want affairs, I wanted relationships albeit very short-term ones. They offer loyalty, security, comfort, and the possibility of forever. Temping felt too sleazy.

Chapter 6
A JOB IS A HOME

By this stage in my life I was battling uncertainty about the future and deciding what to do next caused me a little anxiety. Why did everyone around me seem so settled?

I wished I had gone to drama school. I had all these legal qualifications and the last thing I wanted to do was enter another law firm. My friends tried to comfort me.

"It's okay. You're not the first person in the world to change careers," said a friend of the Tweedles who had joined us for a drink at our local pub. As they sat there, dressed in suits and confident about the direction of their futures, I unpinned my name tag, thankfully for the last time, and listened to their condolences.

"Who is Ariel?" Tweedle Dee asked. I looked at the name tag and realised I had been displaying myself as a Disney mermaid for the last two weeks. They all laughed at my surprise. I went to get myself a large wine, keen to catch up with them. All suitably lubricated by alcohol from the stresses of the daily grind. I don't think I was supposed to hear what I did as I returned.

"Anna's mad, walking out on that legal job. I can't understand it. The girl needs to grow some balls and stick at something. I mean from a top law firm to temping? Who actually chooses to climb *down* the career ladder?" A couple of girls laughed.

Tweedle Dee offered some support, "I am sure she will find

her way. Everyone's different; Anna has to move to the beat of her own drum."

Not wanting to hear any more, I approached loudly and slammed my wine down. It was awkward for a moment, though they continued on, assuming I hadn't heard about my lack of balls. The conversation quickly moved on to boys and office antics. I didn't know most of the people they were referring to, still, I enjoyed to hear about it. I tried not to stew over the comments regarding my recent career decisions. Alas, it was marinating with Susan's earlier points and was certainly causing me some emotional discomfort.

I craved something they had; I am not even sure I could put my finger on what it was. It was not exactly a regular job, or a five-year plan. It just would be nice to have an actual idea of what I wanted to do with my life or be comfortable with where I was at. At the moment, I was in career-desire limbo.

So what did I want to next? Where did I fit? One option presented itself during a frantic Google search under "Who will hire me?"

I applied to be an estate agent. Professional enough and not stuck in an office all day, a career in property seemed the perfect anecdote to my dilemma.

"I have an interview with a real estate company," I told my mum, thrilled at how quickly I had bagged that. She never found out about my stint at the law firm. And I hoped she never would, she was already finding it hard to accept I had decided to not pursue law for personal reasons.

"I am your mum! What do you mean, personal reasons? Sometimes I think you forget you spent nine months in my belly; it doesn't get much more personal than that." She had a point, of course, though my secrecy prevented her disappointment so it was best for both of us in the long term.

"So, you will be selling houses?"

Her response reminded me of the time I told her my GCSE results. Despite my desire for her to show enthusiasm in my news, she wasn't quite jumping on board. I could understand her lack of support. Still, it could always be worse. It was not like: "Hey Mum, I am going to become a refuse collector!" Which, for the record, my dad had once suggested. His practical approach to life knows no bounds. I had been dreaming big after a shift in my waitressing days when he knocked me back with:

"Well, best to do something society will always need. What about refuse?"

"Refuge?" I asked, confused. I thought he was talking about some form of humanitarian intervention.

"Yes," he bellowed, like I was an idiot. "You know—a bin man or woman, whatever, it's well paid. My mate John does it and he can get you a job."

I guess it was always an option. The entry-level requirements are minimal which is one thing it has in common with estate agency. Unlike America, in the UK you do not even need a license or to pass an exam so, yes, property vendors: a complete moron could be selling your home. Saying that, I know a few real estate agents in America who are morons and they passed the exams, so it really is luck of the draw.

Back to my good old buddies, the recruitment consultants, who were clearly skilled in search engine optimization. I wondered how many other applicants they had picked up using that all important question, "Who will hire me?" The firm I would be working for was called Cherries and Co., and they specialized in selling gritty council buildings. What they liked to call, "the bread and butter of real estate."

So, I went from selling handbags to selling council houses

in Brixton. For those not familiar with council housing in London, let me paint the picture. Imagine dated blocks of space often decorated with laundry hanging out the windows. Layer that with apartments that had been practically given away to their tenants. The conditions varied from very okay to dire. Regardless, they were now being sold triple the price thanks to a speedy acceleration in the market. We were mere vehicles for the lucky devils to cash in on their luck.

One thing my life certainly had is variety. And that, they say, is the spice of life. If there was one thing I loved about being an estate agent it was the people I met. Sure, there are a few arseholes, though there are arseholes everywhere. You get used to them, like anything. Let's not be too harsh on them. You're not born one, are you? You become one, probably as a result of having to deal with fully-fledged arseholes every day. Before you know it, you have morphed into one. Then these arseholes go around and label one another arseholes, though I guess my point is—it takes one to know one. Apparently bus drivers are forced to encounter the most arseholes every day, so next time you board give the driver a smile, I am sure they could do with it. Every little bit helps.

I do appreciate a company that throws itself into training. It's vital to create the best work force possible. I may not express my gratitude by staying for too long, but at least I pay my dues by doing a decent job while I'm there. Fuel me up with some good training and like a little rocket, off I go. This kept my new manager very happy indeed. She was all a jobslut could wish for in a manager. Hence the reason why when I tried to quit after a month—usual jitter—we ended up just working our way through the cocktail list of the bar next door and celebrating the fact I wasn't going to leave after all. Lasted another six months, which is not bad.

"You're not ready to leave yet. Stay and sell Cornflake Estate with me," she pleaded, and my fifth long island ice tea encouraged me to accept her challenge.

Cornflake Estate was an aptly named deteriorating council block where a young boy had recently thrown a bowl of cornflakes from the tenth floor over my prospective client and me. The incident confirmed my view that this was a friendly place to live, the neighbours even serve you breakfast. Unfortunately my client was not a cornflake guy.

Another reason I did not leave at that point was due to a wonderful work team. Take Grace, our lovable Taurus. She loved oats and horses, as most do. One endearing quality about her was she feared her personal trainer boyfriend might find out she actually loved McDonalds. If we caught her chowing down on a Big Mac for lunch she would literally hide under the table so no one could take pictures. Which we still managed. And sent. Sorry. A fond memory was when she called me in a state of distress to tell me she had locked herself on the roof of a development with some Chinese buyers who spoke no English while it was bucketing it down. I did rush to the rescue, after pissing myself on the floor for about five minutes and informing the whole office, of course.

Once I had learnt the important stuff, like who I could easily delegate the more mundane tasks to (sorry Andrew, old sport), I was selling houses like hot cakes. This initially involved replacing the receptionist with S, my new best friend whom I'd met the morning of my interview.

I was sat perched by the window in the only cafe I could find where they knew what a cappuccino was and was within walking distance. The big coffee chains or even chic independents only bother to establish themselves in the richer postcodes of London. Still, the place had character, the vibe was trying its best to be Italian and had some really enthusiastic staff members.

I was trying my best to stop thinking about how my recently washed hair was absorbing the thick air of bacon grease and enjoy my very okay cappuccino when I heard a loud voice bellowing into a mobile behind me. I turned and saw a bed of red curls bent over a coffee and a bacon sandwich.

"Yes, Dad, I was bored to death, and if this job bores me too I am going back to Australia." She paused. "Yes, I have the interview now. Okay, love you, bum."

Intrigued as to whether her interview was the same as mine and who the bum was, I went over and joined her.

"Are you here for an interview with Cherry and Co.?"

"Yeah, mate, are you? This coffee is shit, isn't it? Nice bacon sarnie, though."

"We better get used to it; looks like it's going to be our local," I replied.

"Looks better than our local pub." We both stared out the window at The Brown Donkey, which stood on its lonesome. A worn-out little pub, which was missing the K. You could just imagine its owners trying to save on refurbishments, *Oh, no need to replace that, no. People can improvise.* Which was fair. The little grey chalked donkey on the board listing some unrecognizable ale also helped.

"It will do. Did I hear you just got back from Oz?"

"Yeah, last month. That was my dad. He's having a mid-life crisis. He's a Cancer and terribly dramatic. I came back because our dog died and now he's having a meltdown."

"Sounds like a familiar story. When's your dad's birthday?"

"22nd of June."

"No way! Mine too. He's also very dramatic, other than when he is drinking beer—his favourite thing to do."

It is one of the best and most rare feelings in the world when you meet someone and you breathe a sigh of relief they exist.

Shan had returned to her family's rescue. They lived in a little town just a few hours from London, though a totally different world. The people were friendlier, the air was fresher and life was slower. Yes, here the people were ruder and pollution levels high, but at least it was London. As we talked our heads off about our lives, our dads, and our extremely low boredom thresholds we learnt more about each other in ten minutes than most people would in a lifetime. From that very first meeting, our friendship was born. Finding Shan was a lot easier than finding The One, in terms of career or romance. And having a best friend is not something to be underrated. It makes life a whole lot more fun.

"I knew I shouldn't have worn these tights today. It puts me in a bad mood. So uncomfortable."

"Go take them off." I pointed to the tiny little toilet door.

"I haven't shaved my legs."

"You can nail this interview with hairy legs far easier than with a bad mood. And let's face it, we both need to get this job and then go over to the Brown Donkey for our first knee's up."

Shan looked at the pub. "Right, I am doing it."

Thank goodness, we both indeed nailed the interview. Alas, we were sent to different offices.

Our friendship deserves a book of its own, an adventure in nonsense. I will share as much as I can with you. I got Shan over to my office soon enough. She had a horrific manager and needed to escape, so I landed her a role as secretary when I attempted to quit. Thankfully, my manager didn't want me to leave and was a smart cookie—she knew if she hired Shan I would stay. So, hire her she did and it was a comfy fit. Though she was a pretty shit secretary, my manager accepted her lack of organisation skills as she was awesome in every other way. Like having her back when she would turn up hours late due to unexpected hangovers and even do her dry cleaning. Life admin was Shan's USP. And she even got to join in on our priceless head-to-knees. Everything was so much better than she was around. She even increased my productivity. We topped up each other's self-belief and grew some balls. Together we were oblivious to our usual sensitivities about life, encouraging our inner children to come out and play. When we were together, anything was possible.

Shan was rather baffled when I first explained to her the concept of the head-to-knee. (Just to recap: the process of laughing so much your head falls to your knee.) So much so that one day I caught her with an unusually serious expression whilst intensely typing on the computer. When she took a toilet break I sneaked a peek at what had been the cause of her deep concentration. I found "head-to-knee" and "star signs" typed into the Google search box. And that in itself is a perfect example of why she's my best mate. She took to the concept like a duck to water and has used it as a measuring tool for how funny something or someone is since. The shorthand when explaining when something was really funny to one another was: "Was it a head-to-knee?" An interesting development has been the "head-to-boob" which indicates a mediocre level of humour.

Shan is a Gemini, my most well-matched sign of the astrological matrix. Gemini is an air sign, the other two being Aquarius and Libra. Naturally, I love them. Do not fret if you are none of the above because each star sign has its good points. One of my friends, a Virgo, actually cried when I tried to explain she wasn't an air sign—bit dramatic. She *was* a Virgo. I could write a book on star signs. What a great idea! I promise to finish this first and I don't often make promises.

I was cruising along quite nicely in this position. Well, actually, while on the subject of cruising, I ended up with three points on my driving license and about three trips to the pound when the bastards kept catching me parking in the wrong bays. Ho-hum. Such is life. The way I dealt with such dilemmas was generally chocolate. As you do. Still those £200 release charges did put an undesirable dent in my salary. There were far better things to spend my money on, like wine, coffee, and petrol. You know, the important stuff.

Things were ticking over nicely for a while with Shan in the office and plenty of entertainment with all the affairs going on. There must be something about working in property that pumps up everyone's sex drive. Seriously, everyone was shagging everyone. The biggest shocker had been the director (aged fifty, slightly grey, and creepy—think Mr Smithers from *The Simpsons*) had been shagging Nadine from the rental department. She was twenty-one, blonde, from Sweden...and the Swedes tend to hit the jackpot in the looks department. The affair was part of her master plan to become manager. Why is beyond me. All that responsibility for a slightly bigger and more regular pay packet? To me, that's like exchanging the hotel room with an ocean view for a guaranteed view of the wall. It's going to be shit, though at least you have it forever. She was sitting proudly on her manager desk before his wife found out. At which point she resigned. Shame, she was good at rentals.

A dangerous side effect of living in London is undirected ambition. You feel in a big rush to achieve something with no connection to whether it's even going to be good for you. I saw a lot of this in real estate. Making lots of money scores highly on the list as does acquiring a position of power with a casual disregard for health and happiness. Not that you can't make money and be happy—I mean, look at Richard Branson, he's hardly miserable.

I can give you a few tips for the road regarding office etiquette. If you are going to joke about anyone, do not do it on email—I've done this. Got caught. The subject of my joke did not find it funny to be called "a slime ball," (my insults never matured past age eight,) nor did he find it funny having to explain the reason behind my joke to the company directors. *I was only joking*, I told them. Alas, the furious faces told me they did not get my sense of humour. Especially the one I had called a slime ball.

Somewhere during my fifth month, I started to feel the fun had been rinsed out of my job sponge. In this particular role, I am proud to say, I stayed a whopping six months. What pushed me off the edge was a guy called Paul George Wood. He came along with his obnoxious attitude and made me want to run for the hills. He referred to women as "skirts," which gives you an idea of the level of vulgar we were dealing with. He was employed by the directors to increase sales with his track record of having that effect on three rival firms. Increasing staff turnover threefold in the process, no doubt.

"Right, all on the phones from nine. till lunch. Anyone that hasn't booked ten appointments has to work bank holiday." Pass me the vodka. The dictator approach was not for me.

So Paul got a big, "See ya later."

Shan decided to leave with me. We decided to stick to working with property. She had an idea about going to a new office in Westminster. So we kick-started new jobs where a whole new world of nonsense awaited. We actually liked it. We just needed fresh faces and scenery. Westminster certainly felt more

London than Brixton. I traded in selling run-down council properties for modern apartments with concierges, in brand-new buildings representing the changing landscape of London. Still, it was much the same. I was pleased to discover my love for the industry and the London property market ranged whole-heartedly from postcodes SE11 to SW1. Nonetheless, my distaste for arseholes remained the same and reality has taught me they are particularly dominant in the world of real estate.

Fresh office. Fresh nonsense. Shan and I melted into the new company Jones and Co., like the smiles on our faces. We realised we had hit the jackpot when we met Linda the receptionist. Think the humour of Joanna Lumley, the fabulousness of Coco Chanel, meets years of keeping it real. Linda was a massive part of what made Jones and Co. feel like home so quickly. There's a lot to be said about the importance of arranging team bonding (drinking.) From fishing trips in caravans to boozy picnics in the park and regular pub visits, Linda has it covered. Getting pissed with your colleagues on a regular basis is a good way to prevent any ongoing feuds. Get drunk, make up, and move on. Simple, yet it works. Maybe that's why my dad always told me not to trust people who don't drink—those guys must be way harder to make up with.

From time to time things got a little out of hand, like when Shan took the title of this chapter a little too far—and ended up sleeping in the office. We had arranged an extreme night out, masterminded by—let's call him Trouble. His extreme nights were a bit of a legacy in company history and it seemed an essential part of becoming a member of the club. They started with cocktails followed by frequenting more clubs in one night than I normally do in year. I woke up in hospital and Shan somehow ended up in the office where luckily Linda found her before the manager did. She cleaned her up before anyone else discovered her messy face.

And me? Trouble had the decency to come and hand collect me from hospital and even took me for breakfast. He felt a tad guilty about plying me with more tequila than I could handle under his strict rule of "go extreme or go home" (or to hospital, as the case may be.)

I sheepishly arrived back at the office in the afternoon. Most wouldn't have spent the afternoon anywhere else than bed, but I managed to neck a couple of Cokes and soldiered on. Seeing me in my fragile state, my manager went easy on me knowing the hardest lessons in life we have to learn for ourselves. Don't drink on a school night. Yet, according to my dad, it's the ones that don't drink that I shouldn't trust—go figure!

One game Shan and I liked to play was to make up a story about our workmates likes that we thought suited them. Take Simon, our office manager. Think Winston Churchill. The man has prime minister oozing out of him. We gave him a wife called Pat, who had dinner on the table when he got home and the coffee brewing when he woke up. He has his three grown-up children over every weekend with the six grandkids. Married for more than fifty years. We got it a tad wrong. Three marriages. Three divorces.

So. In the grand scheme of things, I was learning a lot more than the average price of SW1 by square foot. I was learning a lot about people, and working with a funny bunch of people from all different nationalities and backgrounds. They came from banking and politics; from Romania and Japan. My new company seemed to offer refuge to pretty much anyone wishing to forge a career in real estate.

Certain traits served me well as a property agent. Namely

my relentless optimism to match people with their desired properties no matter what stood in my way. Worried about a mortgage? Oh, you'll get one of those. Can you have the fridge? Yeah, sure, I would say, without checking with the vendor of course. I mean why let a little thing like a fridge negotiation stand in the way of a man and his home? Patience and attention to were still things I was working on. These skills would probably prevent things happening like nearly selling a flat that was never actually for sale. Joking? No.

Being patient and organised can make you are a very helpful human being. Perhaps I will become one some day. Work with what you got, isn't that what they say? So I was doing my best to fit myself into jobs as efficiently as I could, though I often wondered if those organised types that seem to have it all together were actually just pretending.

At least my deficiencies have prevented me taking a bash at certain jobs I would have tried if I thought I could have gotten my foot in the door. Accounting, architecture, secretarial positions. I take my hat off to them. Beauticians, massage therapists—I even find having a manicure a chore. It's the waiting for them to dry bit that really gets me, stuck there with your hands under the dryer is painful. And I always leave that little bit too soon and chip one. Normally while rummaging through my bag. Worse, I try to do them myself, impatience tapping me on the shoulder telling me *You don't want to go and sit in that nail salon for over an hour.* So, what do I do? I do a terrible job which normally results in nail varnish over my body and home, taking the whole lot off and rocking the natural look till I take my sorry arse to the nail salon.

As for accounting, I could have found myself responsible for another recession—which actually helps me put my mistakes in perspective. My point is, if you are shit at something, God made you that way to protect you from a major catastrophe. What a comforting thought.

I sort of want to be more organised, though not enough to actually do anything about it. I go through phases of using diaries and half-heartedly making folders though my enthusiasm for such tasks is soon dissolved by the mundaneness of it all. Shan summed me up wonderfully one evening over a post-work vino when I was declaring myself useless. I had lost a load of pictures, that I had spent the day taking of a new apartment, by pressing the wrong darn button on the camera.

"Oh mate, you're not useless. You're just an organised mess with massive commitment issues." She delivered the news so chirpily it sounded like a compliment, I think we may have cheered too. It did underline the problem I find with being an employee in most situations. How is that for a CV bio?

To a degree being organised requires dedication or a really good PA. Until I can afford the latter it's something I am going to have to get by without.

Selling houses is a very chaotic business. Every day presents new challenges. Shoes breaking on the way to viewings, wrong keys, no keys, tenants shagging during viewings, estate children throwing cornflakes on your head whilst with clients. You know, that kind of thing. I was not the only one who suffered from real estate problems. Take the day Chloe, a top friend and top negotiator rocked up in the office with mismatched shoes. Poor love.

The daily grind eventually takes its toll. There comes a point where the above average amounts of caffeine, emergency weekly piss ups, and the buzz of doing a deal are no longer getting you through. Once this point is reached, what you going to do? Move to L.A. and try and become an actress, of course!

Chapter 7
TAKING ON HOLLYWOOD

Decision made, flight booked, Shan in tow. I was good to go. Emotions ran high the week before leaving, it was rather overwhelming. You do not realise how much you mean to people till you decide to leave the country. And you do not realise how much they mean to you till you get to your new one. Though sunshine, beach, and meeting a whole load of awesome new people goes some way to helping you cope.

Landing in Los Angeles felt so natural. As we breezed through the city to our new apartment, chatting along to the friendly cab driver, I had the sense this was something I was meant to do. Like leaving a really bad boyfriend or, in my case, job. Or you know, brushing your teeth before bed. Something you will later thank yourself for.

"Are you an actress?" The cab driver called back. "You look familiar."

I imagined what it would be like to answer back with a *Yes, have you seen my new feature?* My first L.A. daydream.

Instead I told him, honestly, "Right now I don't know what I am." Shan laughed at that.

"You're a very nice, beautiful lady—you both are. I love your accents. Are you Australian?"

"No, one hundred percent British," Shan piped up. Though if I had a dollar for every time I got asked that in L.A., I would be sitting in my Malibu beach house. Funny thing is,

I was actually rubbish at doing an Aussie accent, go figure.

L.A. felt electric. At certain times my reckless decision making process serves me well. This one was made with a prayer and complete faith in my last six-months savings. I would have to be careful with my spending. Though how expensive could it be here? I would live on sunshine if I had too. I had said goodbye to buildings drenched in history, coating London in its cultural depth. I had bid farewell to Tesco, Marks & Spencer, and see you later to the M25. Hello Hollywood glamour, beach vibes, the freeway, and Trader Joe's. The landscape of L.A. was as refreshing as an ice-cold drink on an unbearably hot day. My new commute involved a twenty-minute bike ride along the ocean with views towards Malibu, dodging through the chaos of Venice beach. A vibrant mix of pop-up shops, work out stations, hotdog and Shake Shacks which offered hospitality to all—from celebrities to the homeless. You could literally buy anything along the beach—coconut water, weed, even puppies. All of which were purchased in due course.

Our new pad was styled by someone who may have purchased a lot of item number two on the list above. This would explain the inspiration behind the décor. A feminine hippy vibe we meshed with. Santa Monica was scattered with vintage shops allowing you to dress in a way you could only get away with in L.A. Soon we had purchased flowery dresses, straw hats, slogan t-shirts and even rucksacks. They were far more comfortable than handbags when cycling up and down Venice beach, the sunshine-drenched trail to acting school. Shan had decided to give a few classes a bash too. In L.A. acting was fair game to anyone who had the balls to give it a go. I loved hearing stories about rising stars and established actors who had turned up to try their luck and made it against a backdrop of varying adversity.

The crowd was a diverse blend of cultures and imaginations. Many women simply strutted around in their gym wear, with no intention to go to the gym or to deny that they hadn't been. All the pressure of being a certain someone, or doing things a certain way, dissolved as La La Land happily became our home.

We filled our apartment with flowerpots, pastel colours, and random things we bought from artists on the beach. I felt like a different person, now safely enveloped in the dreamy aura of Los Angeles.

One morning as we cycled on our blue and white bikes towards Malibu, the ocean breeze blowing in our hair, Shan called back, "Mate, this is the happiest I have ever been." It was the perfect moment to sum up how L.A. made me feel. A place where anything was possible, a place to find yourself, if you don't get lost that is.

Speaking of lost, our landlords were a little bonkers. They had been waiting to greet us when we arrived and openly informed us they were just back from a retreat to work on their marriage. They had been married only six months. He looked like a model, as a lot of the men in L.A. did. He had a casualness about him that made him seem a bit vacant. She was a fully-fledged hippy enjoying a joint as we went over the paperwork. We declined to toke up despite the generous offer. The misshaped, chunky, wax candles that were dripped around the lounge smelt a delicious lemony vanilla. Not quite as delicious as what sat directly over the road: The Cheesecake Factory, foot-sized slices of cheesecake, seriously good appetizers, and a great wine list. Just what you need when your competition are size-six actresses competing to work for free. The choices of travel— sitting in traffic for hours or risking the bus full of fruit loops—made walking and cycling so appealing. Shan and I shuffled off our arses on the daily back and forth across Venice Beach. I could not think of a better place or way to lose your butt.

So, what was it about L.A. that Shan and I liked so much? Well, it was full of our favourite thing—nonsense. The first day of trekking down to school on Main Street (love the way Americans refer to every learning institution as school even though it is full of eighteen- to fifty-year-olds), I casually asked one of the world's best-known male actors for directions. I played it so cool he actually laughed at me as he pointed out I was practically at my destination. Nice chap and he was wearing orange trainers that inspired my lifelong love affair with Nike footwear. The school was tucked away behind a Coffee Bean and Ben and Jerry's. An open bar was on the left where a handful of aspiring actors were having lunch and beers. I took a moment: a bar, coffee, *and* ice cream? I couldn't believe my luck.

As I entered the building a short blonde-haired girl smoking at the front informed me that this acting school had played host to training the likes of Gerard Butler and some other guy who's name I forget—the Gerard Butler reference got my attention.

"Really?" My impressed expression urging her on.

"Yeah, Gerard I hear made it high up the ranks in law before tossing it all in for the stage. I take my hat off to him." She told me in a warm American accent as she flicked her cigarette butt into the bin.

"Have you acted before?" She studied my face, an intense curiosity about her that no amount of questioning seemed to satisfy. For every answer I gave she lined up another enquiry.

"Seriously, you have never been to L.A.? It's like trying strawberry bubblegum for the first time, isn't it? You can't imagine life without it."

"Are you not from here?" Shan piped in from over my shoulder.

"No, not originally. I ran away from home. Boston girl, my mum told me I was good for nothing so I came here to prove her wrong. I have always known I will be a star." She raised her left hand in the air in utter confidence. I was blown away by her bluntness and amazing comparison between L.A and strawberry bubblegum, if you pardon the pun.

"I'm Betsy." She curtsied and told us to come inside to meet some others.

I loved how homely it was. A little office for reception manned by the students wanting part-time work. A few chairs and tables outside the teaching rooms where students would hang out and rehearse lines. The main teaching room was dark, rustic, and set up like an old cinema with fold-up chairs surrounding the wooden stage. Here students would put in hours of work: breathing classes, on-camera sessions, voice work, and scene practice in hope of making it to the big time.

The students ranged from American to Australian and everything in between.

Shan and I slotted in nicely, adding a good dose of British to the international scene.

We quickly established a group of friends including Betsy.

Dean was our coach. He deserves a mention, for being not only the first, but best coach I have encountered. He had the ability to make us feel like he was one of us. He was totally in on all our jokes, understood our fears, and appreciated our journeys.

He taught us to respect and support each other instead of competing. Telling us to remain humble always. Once he auditioned for a part to realize the director was one of his ex-students. He never mentioned if he got booked; still, it taught us there is no hierarchy in acting anything is possible.

Watching yourself back on camera was sometimes torture and sometimes hilarious. Alas, it was the only way to get rid of all the bad habits that can disrupt a scene. Did you even realise how much you raise your eyebrows when you speak? Are you an intensive blinker? Go and have a chat with yourself in the mirror you might learn a lot. We certainly did. And the results were there in front of us, as we moved through the course it was great to see how Betsy's brows calmed themselves down, everyone slowed down their talking, I became less intimated by a camera and Shan definitely lost some facial weight.

After putting herself on a diet, she proudly told Dean, "I replaced beer with wine."

Dean pushed us out of our comfort zones. He formed an improv group where he would throw us on stages around L.A. with a variety of audiences that we tried to make laugh. We wouldn't even question waiting around till late in the evening for a fifteen-minute set. The feeling of being on stage with no idea what was going to happen next or what the audience might be like was a situation we became familiar with. Yet it never became less exciting. To hear a laugh gave you the best natural high. On the drive home we would breathe in the city lights, charged by the electricity of the starry night. On those nights, it was so hard to sleep.

A good coach is like a painter with a palette of colors who darkens and lightens your shades. Dean was an exceptional painter and we were his devoted colours. We were comprised of Emma and Rox, our French flags. Then there was a feisty German with her travel companion (the only girl to have flown her Chihuahua halfway around the world with her.) Also, a great girl from Texas who solidified my view that everyone that comes from down south is nice with bells on. She was like the social glue, making sure we all stayed together. Always arranging movie nights where we would gather at someone's pad and binge on our favourite classics, order pizza, and talk till the early hours with our ideas for pilots, auditions, and the like. We became like a little family, which was nice. We all genuinely supported each other which was a nice blanket of comfort in the bigger picture that was L.A. We kept an eye on each other, though most of our eyes were on Betsy. If there was a girl that would go the distance to get the part, she was your girl.

Once, Betsy told me that her mum thought she was good for nothing, and that barely touched the surface of what the poor girl had been through. She had been badly beaten by her mum and various boyfriends, both physically and mentally. She opened up to us slowly about the awful past she had left behind.

"Mum loved crack more than me," was the way she summed it up. The deep damage made me wonder if acting was the best place for her; she had a worrying detachment from herself masked in an over-the-top confidence. You scratched the surface and were met with a tender vulnerability—it was something directors took advantage of.

One particular time she called me in the middle of the night, having been partying after an audition with a director who then left her in a hotel, off her head, and in the middle of nowhere. Shan and I figured out where she was and went to collect her. We had to nurse her back to normal at the hippy flat. We still don't know the full extent of what went on that night.

"What does it matter? I can't change a damn thing about the past," said Betsy.

"Yeah, you can start changing your future, though, and you will. Stop treating yourself like you don't matter. You are going on this." I held out a brochure for an "Emotional Release" course in Santa Monica that one of my friends had been though. The course leader had such a phenomenal heart and reputation that she had her students talking about her for the rest of their lives, it seemed. Betsy resisted at first, though after enough encouragement she went.

Seeing her after the four weeks was as if a magic wand had been cast over her. She was filled with a new type of energy, and a smile that finally looked like it belonged on her face. Betsy's new smile had everyone talking. Her engine was refueled now with the right type of energy, the kind that could take her anywhere.

"For the first time, Hollywood, I am really ready for you," she said one night as we finished milkshakes at a diner on Sunset Boulevard. And for the first time, we believed her.

Studying and slogging one's guts out in L.A. with castings, late night shows, and intensive study sessions taught me there is a lot more to acting than remembering your lines. I can understand very easily how people can lose themselves in a whirlwind of false hope and bullshit. It requires a thick skin, a lot of determination, and a high threshold for criticism and rejection. (Yes, some criticism is constructive and some is at the total discretion of a director who can be an arsehole—I have never been a fan of either.) This is the one field in which you will get a lot more criticism than the average human is supposed to tolerate. I remember, after a particularly trying day, being told Dustin Hoffman still takes classes and finding unexpected comfort in that. I like the idea that you're never too old or advanced to stop learning, even when you think you have seen and learnt it all, someone can offer you a new perspective or new idea.

The setting of L.A. provides the perfect backdrop for the actor's dream. An abundance of tarot card shops, endless beach, bright lights of Hollywood, and beautiful mansions decorating Beverly Hills inspire the notion that anything is possible. Perhaps this setting is a massive reason why there are so many artists still hanging on to their ambition. The directors with the golden tickets to transition you to an overnight success can be found at their familiar haunts. Smug and surrounded by pretty young waitresses hoping to get noticed for more than her server skills. Not all of them, of course, thank goodness. This occasionally happens. One girl I know after a year of circuiting the L.A. cattle market bagged herself a job at The Rose Hotel and three weeks later a director asked for her card and she booked her first feature. You just never know, eh?

Having met a few working actors whilst in L.A., each with varying degrees of success, I found that, like a lot of professions in life, people can range from amazingly nice and humble to utter twats. Some have allowed curiosity to lead them in the wrong direction. Obviously, I preferred the nice ones.

Whether you want to be an actor or not, going on stage and performing in front of a room full of strangers is something I would advise everyone to do at least once. The beauty of a live performance is it's a bit like life, raw, unpredictable and full of possibility. You do not know what is going to happen. Will you remember your lines? Will your co-star forget theirs? Yes, it happened to me. I guess this is where improvisation training as an actor is essential. Though life in itself gives you a daily practice. The key skill learnt from failing in improvised scenes, as an actor, is the ability to embrace awkwardness like it isn't a thing. Case in point, when my stepmother forgot her lines, leaving me hanging like a load of laundry. (Did you notice the pun?) I think by breezing over my co-stars absent memory into the next scene, I kind of saved the day, or play. Not sure if the audience noticed—unfortunately you cannot run on stage after the curtains go down and say, "Hey guys, how did I do? Notice I fluffed my lines?" Nope. If you hear applause, bow and run.

Still, I guess my early days as a waitress on display to the world and their dog stood me in good stead for embracing the awkward. Just like a day running a busy cafe. No matter what happens the show must go on. And it did.

So what should the aspiring actress prepare herself for? Well, regular headshots, attending events, and creating your own material is essential. Or so everyone tells you. Don't get me wrong though, some people do get lucky. I heard one world-famous star went from model to actress in one audition with no previous experience, booked her first feature and the rest was history.

My advice for anyone who really wants to make it as an actor in L.A.: find a good coach, surround yourself with positive hard workers who are actively writing their own material. If you are going to work for free it might as well be on your own stuff or for credit-worthy show reel material. Oh, and avoid sleazy directors.

My first role was in a cynical take on Walt Disney's version of events called *Happily Whatever After*. And what a colourful cast it was. I was a contemporary Cinders who was not so fussed about Prince Charming. Sleeping Beauty and I were more concerned with wine than romance. Who could blame us? In this unfortunate version of events, Cinders's lousy father abused her. As for my co-star Ariel, she was head over heels (or fin) in love with Prince Eric. Happy ending? No. It turned out he preferred princes himself. Poor love. She took getting into character to the extreme when she turned up on stage totally wasted.

And did I meet any real-life Prince Charmings? Did I not mention Tom? He came to my acting scene class. There was something about him from the first day we met. He asked to borrow a pen and sat next to me on my first class, much to my delight. He was the kind of gorgeous you couldn't stop staring at, which is why I kept expecting him to be an asshole. He just wasn't. He was so nice to everyone, and me in particular. We fell into a casual friendship; I would provide pens and he would help me practice lines, always looking to help me improve myself in any way possible. He had a way of delivering gentle constructive criticism that motivated me to do better.

The downside: he had a girlfriend, Stacy. Of course he did.

She was a bossy boots. Always pulling him away from class early or demanding he do things for her, she would snap her fingers and he would come running. I had no idea why, there seemed to be some hold she had over him—because, seriously, why else would you miss out on watching your favorite scene to go get your girlfriend a milkshake? That actually happened. He missed the final *Pride and Prejudice* scene a group had been performing as she claimed if she did not have a strawberry milkshake within five minutes she would have an anxiety attack. Yes, L.A. can be that ridiculous.

Tom seemed gutted when he returned.

"So did they do a good job?" he had asked, eagerness in his eyes.

"They were okay, and I took notes for us to work on." He had such a talent and would do anything to work on his craft. He worked every shift he could get at a coffee joint on Venice beach to pay for his classes and the studio apartment he rented nearby. Stacy didn't work. Her dad was a producer, so she was safe in the comfort that she already had a foot in the door if she actually wanted to act. Did she use that to help Tom? No, she didn't seem to give a monkey's ass. I once heard her tell him he might as well get a job in finance.

"You're never going to be the next Brad, let's face it". He never told me why he was with her, though it seemed there was a secret he was keeping. I guess my acting lessons were teaching me to read between the lines.

Tom and I never even kissed, though there was a feeling more than friendship when we looked in each other's eyes and an electricity around us when we were together. We spent gorgeous nights on the beach practicing our lines and watching the sunset. The closest we got to intimacy was him putting his hand on mine one night as we sat in silence after a scene from *Down with Love*. We had finished the romantic part yet he didn't let go for long after. We both pretended it wasn't happening. As tempting as it was to kiss those soft lips, I resisted. It was easier that way.

Tom made me realize that when we find what we really want, we go for it one hundred percent. He was so focused on his craft. And he was seriously talented. You may get the odd Stacy, sure. The ones that get a lucky break because their dad's a producer. Though real talent, determination, and hard work is what you need for a long fulfilling career. I just wasn't sure I had it in me the way Tom did. I certainly didn't have Tom's stamina.

My enthusiasm for the profession came to a halt halfway through an audition for a chewing gum advert. I was finally called in after waiting more than an hour while listening to some hopeful American beauties chewing gum and repeating the one line for the advert—I felt drained before my first foot entered the door.

As the three directors looked at me and told me to introduce myself, I managed to spit out my name. I then rushed my lines and left with a half-joking, "Call me." And you know what? They did! I declined the part. Funny, weeks later I saw one of the girls from the audition smiling proudly on the advert and billboards displaying the now internationally famous gum. It went to the right girl. I don't even like gum. And didn't fancy having to be contracted to chew it for an indefinite period of time. My energy and enthusiasm for becoming a Hollywood Star had dwindled over the last few weeks. I was pretty sure Tom had something to do with it. My feelings for Tom left me feeling frustrated. I had a serious thing for him, and at the same time I envied and admired how career-wise he knew exactly what he wanted. Shame he couldn't be so certain on the girl front. His dedication to the profession forced me to self-reflect. He would sacrifice anything to make his follow his passion and make his dream come true. Would I? No, probably not. I was bailing again, chasing a dream then running away from it the minute it stands a chance of coming true. It threw me into a very confusing place. When would I find the thing I wanted to run into and not from. When would I find the thing I could throw my heart and soul into like Tom? How could I not know my passion?

Ironic, I admired those who followed their passion so much and always had. Coach Dean especially. From maths to acting, I gravitate to passionate teachers who are doing what they love. You soak all that up and it shines out of you.

Years of research have proven the effects of the energy we surround ourselves with. Friends, family, teachers, work colleagues. It is so important they make us feel alive, good and passionate. Negativity is a disease that can spread like wild fire. And quite frankly, I do not know what's worse. I believe negativity is responsible for a whole host of problems people try and blame on way more complicated stuff. Take addiction. Tests were done on rats that, when put in a negative environment, chose to continuously consume morphine-laced water. Rats put in a happy environment chose the regular water. Just saying, all those negative people out there, y'all: keep that shit to yourselves and we might have a lot less people in rehab.

So perhaps the reason I have not landed myself with any major addictions so far is all that positive energy I surround myself with. And for that, I am thankful. Though life without ice cream and chardonnay would be incredibly testing. We are all born with beautifully simple souls. The social, family, and logistical situations we find ourselves in slowly erode at this in different levels with different effects. Gradually as we cover up parts of who we are as a means of avoiding rejection, abandonment, and disapproval we develop unnatural behaviours to help us deal with not being able to express our true selves.

Having been exposed to different levels and types of criticism I quickly realised unless they are truly constructive it is normally an expression of other's fears and insecurities. Not everyone is going to get you, but so what? As Oscar Wilde said: "Be yourself, everyone else is already taken." Another wise person once told me to go where you are celebrated, not tolerated. These are words I've tried to take to heart.

For my dream career, there were no wedding bells yet. I had fallen in love with L.A., though. And Tom a little bit. The gorgeous sunrises and sunsets, laidback vibes, and endless beach drenched everyone with happiness. L.A. broke off a piece of my heart as I cycled home past the ocean one evening. The gentle night sky was decorated with bright stars burning with hopes, dreams, and wishes. I blew mine into the air and imagined it drifting up like a balloon as I pedaled faster.

Sadly, after only six months, a stubborn visa situation forced our separation. Shan had been accused of trying to mess with the system and was forced to book a flight home or be deported. My visa was due to expire in less than a week and faced with the decision of actual marriage to an American citizen or returning home with my best friend. I chose the latter.

I spent my last night with Tom. As we shared ice cream on Venice beach and said our goodbyes he promised the next time he saw me, it would be in London.

"You can take me to all you favorite places, Anna." He wiped a hair away from my face and cupped my face in his hands. For a moment I thought he was going in for a kiss, instead he took a bite of my ice cream. We really wanted a bite of each other, I felt. That would have to wait; another lifetime, maybe?

Chapter 8
BACK WHERE WE STARTED

Arriving back in Heathrow on a grey morning wasn't as painful as I'd imagined. Surely I should have been more disappointed I wasn't returning a fully-fledged Hollywood star?

Maybe it would hit me like a brick later. Right now, I had butterflies to see all the people I had waved goodbye too not so long ago. I couldn't wait to see the Tweedles's faces when I presented them with their personalized Venice beach T-shirts. And the suitcase of candy I would use to bribe them to wear them. The happy thought occupied me as I waited for my suitcases and rushed through customs.

My mum had insisted on collecting us, but neither of us dared sit with her in the front. She was far too energetic for our jet lag to tolerate. She chatted away to herself while we intermittently listened. Here we were back where we started.
"Take me back, mate." Shan looked far more miserable than I felt. She suffered terribly with holiday blues. Returning from a week in Benidorm could leave her believing she had mild depression so you can imagine January wasn't the best month after six months of L.A. sunshine. Also, it didn't help she had been asked by her dad to come home and help with the family business which, given a lack of other options, she accepted. Still it was nice to know you could always go home.

Obviously, I was coming back to no job. I have friends who have proper jobs like teachers and accountants who take holidays off then return back to work and carry on like nothing happened. I can't quite believe it. One particular crazy cat went backpacking for six months, all planned and agreed by her employer then returned to her position as PE teacher as if nothing happened. These are proper people. Perhaps I am not a proper person? I remained hopeful that one day I could become one. Another ladder I would probably take a jump from still would be interesting to see how it felt.

I awaited a barrage of questions about how I had taken Hollywood by storm. Honesty was the best policy. No Oscar, no Golden Globe. I was already secretly fantasying, and had been on the plane home, about what job I could try next. The rebound. I was taking refuge in that I had now covered a fair bit of ground. I was at least getting to know myself a little better. Maybe I didn't have to rule things out the second they didn't work out.

"L.A. isn't the only place to act," Shan told me on the plane home. She had a good point. "Don't be too hard on yourself, you don't have to be perfect or the best. You're good enough as you are." The verbal pat on the back came at a good time. A reminder I could only try my best.

Shan was the best. She had stood by me through every crazy decision I made. Cheering me on with unconditional support—friendships like ours were hard to find. We all get sent that one person in life that makes you feel less crazy. They get you, you get them and you know that they will always be in your life. I loved her frizzy hair she refused to straighten, as she simply couldn't be arsed. I loved the fact she took less time than me to get ready. I loved how she was wearing flip–flops and shorts even though her feet were already turning white. Finding each other was such a relief. And I was so lucky to have a friend that really cared about my happiness. Case example, she took a second date with a guy she would rather never see again because the most amazing carrot cake we had ever tasted was his grandmother's recipe and she forgot to get it from him the first time around. And trust me, that carrot cake makes me very happy

Shan was right. Perhaps I should give the London scene a bash before ruling that out. It was an option and meant I didn't have to compete with half of America. I tried to keep an open mind. I forget so quickly what drew me to a job in the first place when I feel it's time to move on.

I bounced a few other job ideas around whilst bobbing through air turbulence: maybe luxury travel consultant. Hey, I know what you're thinking. *Who does that? Who goes from actress to travel consultant in one idea bubble?* I do, guys. That's the problem. It was the strict office hours that put me off. Also the sending others off to exotic locations—that was bound to piss me off after a while. Running a dating agency? Did that require a good romantic track record? I really wasn't sure. Shan was snoring next to me after making sure she got her fair share of free wine, demonstrated by the red stains decorating her peacefully poised lips. So, without anyone to further discuss the whirlwind of options in my brain, I had decided on a vague plan. I'll see what acting work I could find while I further pursue my next career.

It would satisfy my mum's inevitable, "What are you going to do now?" and make me feel slightly less lost.

Guess what? London wasn't the place my acting career would take off. I am not even sure I hoped it would, despite that being what I had told my mum.

"So you are going to carry on acting in London, aren't you?" Poor thing. She had by this point got quite excited at the prospect of having an actress for a daughter. I felt a tad bad building her hopes up if next thing I'm a waitress again.

"I do hope so," had been my hesitant reply. Still there are worse places to put you hope, I guess.

Do not get me wrong, I managed to find more work than in L.A. I found myself in a few strange situations that became a tad off-putting. Like when I got offered the apparently once-in-a-lifetime chance to become a porn star. Some director making shorts exploring personality types calls me in for an audition, which involved crawling along the floor then posing against a number of backgrounds. So that was his beat around the bush, if you pardon the pun. Next thing I know he's trying to put a deal on the table. After telling the short little shit he was no Hugh Hefner and should be clearer on the explicit content he was calling people in for as to not waste the time of those who don't fancy following the careers steps of Linda Lovelace, I was off. I think I will stick to the Porn Star martinis if it's all the same to you, love. Which are, for the record, definitely worth trying. Maybe if the douche bag served a load of those before delivering his pitch he may get a few more signing on the dotted line. Even if it's down to intoxication.

Oh, bad decisions. We have all made them, haven't we? I was recently sent a video clip featuring an ex-porn star who was trying to break into the nursing industry and was terribly upset no one was taking her seriously, as she would always be tainted by her past. It was from Tweedle Dee, with a text that followed saying "Probably best you turned down the porn, imagine if you wanted to go into nursing?" Her intentions were good. I guess the reality is the only person your past taints is yourself, and this influences how you think people perceive and judge you. Working on self-belief means letting go of past decisions. I am reading a book about it.

My passion for acting had started burning bright and was now a flickering flame keeping me auditioning in London. By the time I did actually start getting offered roles I had thoroughly had enough. My friends and family thought I was insane to say no. But, I had to follow my intuition. Which was telling me: keep going, you'll find what's right for you. All you need is belief, trust, and maybe a little vodka. In fact, those three ingredients can get you through a lot of life's hardships. Though it's good to get focus of the first two, as they will see you through anything without the hangover.

Enjoying oneself is a fundamentally important part of life, it does seem society tries to persuade us otherwise. Moments of enjoyment should be reserved for the weekend, break times, and holidays of which you are granted ten to twenty days per year. And we wonder why there are so many poor souls suffering from anxiety, stress, depression, addictions, and nervous breakdowns. Pressure manifests itself in the foundations of many corporations. It is passed down from the hierarchy of people at the top to the lesser-paid employees at the bottom. At least those in the higher paid positions signed up for the pressure and are rewarded accordingly. Further down the company the more unjust the pressure cooker becomes, and they absorb it all in the hopes it will get them to the top. Or they are too busy to notice. I guess at least if you're doing something you're passionate about, whether that is making socks, taking care of the sick, or making coffee, if it all goes tits up you can somehow justify how you spent your time. We have to try our best to find enjoyment in as much of the day as possible.

This can be challenging, finding your passion. What was mine? I felt like *Sex in the City*'s Charlotte did about dating when she declared, "I've been dating since I was fifteen! I'm exhausted! Where is he?" Though she did eventually find her true love, so I felt optimistic and hopeful my future career was out there too.

I decided it was time for me to figure out who I was, before losing myself in pretending to be someone I wasn't. And being away from the camera allowed me more of the opportunity to do so. Confronting myself definitely proved a challenge. Shan called me one morning I was feeling particularly overwhelmed. She had been with me through my box of life experiences, which made her the easiest person to talk to. Different people in my life only know one side to me, and so they expect you to only reveal that side. There are only a few people I know who get the whole combined self. The Tweedles, for example, can only relate to my relentless optimism, my "everything will be okay" side, despite my constant career break-ups. They wouldn't know how to deal with me if they found me wanting to pour my heart out over the fact I am beginning to question if, for me, "the one" even exists—and it would also be nice to have a boyfriend or at least a consistent date. And that I wondered if I was a lost cause. Shan, however, I could talk to about such life concerns, as I know she just gets me. And when all else fails, we turn to our horoscopes.

She must have sensed my low mood.

"What's up?" Being straight to the point was one of Shan's best traits. "Do you want your daily?" By "daily" she meant my daily horoscope.

"Go on then," I replied. I didn't exactly have any other guidance knocking at the front door.

"It's time to start putting the wheels in motion to achieve what your heart desires. Be prepared for some opportunities coming your way that way you can make the most of them. Many dreams come true just before you give up, keep going and focus on your goals."

"Thanks, Mate. That helped. I need to start working hard on my dreams and not expecting things to just land in my lap. I seem to start running after them then running away from them. A bit like Julia Roberts in *Runaway Bride*, but more like the Runaway Employee."

Shan agreed. Another of the many things I loved about her was her contentment with the simple things in life. She could always be cheered up by some good food and a few beers no matter how grave the problem. And as long as she could pay the bills, doing something not too demanding, she was happy as Larry.

"I'm sure you'll come across something. And I bet it'll be weird this time." Boy, did Shan turn out to be right.

Chapter 9
PREPARING THE DEAD

There are a few times in life I ask myself quite seriously, *What is wrong with you?* As I pushed my way through the doors of my new office in Shoreditch and breathed in the dusty atmosphere that complimented its theme entirely, this is precisely what my inner monologue was asking.

How and why had I found myself here, in this small little funeral parlor sprinkled with a few surprisingly perky-looking coworkers ready to get all trained up as a mortician? Good question. Well, it all came about last Saturday. I had coffee with an old friend who had just had a member of their family pass away and the funeral director managing the departure arrangements had dropped by to go over the final preparations. His name was Percy—what a brilliant name. His face reminded me of the little pink pigs you find in pick-and-mix. He was so calm and collected yet oozed a peculiar enthusiasm for his work which, if nothing else, intrigued me. Much to my friend's bemusement Percy and I fell into a long conversation about everything from how to take a phone call from a person arranging the funeral of a loved one to what make up you apply to the deceased. I was so thrilled by his profession; thinking back, I was quite sure no one had ever expressed as much excitement as I had over his involvement with the departed. So, it was likely a mixture of my sheer flattery and his pity for an out-of-work actress that led him to offer me the position.

"You would not believe it, but our receptionist has just left. We are looking for someone to start ASAP. Someone who is happy and not afraid to be hands-on. You would be perfect."

I did stop for a second and contemplate my decision. I stared briefly at friend then back to Percy.

"Yes!"

I had a friend at school whose dad owned a funeral parlor. I remember asking him one day what had inspired his dad to start the company. It was an old business passed down by generations. Figures. Really, who wakes up one day and thinks *Let's become funeral directors*? It seems life just takes you where you're supposed to be and if that is death's doorstep, then best just get on with it.

On Monday morning I arrive and am pleasantly surprised with the joyful atmosphere at the funeral parlor. Very happy indeed—and then in walks Jen. With Jen came a force of energy that made you want to hide. Or get into Child's Pose. She exuded authority. She was responsible for the most important part of the business, preparing the dead bodies for their funerals. I noticed the general background banter in the office dissolve as she went about banging a few files on her desk and changing her dark cherry Mulberry coat which matched her handbag nicely, though I think she was pushing it with the matching shoes. She stepped into brown overalls. Charles, who had been running me through introductions, spat out a hello like a fart that needed releasing. Jen acknowledged, said hello, then pushed through another door at the back of the office with the same sense of urgency that she had entered the office. It still took around ten minutes for the office to return to its previously calm equilibrium, enveloped by the safe knowledge, I later learnt, that she was unlikely to return till lunchtime.

Percy had ever so kindly offered to shout me lunch as a welcome gesture. When he asked what I wanted, I told him to surprise me. My only condition was no meat, as I had decided to become a vegan for a week. Or a day, at least, but he returned with stinking KFC. Chicken burgers for the team, and a tin of cold beans for me. I regretted my decision immediately. Five minutes after my little tub of beans were placed in front of my desk, a corpse was delivered.

I had never seen a corpse before. Given the option when my Grandpa had passed away, I opted for not participating in his viewing. I preferred to remember him alive, full of color and vitality. As I looked at the dead person now, I was very happy I made that decision. I was mesmerized by how still it was. I had never seen a body so heavy and still. The dead person did not look as old as dead people should look. He was only in his forties and his mouth was open. My skin felt prickly and arm hairs stood to attention as I tried to stop looking at him.

Suddenly Jen appeared from the backroom like a real-life Powerpuff girl. She ushered the guys to transport the corpse to her back room where it would undergo embalming. I was left quite disturbed. It was easy for me to sit on the receptionist desk and write Jen off as a hard-nosed cow though she needed a tough edge to numb her to dealing with the dead. How scary. I wondered whether our jobs set the tone for how we handled all other areas of our lives. Did Jen go home and leave her Powerpuff powers behind? Or did she need them to sleep at night?

I hadn't ventured downstairs to where the bodies went. I wasn't sure I was brave enough. I did want to see what Jen was doing down there, though. There was only one way to find out: I was going down. It had been about thirty minutes since Jen had ordered the corpse to be taken down. I wasn't sure I was even supposed to go down to the embalming and viewing rooms. I took my moment while Percy and the office were busying themselves with their computer screens. Ask forgiveness, not permission was my go-to approach in these kinds of situations.

I followed the noises, taps and splashy sounds came from the room on the left. I knocked on the door, warning Jen of my unexpected visit.

"Come in." She sounded distracted.

"Anna, what are you doing down here? It's out of bounds." The room stank of anti-septic. It felt suitably depressing.

"I was seeing if you wanted a coffee."

"I am fine. I think Mr Cook is, too."

I looked at the dead body draped over the table from which Jen was working. Giving him a name was a harsh reminder this was a real person, who not so long ago had been a fully functioning person. A person, who may have said yes to a cup of coffee, a dad, brother, son and friend.

He didn't look old enough to be dead. I had read about people dying, heard about it in the news, read about it in books. Though to see death right in front of my face it became a reality for the first time. Jen sensed my processing and softened her sarcasm.

"Is this the first time you have seen a dead body?"

"Yes. In real life, it is."

"Okay, it can be a bit of a shock."

"How did he, er, how did he…" I was finding it hard to get my words out, my gaze fixed on Mr Cook.

"Cardiac arrest. Trust me, I have seen a lot worse." Jen was calmly rubbing some balms into his face.

"Wow," I was lost for words. Mr Cook's arm flopped of the side of the table, making me jump. Jen noticed my flinch and

I could have sworn she smiled beneath her paper mask that covered her mouth and nose. "How do you deal with this, Jen? How do you sleep at night?"

"Same as I always have, in comfy pajamas." She said. "The hardest part of this job is not making them look like this. It's meeting the family. I once had a young girl thank me for making her mummy look like a princess and give me a letter she wanted to put in her hand when her mummy goes underground."

"Did you read the letter?"

"Yes."

"What did it say?"

"Daddy told me you have fallen asleep forever. I will miss you, Mummy. I hope you wake up one day. Love you always. Grace."

I felt a tear trickle down my face. "That's so sad and so sweet."

"I know. So, no, this job doesn't affect my beauty sleep. Though, honestly, dealing with the emotions of their loved ones is the most rewarding and exhausting."

"I can see that."

I had a newfound respect for Jen and was suddenly intrigued by her. I wanted to know more about her. How did she become a mortician?

"Since I have never seen a dead body before, I for one could certainly do with a glass of wine to recover from the experience. Would you join me for one after work?"

To my surprise, I got a casual "Sure."

"Where do you live?" I realized I knew nothing about her other than in my eyes she was a hero.

"Old Street."

"I know the perfect place. Let's walk together after work."

Jen would love the Wine Box, a trendy yet quiet bar a short

walk from the tube station so she could hop on and get home easily. Jen struck me as the sort of woman who appreciated drinking logistics. Percy tried his luck for an invite. I gave him a stern "girl talk." Why is it those words petrify men? I wonder what they imagine we sit and talk about. Periods? Beauty products? Them?

Jen walked at a pace I admired. Swiftly. She really knocked me for six when she pulled a packet of Marlboro's out her Mulberry.

"Oh, you smoke?"

"No, I do not." She was adamant about that. Here I was thinking they were her vice for dealing with the dead every day, though it seemed the living were causing her more problems.

"He is such an idiot," she muttered into her purse as she looked at the cigarette packet. I tried to display surprise at hearing "he" and "idiot" in the same sentence. I just wasn't. Not one little bit.

"Who? Your boyfriend?" I took a wild guess.

"Not for much longer if he carries on like this," she said. She then proceeded to have the coolest little tantrum right there on the spot. It was very dignified, not too over the top, simply airing her emotions. I allowed her to get it out of her system. It shocked me Jen was in a relationship; my assumption was she was single with a couple of cats. I must stop being so judgmental.

I was glad she had a boyfriend. It always makes me sad when women just go through life wasting their vagina. Not that I am overly promiscuous. Still, it could be worse: one of my mum's friends admitted she was still celibate at forty.

"I don't see the point in starting now, it's a bit like gymnastics better to start young or not at all." That was her exact declaration. I hope wherever she is she has at least found a friend nice enough to treat her to a vibrator.

Before I knew it, we were seated at a window table and had agreed on a bottle of Sancerre to get the evening going. The fact that she had found the cigarettes in the bag meant, to cut a long story short, her boyfriend Graham was cheating on her. The long story was, as this nosy parker demanded, that his bit on the side was a devious little monkey who smoked Marlboro Reds and had popped them in Jen's bag when she had been over for an afternoon rendezvous. Her intention in doing so was to bring poor Jen's love life crashing down. Without so much as raising a cowardly finger. Girls could be the worst kind of evil when lusting over a stupid guy.

So far, the things I knew about Jen: 1) She swore a lot when angry. 2) She loved wine. 3) She made me feel brave. She was a lioness with a big heart, and I had hardly scratched the surface.

I had only had one glass of wine, it had gone straight to me head, lubricating my thoughts.

"I must say, seeing you at work today completely changed my perception of you. I got you all wrong, Jen."

"Most people do. Especially when you tell them you work with dead people all day. They tend to put you in the weird file and distance themselves from you."

"I am beginning to realize how easy it is to be judgmental; definitely something I am working on. That and believing in myself more."

"Admirable goals. I wish I had more self-belief at your age. We are capable of anything yet we absorb other people's insecurities, criticisms, and fears to the point they become our own. So what would you want to do if you could do anything?"

"I want to do something that makes me feel free and inspired."

"Receptionist at a funeral parlor not cutting it for you?" We both laughed.

"I don't see it being my forever job."

"Do you think dream jobs are like dream men?"

"How do you mean?"

"They don't exist." Jen must have noticed my look of despair as she continued, "No, of course they do. And you, Anna, have a sparkle and enthusiasm for life. You have plenty of time to find what's right for you. Whereas I am in my forties and can officially say I am giving up on the dream man."

"Behave. Life begins at forty," I told her, thinking of Susan. "How did you meet your current douchebag?" As the wine had flowed so did the backdrop to their unenviable love story. Graham, who looked like John Travolta on a really bad day, had met Jen at a dinner party held by her friend. The friend was one of those who insisted that her two single friends must date. Jen had agreed to several dinners and, cut to three months later, he had moved in. Cut to now, she had realized he was a cheating arsehole. Poor Jen. This amazing woman who could handle a job that involved not only the trauma of physically seeing, touching, and preparing dead people for their last goodbyes, but also the emotional suffering of the ones they are leaving behind, was wasting her greatness on an idiot that couldn't appreciate he was punching above his weight. Jen was gorgeous, funny, down to earth, and clearly had a heart far too big for her own good. Hopefully not big enough to forgive him for shagging the receptionist at work. That behavior deserves instant dismissal.

"Jen," I said grabbing her hand. "You walk away from this with your head held high and let good old Karma catch up with them. Sounds like they deserve each other."

She nodded as the words sunk in.

"Let's talk about something far more interesting. You!" I

wanted to know more about Jen's career history, naturally. "So why dead people?"

Jen wiped a hair from her face and took a sip of her wine. The energy shifted between us, it felt edgy. She gave me this look, it reminded me of Tom in L.A.—like he was on the verge of telling me something, unsure of the outcome.

"I studied forensic pathology for three years and…" She paused and huffed before continuing, "…things happened, unexpected things, and so I decided it was best if I pursued a different line of work." I looked at her, perplexed, her response seemed so defensive. She threw me a look that told me to stop pushing. Alas, my curiosity was burning a hole in my mouth.

"What do you mean unexpected things?"

"Why are you so easy to talk to?" Jen looked annoyed and happy about this at the same time. Like when someone you don't really want to see shows up, yet they brought pizza so it makes it okay. "The last case before I left was a murder involving a well-known QC. You probably saw it in the news. Listen, Anna, I cannot tell you exactly what I discovered. I decided to leave on moral grounds and it taught me a lot about myself. The reason I got into forensics was to reveal the truth. To help people answer questions, so there was no way I was going to be forced to lie. My work had become a bit mechanical and it reminded me I wasn't there to go through the motions of dissecting the dead. I felt passionate enough about my morals to walk out that door and tell the arseholes I would not be involved. Do you know how that felt?"

"Euphoric." I stated, imagining the combination of walking out the door to a world of possibilities leaving behind a bunch of crooks who were trying to force you to become something you weren't. For a moment I wanted to be here, a strong, clever woman with integrity, guts, and great hair. Not that my hair's that bad, though the other stuff I could do with more of. "Haven't you ever thought about reporting whatever you know to the police?" I asked.

"Yes. Every day for the first few months. The circle of corruption is a hard thing to fight on your own. Then again, living with what I know has been harder. As time has passed I have let it go. It may be best not to open that can of worms again, you know?"

"I know a great lawyer if you ever need one, I am sure she can put you in touch with the right people."

"Please, keep what I have told you to yourself. It's my decision to make and you're the first person I have told as much about it to."

"Say no more." I decided to move back to lighter conversation. "Okay. Well I guess you're still working with the dead, replacing the autopsy with hair and beauty."

Jen laughed. She looked even prettier when she relaxed. She waved at someone at the bar so I gave her a questioning look.

"Oh, that's just Stacy." She told me as if I had a clue who that was.

One thing that has always baffled me is the fact that despite feeling like I know a fair few people in London, I never bump into anyone I know. The amount of times whoever I am with has had to excuse themselves to say hello to a so-and-so who they used to work with, or introduce me to this exquisite thing they used to date, or even some boring bastard from the account department…but me, nada. It was so effortlessly cool. Well, there I was with Jen, second bottle into our wine, which was really strengthening our bond when who would display themselves a little too close in front of my face, squeaking my name in a slurry high-pitched flurry of excitement. Susan.

She pulled up a stool, perched on it, we got her a glass and another bottle and whole-heartedly pulled her into the conversation. So, there we were, an embalmer, a lawyer, and a jobslut. I couldn't wish for better company. Susan had, since we last spoken, started to date a string of unsuitable tomboys. The sex was doing her good, she looked like a weight had been lifted off her shoulders physically and mentally. She was so refreshing to be around and her and Jen really hit it off. I was happy for them.

"How on earth have you ended up working at a funeral director's, then?" Susan tapped her hand on the table genuinely excited for my response. "Still running away from your potential?"

Unsure if that was a compliment I resulted to my default persona. Even though I was learning some people didn't believe the perception of self I created and Sus was one of them.

"Because, Susan, I am a total jobslut who will try anything once." She gave me a meaningful smile. It represented a deep understanding. She had got to know me quite well in my stint in the jungle. "I love the thrill of a new career," I continued. "Alas, it's incredibly challenging to stay past the honeymoon period." She nodded and smiled.

Saying it out loud was like therapy. I wanted to stay and offload the mental thoughts that had been exhausting me about my relationship with work. All of the things I hoped yet to try. And the longing I had to find the one I could settle down with. Alas, I was drunk and tired and would probably just grab a cab home. Tomorrow I would continue with my job merry go round.

"Anna, the last thing you want to do is waste the best years of your life in a profession that's not right for you. I just don't want you to waste your life running from one thing to the next when I know if you stuck at something you would make it a massive success. I want that for you. Sometimes I lay awake at night and think. 'Fuck, I wish I had become a professional tennis player.' I was pretty good you know. Everyone tells you to do the sensible thing and you do it. Suddenly you're knee-deep in a life you never even wanted. Well, I say fuck being sensible."

She slammed her glass on the table, a great end to her shocking revelation, Sus fancied her luck at Wimbledon. Who would have known? Jen and I sat in admiration, briefly stunned to silence.

"Wow. Well, that's affirmed my decision. I do not want to be knee-deep in dead people when I reach forty. Thanks, Susan."

I filled her glass up. She deserved it after dishing me up some of her finest advice. Her and Jen were not so different, I thought as I watched them both pondering their life decisions. They had a lot in common. I felt it a good time to leave.

They decided to stay and have since formed a very strong friendship. I felt kind of nice for introducing them, like I had gifted them both each other. Perhaps there's more to your purpose in life than finding the right career. What about the life stuff you're just good at? Why can't we just be paid for that? Like drinking lots of coffee, telling people who they are astrologically compatible with, getting over-excited about Chinese food. I had a lot of potential in those fortes; alas, they did not come with a salary.

I wondered if Jen would confide in Susan about what she had told me that night. True to my word, I would let that be a decision she made on her own. Right now, my purpose in life was getting Chinese food, going home, and preparing for tomorrow. I felt it was time to embark on my new quest. Which was over-sharing spring rolls with the Tweedles and over some post-wine brainstorming, we jointly decided was to become a teacher.

Chapter 10
IF YOU CAN'T DO, TEACH, THEY SAY

What a load of bollocks. And more fool me for attaching any significance to the above statement. That's the thing with words, when put together in the right way and coming from some form of authority figure our default position is to believe it to be true. Well, I did the legwork, and can confirm the above statement should be amended to, "If you can't do…definitely do not teach."

So, when I got back I came across an ad for a week's course in teaching English. The only requirements being 1) you spoke English and 2) you had a few academic qualifications. Technically I was overqualified.

As I looked around the room I felt reassured. Reassurance confirmed by introductions. I was in a room full of professionals looking to further their skill set and two little darlings looking to head over to Asia to teach. The darlings were Ally and Sam, and they saw this certificate as their green card to jam around the world and postpone the rush to university. Pretty good way to spend a gap year, if you ask me.

I had done a bit of research into the whole teaching thing prior to embarking on the course in the name of a new and improved me who thinks before she works. The course teacher was a lovely lady named Carol, who reminded me a bit of that Aunty everyone has (or should have) who has had at least one divorce, likes wine a bit too much, and lives for a party. Carol, after divorce number two, (which she did not mind discussing with us all,) had nipped off to Spain and fell in love with the country, local tapas, and probably a few young Spaniards. She had made friends with a few women who taught in the local schools and to families. Seeing this as her way to plonk herself there for half the year, she cracked straight on with the TEFL course and now comes back to the UK to teach a few months of the year so she can basically buy more vino. Carol taught us how to structure a class. And there was me thinking teachers were making it up as they went along. Oh no. They spent weeks preparing those maths lessons. It was all a bit much, though doable. Deviating from the structure was not advised. Then there was marking of homework, and monitoring students' progress.

All this preparation and marking made for a lot of paperwork and files. Two things I have always considered a pain in the ass and tried to keep to a minimum. Ho-hum, I would just get on with it. If the two young girls bombing around Asia could manage it then I am sure I could. Besides it was only teaching a bit of English, how hard could it be? I passed the course and got the certificate. I set up an advert that I was teaching in London, home visits and such, a few private clients seemed a lot more appealing than whole classes. And pretty much waited for the phone to ring and those emails to fly in.

Oh, Christ.

It seemed London was flooded with people who couldn't speak English. Or could do so, albeit not very well. I had three lessons requests for the next day. The first was in Muswell Hill, a home visit for a Chinese boy who was doing his GCSEs and in the words of his mother, "He English very bad." Well, the apple never falls far from the tree. Second, an Arabic-speaking boy who wanted to come to me. I arranged to meet him at the Costa coffee chain conveniently located under my flat in consideration of the flatmates. And the third, a French student whose English was pretty much perfect and who just needed some help with her CV and the like. Another Costa meeting—proximity to caffeine is a must when embarking on a new job venture.

Client number one was the Chinese young boy with a very English name, Henry. His mother pretty much threw me into the room where he was eagerly waiting with his pen and pad on the oak living room table.

"Hello, Henry."

"Hello," said Henry as he offered his hand for me to shake, and pushed his glasses back on to the top of his nose.

"Let's get you ready for these GCSEs, then." I offered brightly, hoping that his mother who was still hovering behind me might go get me a drink or a cookie. Was it rude to ask?

I sat down and made a start with my carefully planned lesson on active verbs. Hoping his mother might use one and leave the living room. Which she didn't throughout the entire lesson; it seemed I had two students. Henry seemed to absorb some of what I was telling him. He looked at me for clarity, his literary angel sent to guide him to an A-star in English. The pressure was immense and not made easier by the mother's entirely inappropriate and unrequired presence. I mean a glass of water would not have gone amiss. I have to say, I was already considering dropping Henry as a client as we scheduled another lesson for Friday morning.

Costa was far less risky in terms of venue, I decided as I spread myself onto a comfortable table with my large coffee and pastry. It's one of those spots that never gets too packed other than Saturday afternoons. Outside of which I have never had more than two people in front of me in the caffeine line.

I didn't know this client's name though my guess was the guy who walked in with headphones looking a bit spaced out as his eyes casually circled the room was probably looking for me. I raised a hand and pulled that face that says, "It's me. I am her." You know the face I mean—eyebrows raised, hand still in the air smiling and looking moronic hoping it wouldn't last too long. And it didn't. Pretty soon Asaf was sitting next to me with his very strong scent of sweet aftershave.

His English was far worse than the level two he had rated himself in my email. I would say closer to a minus twenty. There was just a smiling smugness to him that made me feel uncomfortable. He spent most of the hour half listening to me and half sending Arabic texts to his buddies. Once I gladly told him his hour was up and he had left I realised I had totally forgotten to get paid and he had left me the bill for his hot chocolate. Sometimes I just have to laugh at how totally and utterly ridiculous I was.

Teaching was unlikely to be the career I would be bringing home for Christmas, I would have just rain-checked my third and final student though it being only half an hour before she was due to arrive I thought, *What the heck, it can't get any worse.* And it didn't. Gabriella was lovely in every sense of the word; she oozed French elegance with a respectful attempt to blend in with the British. She placed an envelope on the table on arrival, apologized for being two minutes late and offered me a coffee.

Her English was as good as mine verbally; okay, she needed a bit of accent work. Her written work just needed tidying up. Her main concern was perfecting her CV for a job she wanted desperately to apply for. Well, she had come to the right girl. My forte! Years of experience! We chatted over coffee about everything other than English. Like how her shithead of a boss fancied her (and hence her wanting to leave her current job,) and our favourite French wines. I upgraded her CV to a standard that would blow Lord Sugar's socks off. She left my most satisfied customer and despite having to refuse future lessons based on a loose lie that I was likely to be leaving the UK at the end of the month, I made her promise she would write to me and tell me if she got the job.

I decided to end my day on a good note and, taking my teacher's hat off, I popped myself down at the bar across the road and greeted my flatmates came to join me for a few drinks. One day of being a teacher had been enough for me.

We debriefed on our respective days; Tweedle Dee had been sexually harassed by her lesbian manager, and Tweedle Dum had tripped over the escalators, bottom up, at the top of her office on the one day she had finally decided to take Clara from Accounts's advice of "going commando." So, as you can imagine, it really put things in perspective.

Chapter 11
UNDERCOVER ANGEL

After my fling with teaching English, I needed something to turn me on again. Never having wanted to learn another language, I now understood why. One is enough for me. I took a little break to assess my options. I was having an internal panic about what they were. So far, I had already exhausted a fair few dream careers that I had really envisaged settling down into—why had none of them taken off? Law, acting, selling houses. I had even tried working with dead people and teaching my native language, but neither stuck and I was feeling a bit useless. Part of me wanted to open the flood gates and have a good old cry to the Tweedles or anyone that would listen. Usually I decided it was easier to hide behind my default attitude of not giving a toss that my career life is a bit of a joke, but the tears needed to come out, and they did. Instead of comfort and reassuring encouragement from friends I chose Ben and Jerry's and my pillow. A week of hiding as a recluse wallowing in self-pity, bad food, and *Sex in the City* and my brain felt like mush. I had to pull myself back together or I would be crying on a bench. Tears do not pay the rent.

I woke up one morning and decided my heartbreak period was over and I was ready to get back out there. I didn't need long to recover and replenish my relentless optimism. A few phone calls to Shan and reengaging with the world reminded me there was more to life than having the perfect career by a certain age. It goes on regardless and so would I. Even Winston Churchill supposedly said success is going from failure to failure without loss of enthusiasm and, thankfully, that was something I always managed to summon up.

Is the brain a muscle? If so, it was ready for a good work out. My single career status gave me time to ponder what the decisions that ultimately end up shaping our lives are based on. I put it down to a mixture of logic and inspiration. Logic being the safety net for when inspiration gets a bit wild, alas I do not believe it is distributed equally. I am particularly deprived. I cannot imagine any of my ex employers sitting around the table mourning my logical ability " Anna was such a logical girl" No, to be honest I wouldn't want to be a fly on that wall. I guess that's why they say oblivion is bliss.

You may even be a source of inspiration yourself. A delightful colleague once told me my mere existence inspires her. She took on a job based on a conversation we had one night after a crap day in real estate. In fact, a lot of people take advice for their futures from me. Which is ironic considering I have no idea how to create mine. One thing I had to appreciate I was developing the ability to flow with life.

As my dad once told me one day when I was moaning about a boring day at a forgettable office. "You are not a tree, move on."

I sense I have digressed despite my best intentions not to. Where were we? So, I was searching Google for fresh inspiration in Costa over a strong Americano.

While verbally affirming, "I am not a tree," the guy to my right looked a trifle confused, but still, my dad would be proud. I had just come across a very interesting job advertisement. I bravely say, "interesting" while I was shielded by the gloss of safety that everything has when you're only viewing it from your computer screen. It was an advertisement reading SEEKING DISCREET INVESTIGATORS FOR PERSONAL MATTERS.

The ad had been simple and to the point. 1) Are you attractive? 2) Are you discreet? 3) Are you educated? 4) Are you based in London? 5) Are you flexible? Hoping the last question referred to my availability and not my body, I ticked all the boxes. And when I did I wasted no time in filling in the application form to become a Marital Affair Detective. The response was super-fast. Based on my profile picture and brief bio I was invited to two weeks of training after which, they hoped, as I did, I would be ready for assignments.

What is a marital detective, exactly? Well, I had been reading a lot in the press of late about the rise of marital dating websites and the crippling effect they could have on people's hearts. Having been of a generation where it was far more common for your parents to have separated than be together, my default attitude towards men was not to trust. Which I know is totally unfair based on the actions of a handful of people, albeit a rather large one.

My mum was on the receiving end of this particular crime. It seemed a bit like a kidney stone being the closest thing in terms of the pain. Yes, it passes and you move on, although let me tell you, every time you feel a pain in your belly you feel like running to A&E. My sister and I would sneak down the stairs many times when we were young to earwig on Mum and her lady friends discussing the latest cheating scandal, one of them crying into their vodkas. One night, which we still refer to as "Oh Carol," we both remember vividly. We were around twelve and ten years old and laying in our bunk beds. She was conveying her dismay at finding out Mum had eaten half of the box of chocolates she had gotten for her boyfriend for Valentine's Day. He had opened them and accused her of the crime. (My mum is still in denial and to this day I do not know who was truly responsible.) It did leave to my poor sister being publicly dumped. Anyway, that night we were tempted downstairs by three very loud voices. We carefully snuck to the edge of the living room door and peered in. Carol, one of mum's closest friends was crying a river as Flo, Julie, and Mum consoled her. The table was covered with vodka, wine, and chocolates. Apparently just the medicine Carol needed to mend the damage done by her cheating partner. I took it as a warning to be very careful placing my trust or heart in the hands of a man.

Whether it's my perspective, luck, or just where the universe chooses to place me I am very fortunate in the sense that I always seem to meet the most wacky, weird, and wonderful people. Marianne was no exception. She was from Russia, with a cold nature about her. Marianne had set up her agency Undercover Angels in response to a friend's adulterous husband compounded with her own pretty obvious detest for men in general.

The logical side of my brain loves to join links between everything I do. Somewhere in my subconscious mind a link was being drawn that law and detective work are not a million miles apart. I would be technically putting together cases against people. I would be doing something financially rewarding and flexible that didn't require me to sit in an office surrounded by people who made me feel crazy, while counting down the hours till I could escape. Playing with the possibilities of my new venture was all part of the fun. I was with Tweedle Dee and Tweedle Dum when I got the news that I was being hired. They were thrilled at my new position. Okay, so I wasn't supposed to tell anyone what I was doing. That had been Marianne's first instruction. Her authoritative voice had clearly stated to keep all communication strictly confidential. Breaking rules already; I do like to start as I mean to go on. The informal interview was set for a Tuesday morning in a Starbucks on Brompton Road. When I asked where the closest tube station was I got a husky laugh and a, "Take taxi, darlink," in an exaggerated Russian accent. Tweedle Dee—that girl is like a human map of London—later informed me it was right over the road from Knightsbridge tube station.

As soon as I met Marianne, I knew she had never been to North London. It is highly unlikely she had even left SW7. She stunk of weird, alien perfume. If smells were reflections of one's personality she had given my nose an apt warning. Marianne was sweet in small doses.

She was an intriguing woman. Without her ever really explaining much, her story revealed itself. Never was there a cohesive flow of conversation that explained how she had ended up as the director of a marital investigative company, hiring ad hoc jobsluts such as myself. It was more abrupt statements that forced you to jump a few chapters in then ping pong back and forth till it all melted together in a pot of vague sense.

I learnt quickly not to seek clarification as it just left me on the receiving end of a huffy, "Really honey," a husky laugh and a little shake of the right hand into the air as if waving away a useless waiter. Marianne was a character once met but never forgotten. I wondered if this helped her position or hindered it. Surely the human chameleon was more useful in her field. Someone who blends in and doesn't stand out. Forgettable. Silly me. Marianne didn't take part in the investigative frontline herself. Of course she didn't. She just hired morons such as myself who would be doing the honey traps. This is why she liked to meet you; she wanted to assess your level of communication and attractiveness to see where she could place you.

I was delighted and a trifle concerned to hear she thought I would make a wonderful honey trap. Hoorah. This would mean I would not only be following unsuspecting folk around to establish if they were cheating on partners who had pulled the panic cord of Undercover Angels. Her market was, as she put it, "Those lacking in the trust department." What an unusual basis for business, reliant on the suspicions, anxieties, and distrust intrinsic in human nature.

The interview didn't feel much like an interview at all. I believe she was sizing me up from the moment I entered. My quick, articulate responses to her basic questions were enough to convince her to give me my halo. After that it was more her telling me what I would be doing. It took three Americanos, one cinnamon bun, and two toilet breaks until I could leave with half an idea of what the hell I would be doing. That night was my first test, to see if I was up to the role. If I wasn't so fundamentally impulsive, or lacked an odd fondness for putting myself in unusual situations, I may have said no. Besides we regret what we don't do, right? That is what I told myself as I agreed to my evening challenge. So how does this whole honey trap malarkey work?

Well, Marianne received phone calls from distressed wives, husbands, or apparently the more emerging market of concerned relatives, to report the suspicion of a cheating boyfriend or spouse. Quite literally we were the cops for the unfaithful. Instead of the wrath of a custodial sentence, if proven guilty they would likely be served with a divorce or a lifetime of hell. Details were taken and a report was prepared, in which a description of the naughty behaviour of the spouse was compiled.

I was invited by Marianne to her home office following our coffee to sign some paperwork, disclosure agreements, and that kind of thing. Sarcasm is the appropriate tone when referring to the office. She felt that spreading a load of paperwork and stationery over her living room graduated it to such. If there was one thing I learnt quickly about Marianne it was she certainly had her shit together. Her apartment was beautiful. A duplex, two-bedroom apartment in a little mews tucked behind Harrods. It was surprisingly spacious, despite my initial assumption upon approaching the small oak wood door of the thin-looking building. Her choice in real estate was enough to confirm her great taste extended beyond Prada. Not only did the living room serve a dual function, her guest bedroom housed a walk-in wardrobe and a shoe collection that would make Carrie Bradshaw drool.

She had them all lined-up in colour order, making her preference for red, grey, and black quite obvious.

I never once asked how she had come to acquire this particular piece of real estate heaven, though I do remember her quite clearly waving her finger at me and in her matter-of-fact Russian tone declaring, "Darlink, if you are going to be a trophy wife, you must at least walk away with a trophy." Something told me Marianne was not the sort of woman you wanted to get on the wrong side of, which I found intermittently petrifying and endearingly entertaining. Of all the bosses I had experienced so far, I feared her the most. I thought it best to bring my A-game to this role. Marianne demanded it without even having to say the word. So I was all in. I was all ready to jump right into the exciting world of being an Undercover Angel.

A new boy was on the scene around the time I became an Undercover Angel. We will refer to him as D, for douchebag. It wasn't serious; ever since Martin, no one had been. Dating in London was far more casual than the surrounding suburbs where stock was generally lower. Not quite as cutthroat as New York, but still a Londoner was provided a safety bubble of anonymity to get up to as much or as little mischief as one pleased.

We had a casualness attached to the whole thing we were both comfortable with. Our dates were usually the same. Drinks in town, followed by fondles back at his place. He had a much nicer apartment than I. He was living with two colleagues in a fancy flat in Canary Wharf with a wraparound balcony, fully-stocked fridge, and a chic, comfortable interior. He had a thing about mirrors; I was okay with it, although I wasn't quite so keen to look at my naked body as he was. Alcohol made the whole experience seem more fun than it actually was.

One night as we were wrapped post-sex on his leather sofa watching E.T.—his choice, not mine—there was a knock on the door. A knock that demanded answering. A knock that said if you don't, I will keep thumping this door till it breaks down.

D looked a tad petrified. He pushed me of the sofa, tipping his half glass of rosé on me in the process. So there

I was, soaked in rosé on the floor, too shocked and lazy to get up. He paces around in some mad rush to get dressed, throwing mine at me.

During all this commotion, in bursts a whipper snapper red-haired beauty. She starts hurling abuse in an Irish accent at D.

"I knew it, ya lying, cheating asshole. I knew you weren't in Dublin. I had my ma check the pub you said you were at. Well, here's your key and here's your ring. I am done with you. You're welcome to him, you tart."

And with that, she stormed out. I got dressed and also stormed out, leaving D with the mess he had created for himself. He put me off even having a casual fling. I had enough on my plate with my career flinging to be further complicating my life. I would reserve my time, emotions, and vagina for someone worthwhile.

But, getting back to catching other people cheating. Oh, the thrill of starting a new job. You've yet to discover all the things you will love and hate about it. The sweet nervous apprehension clinging to the hope you will do well. I sat perched in a glossy white, dimly lit bar in the West End slowly drinking an espresso martini. My inner monologue loudly reminding me not to have more than two. All well and good while the old logical side of the brain is still functioning. Though after two you slowly increase the limit to three, four, then it's, "What the hell?" I was embracing those very first tingly nerves. So far, I would say this was the best job I had ever had. As I assessed my surroundings I felt secretly smug that I was on my secret mission. Which was what? Well, Jeremy, bless his bones, would be here in approximately ten minutes. It was his usual after work haunt. Kate, his wife of fifteen years and mother of two, was suspicious he was cheating. I was here to see whom he came to the bar with. If, after an appropriate amount of time, he had no female company, I was to approach him and tempt him into making a move on me. Then I'd report back to Marianne verbally and fill in the report card for Kate. I wished I didn't know so much about Jeremy already. What if I let slip something that would freak him out and blow my cover? Another reason to watch the consumption of the awfully good martinis. I felt smug my role allowed me to work in bars.

Despite the strength of the martinis, I ordered another before I approached Jeremy. The fact they were three or four times the price I would normally pay for a drink mattered not. I had an expenses card, courtesy of my trusting boss. I pondered as I waited at the bar where my above-average tolerance of vodka had started. Dad. Good old Homer Simpson had started me on vodka and limes on ice. I remember the sunny afternoon he took my sister and I to the Punch and Judy pub in Covent Garden around age twelve. Tired of having to leave us in random shops, he needed to offer us more than a few cokes and packets of crisps to sustain our interest in pub life. We took to the new beverage like ducks to water and developed an enthusiastic approach to trying all other types of alcohol since. Dad was proud of us. Interesting how the early stages of parenting begins to weave the fabric of who we become as adults. Our attitudes and values, and the older you get the harder it is to avoid the fact you will inherit their traits. The good, bad, and the utterly annoying.

Jeremy was looking down at his watch. His style was atrocious, not that I am an authority on men's fashion. A yucky pale yellow shirt with white trousers was, however, a bit of a visual assault. I was saved from approaching my target in the nick of time. A busty blonde—also terribly dressed—brazenly stormed down the bar as if it were a catwalk and kissed her prey. I kept my gaze as discreetly as possible on the two canary-like love birds with their greens and yellows melting into each other as they smooched inappropriately. Talk about a lush, she had barely made her way through half a glass of champagne and she was practically sitting on his lap, making the obvious age gap between them apparent. Poor bloody Kate. She didn't stand a chance next to this twenty-something dressed like, well, like a boob-implanted twenty-something. As for Jeremy, he was an idiot. I was awash with relief as they ordered another bottle of champagne. For a moment, I thought I would have to follow them. I couldn't really be asked to hotfoot all over London from bar to bar to prove what is already pretty obvious. Jeremy is going through some sort of mid-life crisis and shagging someone half his age. I managed to strategically place myself at the other side of the bar unnoticed and captured a couple of snaps of the crude display of adultery. They flirted outrageously, kissed, and touched each other for another couple of hours at which point I felt my job here was really done. I texted Marianne an update of my situation and she replied, "Well done, go home." Bravo, I thought. Just call me 007. Joblsut 007.

When Marianne was not manning the phone, a man called George stepped in as security should any Undercover Angels need him for anything. I had yet to meet him, though my mind conjured up images of a man around fifty. Tall, sturdy, with a fondness for red wine and fires, and, by the sounds of it, Marianne. I wondered if there were mutual feelings of fondness there. When she had told me about him over coffee, I swore I detected a softening to her usual harshness, providing a glimmer of hope her heart had not completely frozen over.

Her eyes had glazed over as she reassured me, "George is there, anytime." Although I had never met the G man, it made me feel safe just knowing he was around.

After my successful evening, I decided to do the only thing I wanted to celebrate. As I toddled out of the Sanderson Hotel, a suited and booted doorman assisted me to a black cab. I won the black cab lottery that night with a cheerful old boy who was more than happy to chat away while I watched the London night pass by my window. I asked him to stop outside my favourite kebab shop en route home. He waited patiently as I ordered a chicken pita and falafel to go. We continued our journey all the way back to North London. As we moved more towards Hampstead I admired the contrast of the dimly lit road lamps casting a mysterious glow over the beautiful parks. The delicious feeling of London by night was just as tasty as my dinner. I gave him a good tip. After all, it was courtesy of Marianne, and it would be rude not to.

I entered our usual Starbucks for a debrief on my first assignment. I had to hand in to Marianne the report which I had started after my supper the previous evening. I was now rather ashamed of the greasy marks on the pristine white A4-sized sheet of paper. Marianne seemed chirpier than the last time I saw her and, if possible, even more immaculate. She wore a silk, blue-and-green scarf swept casually over her left shoulder and a cream cashmere jumper. Her freshly blow-dried hair bounced as she shuffled with importance through her classic black Prada hand bag. My mood was also lifted. They say people's energies can be contagious and my immune system has never been good with negativity.

I felt like I had taken a big stride towards proving myself as an Undercover Angel. I never used to have this desire to prove myself to people when I was younger. Where does it come from? I suspect it's something we develop as we get older and I am still figuring out why. I love reading interviews from thirty- to forty-year-olds saying they reached the place where they only feel the need to prove something to themselves and I wish there was a fast track to this mental safe house. Proving yourself to others is pretty tiresome at times. Not giving a single fuck seems like quite a relaxing place to be. It is okay to pretend you do not for a while, then you always come back to giving many fucks. Perhaps it is okay to give them, though just not to waste them on the wrong people or events or ideals.

Marianne moves her attention from the bag to my hopeful face as I sit down. I offer her a coffee which she does not turn down. She's the only woman I have met so far who can match me in love for caffeine and wine.

We went through my report. She pretended not to notice the greasy marks and I rolled with it. Fortunately, her satisfaction with the content outweighed her disapproval of the mess left from my post-martini dinner choice. Besides Marianne didn't exactly look like she lived on salad. She had given up on being a starving model (despite her mother's best wishes, as she had hinted one evening.) I did love the feeling of knowing you have done a good job and being recognized for it. What is wrong with being result-orientated? It's great to be told, "Well done, you." Parents always tell children when they do a good gob, why do we have to be deprived of this as we get older?

I can empathize with Anne Hathaway's character in *The Devil Wears Prada*, who ended up running around after the owner of *Vogue* for a year in a constant battle for praise and recognition. It's the perfect demonstration of seeking approval from others is exhausting, and sometimes you are so pissed off by the time you get it you don't even want it anyway. Still, this is such an easy trap to fall into.

I have never forgotten one of my lecturers of constitutional and administrative law telling me in what I perceived as an accusatory tone that I was result-orientated. I wasn't happy with a grade I received for a paper I felt I had done very well on. I had followed every guideline and done all the recommended readings. When I displayed my dismay, I told him outright I was disappointed with the grade, and that surely it deserved a higher one?

"You are results-orientated and it came across in your work," was his reply.

I was confused. He was somewhat disapproving of me wanting praise for a job well done. I did not get it. I tried to explain my way of thinking and thought I was getting somewhere. His silence suggested otherwise as we held an awkward gaze for what felt like forever and I wished I had not bought him those Christmas cupcakes. He gave me this look, which made me question if I was being a tad stubborn. The look was enough.

"I do not see there being anything wrong with giving praise when it's deserved. How else is the student to know they have done a good job? In fact, I think it's crucial, almost a duty, to do so."

"You remind me of myself as a student. I am passing you on a lesson it took me many years to learn. Focus on the work, not the result. You will see what brings the most satisfaction and avoid a great deal of disappointment."

His words have stuck with me and bought me comfort at times. They soothed some result-focused anxiety. I am grateful he shared his wisdom with me. I re-did the paper he had graded me on with a fresh perspective and enjoyed researching and revising my argument more thoroughly, so much so that it really didn't matter what he re-graded me at. I was still pleasantly surprised when he asked to publish it in the research guides for students to refer to.

So, where were we? Oh, yes. Marianne was ever so happy with my greasy report on Jeremy and the excellent photographic evidence slyly taken on my Blackberry. I had no direct contact with the client Kate, for which I was glad. I did ponder what satisfaction one gained from telling these women their suspicions were true. Even with all the mental preparation in the world, it's still got to hurt. Delivering my news and report to the neutral party was altogether far more appealing and less emotionally distressing. I had an alias to protect me just in case shit did hit the fan, which, according to Marianne, was "very rare." This made my role more of an anonymous spy. Marianne told me this would probably be case closed for Kate. My efficiency was what seemed to please her the most. There was no need for further surveillance, as I had gotten a hole in one. The only type of hole in one I was likely to ever get, not being a fan of golf. She was refreshingly forthcoming with her praise. She told me in no uncertain terms, "You have done a very good job."

Her directness was one of the things I liked most. I was certain she would be exactly the same if she were not happy about something. Until she brought it up, I had not noticed we had not discussed how much I was going to get paid. I did tend to do that a lot. Rush into a job with no thought as to how much money I was going to make. I seemed to be in pursuit of something else. Let's just say I was pleasantly surprised when I checked my bank balance that evening, curious to see what amount she had transferred. She'd promised it would be instant. I actually liked the fact she had not told me how much to expect. It added to the mystery of the job. Naturally I was on cloud nine that night. I'd aced my first assignment, and was paid more than I'd had to previously work months for. Most importantly, it was with a job that threatened no sign of the b-word. I know, I know you may have one justified concern here. Once I have nailed a job, I tend to spread my wings and fly off. There she goes the little job butterfly off to her next destination.

When I think about the times when my parents were together and we lived in a far-from-perfect, but united, family home, I can vaguely remember a time when I felt less restless. Something must have happened when that stability was taken away from me. Followed by being rejected from my school, I got used to life throwing me into the unknown and it seems to have become a bit of a thing.

There were two things that counteracted the usual rising to flee at this point. First, I felt there was so much yet to happen and discover here; second, I felt Marianne had not seen the best of me yet and she knew it.

I sometimes wish I could turn off this voice inside my head constantly asking me to think more about what I truly want to do. It causes an internal conflict because the voice wants deep analysis whereas I don't. I don't want to think much, because you think up, down, left, right, sideways and it doesn't get you anywhere other than more confused. At best, it results in a tension headache and the need for a large glass of wine.

Recruitment consultants cater to that doubting voice, the devils. With all their tempting opportunities, they lure you in with their friendly banter and treasure chest of careers. Jobsluts are the perfect prey. They are like Ashley Madison to the serial adulterer. Tempting you with the glimmer of unknown opportunities. As Oscar Wilde famously said, "I can resist anything except temptation." I mean, even the more committal type is likely to be swayed by some of the more aggressive headhunters. What can we do? Stephen from Recruitment calls every day to tell you about the perfect role, that you really cannot afford to turn this down. That you could start next month. We must simply remind ourselves that contentment comes with appreciating what you have. Many come to realise that the grass is not always greener on the other side. Water your own grass.

Back to which, Marianne was very excited about giving me a new assignment. She had thrown me straight in at the deep end, or so I had assumed. Apparently, the deep end was further afield. It all felt a bit surreal as she broke down what my next mission would be, like a really scary dream coming true. I wonder what particular part of my past is responsible for my tendency to thrive on fear and adrenaline. The scarier and riskier the more likely I will say yes, even when the approval comes out of my mouth I hear the little voices in my head saying, *Is that a good idea? Do you really want to do this?* I guess it's that voice that encourage us to make a reasonable decision or weigh things up. Though, for me, there are these over-excited bunch of head cheerleaders telling the other voices to pipe it down and me to just go for it.

So, thanks to my head cheerleaders I found myself on an early morning flight to JFK the following morning. I was clutching my clear blue assignment folder in one hand, underneath a pile of nonsense magazines I could not wait to flick through. I smiled at grey London out the window. I imagined my first trip to NYC might be a cheeky shopping trip with the girls. Perhaps something more romantic—I guess, in fairness, my trip did fall into the romance category. My role a little less traditional I guess, as I am to spy on someone else's romance as opposed to holding the leading role of the love story.

Does adultery count when the object of stolen affection is not a person? For my father, it was beer. His love for ale made him somewhat unreliable in terms of fulfilling any fatherly duties. He was someone who spends more time at the pub drinking and would rather sell a sofa than go a week without booze. That's not too helpful when you have children and want a comfortable life. Eventually my mum came to the conclusion she would rather leave the father category blank for the remainder our youth. To sum mine up, I would say it taught me to understand the power of change. As a child, it threatened every perfect moment. People move and homes disappear just as you're falling in love with the colour of your wallpaper. The more you embrace it, the less you suffer. We all have the same wrapper shaded with the uncertainty of life. The moment is the present. Enjoy.

My current present was a little bumpy. Why does air turbulence always kick in the minute they bring the food? I cracked open my second Chardonnay and finished my rubbery chicken and lumpy cheesecake. To wash away the taste, I ordered a posh box of chocolates from the duty-free confectionary; I was definitely getting used to this expense account malarkey. I propped open the blue folder on my tray and had a mini epiphany. I was working in the air—air working! I must add that to the CV skills list.

Seeing as I was seated next to a French-speaking couple who had struggled to order between the chicken and beef in English, and the extent of my French was *bonjour* and *au revoir*, I was at no risk of nattering the flight away. I browsed over assignment number two. Client Name: James Perkins. Hmm, this was a new one, the husband is suspicious of the wife. Interesting. Settling in with my vino and praline truffles, I found my work proving more entertaining than anything the pages of the magazines I had whipped though. So, James looked a bit like a chef. Stubbly grey beard, podgy in a cute way. His smile was warm and genuine, he looked like your typical English country dad; I bet he loved taking his dogs for long walks, making hearty Sunday roasts for the whole family. And then there was Elle. I struggle to find the words to do her beauty justice. I could just pop a picture in here so you would understand, but I am pretty sure that would breach client confidentiality. Put it this way, I am not even sure I would even want to be that hot—too much pressure. No wonder James was worried. Unless he locked her up in the house I bet she had guys pursuing her left, right, and center. I did feel a tad guilty as I read over the info James had provided on their private lives. I imagined how I would feel if I was in Elle's shoes and finding out my husband of eight years had decided to hire someone to stalk me, and had told total strangers about our routines. Those elements of our lives being kept private was crucial to keeping them special. Sharing them rinses the magic like leading the public to that bit of paradise you found.

Touching down in JKF airport was glorious. Not just because the air turbulence had me bricking it for half the flight, admittedly, that did play a part. I had always known I would love New York, As I wandered through the airport, I blended in with the businesslike bustle of the place. All the hype about this being the city that makes or breaks you started with getting through immigration.

I had been pre-warned they were a tough bunch. And I wasn't disappointed.

"Make sure you are clear about why you are there and be prepared to be made to feel like a criminal even if you just say shopping," my friend, a frequent traveller to New York, had warned me. Marianne had asked me to pick her up the latest Prada handbag, so it was hardly a lie.

New York demands your attention. Cliché as it sounds, it's just like walking into a movie which gives you the weirdest sense of déjà vu. The yellow cabs, rush of energy, promise of possibility, nothing disappoints. While crossing the Manhattan Bridge with your post-flight achy bottom perched on the seat of your cab, you will have a moment to give it the attention it demands, so enjoy it. I have that moment locked in my subconscious to visit when I need a dose of NYC. Which after one visit, you will.

Marianne had done me well in terms of accommodation. I was staying near Times Square in a short-term rental close to Central Park. I had often heard how Manhattan was notorious for shoebox-sized living spaces that came with huge rental price tags. It was only as I placed my fifty-square-foot suitcase down in my four hundred-square foot apartment that I understood.

Alone in the concrete jungle, my "Empire State of Mind" kicked in—well, the lyrics to the Alicia Keys and Jay Z song did—on the sketchy speakers provided by the rental company.

I headed out into the madness of Manhattan to find a Starbucks, which took all of fifteen steps. I felt at home. If anyone appreciated the importance of caffeine, it was the New Yorkers. London does culture, Paris sophistication, and Milan style. It's not that NYC did not offer any of the above, though its forte was definitely "large." My love affair with New York had begun—at least one romance would be making it out of here alive.

One email stole attention in my inbox:

"NEW YORK MISSION."

Darling

When you land buy cell phone—cheaper.

Will email you details of where client will be later.

Please do not forget Prada bag, darling.

M x

So, our business chat was pretty intense, as you can see. I decided to get the shopping out of the way before my working day began and, yes, I am one of those girls who finds shopping a chore. I remember watching *Confessions of a Shopaholic* thinking WTF? Was it not for my girl-crush on Isla Fisher I would have never even tried—she is adorable though, isn't she? I cannot believe she married Ali G. Anyhow, Marianne would choose the biggest bloody Prada bag in NY, wouldn't she? The rest of my afternoon was consumed by shuffling said bag back to the apartment, taking in the sights of the giant buildings, pretzel stands, and honking traffic. The rushing streets lined with glossy shops and homeless people moved you along, a current you'd do best not to fight.

As promised, Marianne had sent me the details for where I would be headed that evening. I had dutifully noted the

Waldorf Astoria on my route home from shopping. I arrived twenty-five minutes early. I picked a good spot. Elle was apparently meeting somebody here and all I had to do was wait and take notes. I pulled my grey jumper dress down to slightly above the knee and relaxed into the leather cushion. It was busy with a few middle-aged professionals scattered around. I sipped my Cosmopolitan and gazed at my nails. They looked like shit. They were denting the sophisticated look I was going for. All of a sudden, the energy of the room changed. I raised my gaze in response and my eyes fell on Elle. She graced the decadent bar with a slow walk and elegantly swirled herself onto a stool. My worst nightmare was confirmed: she looked hotter than the picture. She placed her Yves Saint Laurent clutch bag delicately on the bar's brown ledge. The bartender bowed his head and took her order as other men stared and drooled.

Even my mouth was open. I finished my drink quickly so I had an excuse to get back to the bar and closer to this creature of perfection. She was sipping a glass of red wine, oblivious to the reaction she had caused, and was gazing at her phone. Moments later, another woman arrived. A brown-haired ball of energy bounced her way over to Elle; their delight at seeing each other bursting into a visual and audible display of cuddling and squeals.

"I cannot believe you are here. Look at you—amazing."

"I gained twelve pounds since I last saw you." The girl, who by the looks of it, needed that twelve pounds looked shamefully down at her frame and pulled her sweater over her patchwork skirt. Manhattan has unfair standards on body shape.

"I do not care how many pounds you put on," replied Elle warmly, then ordered another wine as the girl smiled and relaxed, taking a seat next to her. There was a familiarity between them that told me they were more than casual friends. It was a closeness. The way they were sitting, touching each other, love pouring out of them as the wine filled their glasses.

Elle had tears in her eyes as she grabbed a napkin from her nut bowl. I tried to hone in on what the girl was saying.

"James knows, Elle." Elle looked a little taken aback by this.

"He does?"

"Yeah, he called me last week. Probably when he found out you booked your flight. He asked me if you were coming to see me. I had to say yes, if he finds more lying I am never going to be able to fix the mess I have made, and honestly, he didn't seem to mind. I think he was relieved you were not having an affair."

Elle sat silently absorbing the information, and visually rationalizing everything in her own head.

"Well, look at you and look at him. If I was James I would be worried. He's always been a little vulnerable about how gorgeous you are. I remember the week before your wedding we spoke about it. He told me, 'I am more excited and petrified about marrying your sister than anything I've ever done. The way I see it, she has my heart no matter what, so I am going to have to try.'"

"James said that to you? When?" Elle's face expressed the type of happiness no compliment has yet given me.

"Yes Elle, he adores you. The poor sod has always felt he's punching above his weight in the looks department. He's probably lived your whole marriage on edge that you're going to be whisked away by some lothario. I told him the Sweeney sisters go for hearts and minds."

Elle raised a glass. "That we do, angel."

"Anyway," her sister continued, "we had a chat on the phone and I told him I am not angry he sent me away. It was for the best, I was stuck in a terrible rut and would never have stopped drinking had he not..."

"Not what?"

"He paid for my rehab. He never wanted to burden you with the guilt of him having to cop your sister out, so he just pretended I had moved here to get out of London. Partially true, though without the rehab I wouldn't be here now, babe."

"I don't know what to say. It is so James, always caring about everyone else. I love that man."

"And I didn't want to ruin that love. I felt that's what I was doing. I was a mess and you had this great family... you have done enough for me over the years. I was so happy when you got in touch, I want so badly to be a part of your lives again. The last thing I wanted was James worried you were cheating when you were coming to see me."

"It's okay. I'm not mad. You did the right thing. Ruth, you're my sister. We came from the same belly. Life without you is not what I want. And it's not what James wants. He just had to make the right choice for the kids and he knows I am not strong enough to turn you away."

"I want to make things right again. I will pay back the money for rehab. I am clean now and I promise I am going to stay here in New York and makes something of myself."

I was beginning to paint a picture of what was happening here. As I watched and listened to these sisters mending something, I realised I had no right to be doing so.

Is this what this job was going to force me into? I wondered whether Ruth knew James had sent a spy and that would be one piece of info too much for Elle. The thought gave me chills. She could be looking at me. Suspecting that the girl perched at the other side of the bar with chipped nail polish was spying on their intimate reunion hoping to detect betrayal.

The last thing James and Elle needed was to pay someone to confirm they loved each other. Or that they didn't. That is something that needs to be communicated between the two people involved in the relationship and anyhow even if one of them was having an affair was that really enough to throw a relationship away over? At least an organic discovery allows for a more reasoned reaction than news being delivered by a third party. There are always reasons, layers, hope it may not be the end. Other people's relationships are too complex and intricate to ever be known by spying on it for five minutes knowing nothing about either party than a few notes. If someone wanted to leave someone for another that is surely something they have the right to disclose. Looks like I hadn't taken the time to consider these values prior to hopping undercover. My bad.

I walked out. Quickly. Out of the bar, then the hotel, leaving my bar tab unpaid. The cold air hit me in the face straightening up my tipsy wobble. This Undercover Angels mask was coming off as quickly as it went on. In my decision I felt more relieved than I expected. It was teaching me more about myself than I knew. Without anyone to call and vent my realizations I reminded myself it's okay to walk away from something that's not right for you. *You are not a tree*, I told myself, although a little bit tipsy. Still, I meant it.

My phone stole me away from my reflections. It was my mum. Typical. Of all the times she wants to call it has to be in the middle of a secret trip to New York. I screened the call and would deal with any questions when I got home.

I had a whole flight to make up a good story as to why my phone was on international dial. I didn't like the feeling of not telling the truth, it made me feel anxious and edgy. This was the last job I would take which made me feel this way. Perhaps one day I would tell her about my secret adventure, but right now was not the time for her thoughts on the matter. I hope one day we could exchange secrets; I have a feeling my mum has some worth knowing.

My flight was booked for the following day so I decided to tell Marianne in person I was handing in my badge. I allowed myself to indulge in my last night in New York. One thing I was good at was putting everything on hold to enjoy the moment. Dealing with life drama could wait till London. I walked around Times Square till my legs begged for mercy, breathing in the lights and energy. I went to an old-style waffle house for breakfast. I sat surrounded by strangers who were all immersed in their own stories. Stories that neither I, nor anyone else, had any right to intrude upon unless invited. Maybe some were having affairs. Maybe some were saying sorry. Maybe some were just enjoying breakfast. I sure was. Waffles never tasted so good. They alone had made the whole trip worth it. As for my endeavor to become an Undercover Angel, how was I supposed to know what was right for me without trial and error? This trip had taught me a lot more than to keep my nails polished.

Marianne took the decision relatively well. I sensed I was not the first nor would I be the last Undercover Angel to temporarily flutter my wings and disappear out of her life. Though one gesture I was not prepared for. She gave me her bloody Prada bag. I saw a slight sadness in her eyes as we said our goodbyes. I'm not sure if it related to the bag or me, as there was a mutual understanding to the finality of

our departure that required no words.
   And that, folks, was that.

Chapter 12
HOLY SHIT, IT'S NEARLY CHRISTMAS

With two weeks left till Christmas I had to accept the chances of me finding "the one" were pretty slim, unlike my seasonally-expanding body. Still, I was determined not to be both fat and unemployed. If Mum did one thing right, it was put on an irresistible festive spread that would even have my die-hard actor friends in L.A. bingeing out of their size zeroes.

One thing she did wrong, though, was making me feel like a total failure in the career department; well, it was a collaborative effort, to be fair. My siblings with their stable lives only highlighted my lingering status as being a work-in-progress. It was exhausting.

With little to lose I flicked out a few CVs for PA roles on various websites. Tweedle Dee must have sensed my desperation and with a little festive pity offered to get me a job as receptionist sitting at the top of the escalators of her marketing office. As much as the thought of greeting her changing work-face each morning (the closer we got to Friday, the bigger the smile) or her bottom, living and working together seemed a bit much.

Fresh from my decline for Tweedle Dees, another offer was on the table. It was in response to one of my PA applications. It was from a guy named Daniel Brian, whose title read Music Producer, and the ad read:

Need help managing my life—from booking flights to

walking my dog. Must be articulate, flexible, forward thinker, happy, and like the colour yellow.

I was pretty much all of the above and had provided him the following:

> FORWARD THINKING—YES. BY WAY OF EXAMPLE I TEND TO AVOID PLACES WHERE I KNOW I WILL BUMP INTO PEOPLE THAT WILL HINDER MY DAY/ MOOD/ PLANS THROUGH TO A SYSTEM CALLED "STRATEGIC MOVEMENT."
>
> FLEXIBLE—VERY MUCH SO. I HATE PLANS. AND IF THIS REFERS TO THE PHYSICAL I AM PLANNING ON TAKING UP YOGA.
>
> HAPPY—I AM TOLD HAPPINESS RADIATES OUT OF MY ASS LIKE SUNSHINE.
>
> YELLOW—DIVINE AND REGULARLY CHOSEN AS A COLOUR FOR MANCIURE.
>
> I look forward to hearing from you,
> Anna

Daniel had sent me an email requesting my company at his home-based office at Friday afternoon to discuss my application. Great. I booked a manicure immediately and checked the timetable of my local yoga studio. You know what they say about preparation.

The location of my new boss's home was none other than Bishop's Avenue, a road of shameless extravagance. Every home demonstrating the diverse taste of its owners, money really does talk. There's a lot you can tell about a person who chooses to have artificial palm trees on their driveway. Like they probably have a holiday home in the Barbados, which is somewhere I wouldn't mind being right now.

My nerves were of secondary importance to the fact I was fucking freezing. My nipples were begging me to find warmth so the poor little things could thaw out. This was certainly not the weather for the balcony bra, note to self.

I was about to give my best knock on the doors of the mansion, which I was surprised to find had no doorbell. I was pondering how to best make it professional yet loud enough to only do once. I hated that awkward, going in for the third knock just as they open the door and catch your hurry-the-fuck-up-and-let-me-in face. Hence, the reason the genius that created the doorbell is probably lying on a beach drinking exotic cocktails. I wonder how many times he got caught with his let-me-the-fuck-in face before he had his epiphany and blessed households and more importantly door-knockers everywhere. My doorbell dilemma was swept away (as was I) when a roaring engine landed a huge black Range Rover about a metre from my backside. Out jumped a short, stocky, notably agile man closely followed by a dog about his size.

"For fuck's sake. Listen, if you're another one of Becky's friends clear off, I have had enough. I am a nice bloke, though that girl is a psycho and if I was you I would get some new mates before she turns you into one."

"Erm, nope. No. Not a friend of Becky's. Don't know who Becky is, but I am here about the PA job. We had an interview in the diary for…about now?"

I looked at my watch which had stopped working about a year ago and was more of a wrist decoration these days. Still, I pulled my best poker face so he didn't have a clue.

"Oh, the PA thing. Oh, that was just a joke," he laughed as he slammed the car door and walked towards me. "I forgot about that, I…" He stopped. I think he had noticed the yellow manicure and out of pure pity changed the direction on his elaboration of this joke. "I could do with a PA. So, joke's on me. In fact, it was a joke that it was a joke, do you get me?"

I had to hand it to him, he was funny, he had a cheeky grin, and an easy aura that had probably allowed him to do cock-like things his whole life and get away with it. It didn't hurt that he was rich as hell, by the look of things. Fuck me, maybe *he* invented the doorbell.

As much as a part of me wanted to be proud enough to tell him to shove the job up his backside, my sunshine-tipped fingers reminded me if I didn't give it a go it was a total waste of a manicure, the yoga class I had provisionally booked for the weekend.

Besides, my curious nature far outweighed my pride. Yep, I was whole-heartedly accepting a job that never existed based on the pity of a short, rich, arsehole. Though, you have to admit, to gain pity from an arsehole is a mini-triumph in itself.

Daniel ushered me in out of the cold into his "humble abode," and I was soon perched on the most indulgent sofa my grateful bottom had ever met. I was slowly adjusting to the luxurious surroundings and getting used to Jasper his big, fluffy dog (of which breed I was yet to confirm) sniffing my feet. This was perfectly okay by me, since dogs normally tend to sniff my vagina, which is always a bit awks.

"So, what is it you do exactly?"

"I am a producer, babe. And I am a total control freak, which is why till now I never had a PA. See these socks?" He hangs some form of designer-socked foot in my face.

"I sacked my last cleaner because she couldn't even buy the right ones. I just have to have everything exactly as I want it or it messes my head up."

Clearly, I thought, as I looked around and the perfection of everything made sense. A symmetrical theme resonated throughout the house. He literally had two of everything. For example, he had two portraits on opposing walls, facing one another, each featuring the face belonging to a super model.

Noticing my jaw drop open slightly in surprise (something I was working on—it really was not a good look) Daniel told me, "That was my mum."

There was an evident resemblance; they shared the same sharp jaw line and expressive eyes.

"She's stunning."

"She was a model."

In respect of his silent contemplation I did not proceed with a sarcastic comment about his dad being a short-arse that was on the tip of my tongue. The subtle change of tone on the word "was" implied more than anything else he said so far.

"Have you produced anything I know?"

"You mean you don't know who I am?"

"Your ad said Daniel Brian, or was that another joke?"

He laughed so hard it kind of got me chuckling. Next thing I know we are in his basement studio listening to mixes I had been shaking my tush to blissfully unaware of who produced it.

"That job ad may have been a joke after one too many whiskies, but fuck it. Let's give it a shot. I would probably just want you doing my shopping, travel arrangements, sending presents to girls—that kind of thing."

"I reckon I can handle it."

There was a knock on the door.

"You can start by going to tell whoever that is to fuck off."

And so my employment as PA to a mega-producer began with me telling one of his most recent ex-girlfriends as politely as possible to fuck off. It worked, he never heard from her again. A word of advice here folks, never underestimate the power of a Gumtree ad, it could be a drunken mistake by a shit hot producer, you never know. My success in managing other aspects of my new venture as a PA, well they varied. My main tasks included the following:

Travel Arrangements

Dealing with a perfectionist is never easy, but when said perfectionist is musical royalty, the pressure is immense. He only ever travelled first class and liked to arrive at the airport only twenty-eight minutes before having to board. Which actually forced me to do maths. He wanted time only to grab one glass of champagne and check his emails then move on to the airplane before anyone noticed him. I was excused from any flight delays that were out of my control—though endured the wrath of his discontent anyways, so I pretty much prayed every time he was en route to the airport. Though I also liked him to travel; he called it "flying time," while I called it "peace on earth."

Hotel bookings had to be very specific. He wanted fresh orange juice on arrival and the room to have extra pillows, a fruit basket, and dry roasted peanuts. Every. Single. Time. He tended to stay in the same hotels and was mostly in L.A., New York, or Miami so they knew not to cock this up. One good thing about my boss is he tipped fairly when he got what he wanted and the staff knew it. Which was why they turned a blind eye when he wanted to party till the early hours and invite company back which (from the pictures I used to see) looked like he had the playboy mansion on speed dial. He would often flick me over a pic or two whilst I would be drinking a glass of wine, munching on some cheese, or binging on *Sex in the City*. It made me so glad I didn't have to travel with him. My role was more to make sure that everything was in order at home, so that when he got back there would be nothing intolerable to deal with if he was hungover or high.

<u>Buying Presents</u>

Girls, if you are dating someone who is famous, has a PA, travels a lot, or worse, all three of the above, it is highly likely his PA is responsible for every romantic gesture you have received. And it makes me sad you never really get the chance to thank her for it especially when she does such a good job, like moi.

Take Tiffany. My boss had been dating her a while (along with all the others,) and when he missed her birthday he asked me to deal with it. I booked them a champagne boat ride, rooftop dinner with a table covered in rose petals at which he produced the latest Chloé bag every girl was lusting over. Wait. In the bag there were plane tickets to Rome. She was putty in his hands after that.

This did get confusing at times. My boss dated a lot of girls and once or twice I did send the wrong bouquet here or apology there though this was one area he was thankfully pretty chill about.

<u>Fan Mail</u>

Yes, even producers get it. And I was the lucky one that had to deal with these bundles of joy. Sometimes I would let piles build up that would take me hours to get through. Dealing with it as it came in was far easier, though it depended how demanding Dan's schedule was as to whether this was an option.

The way our working relationship developed was pragmatism at its finest. I had fortunately clicked with Jasper who was a certain type of Labrador. Dan trusted me. I never once told anyone who he was as I could not be bothered to deal with the hassle it would cause. For convenience's sake, I stayed over a lot and when he was away I would look after Jasper. This saved him going to the kennels and put Dan's mind at rest since he really loved that dog. And so did I. You really have to meet him to understand. He has this way about him that just makes you smile. Even if you had just had a really shitty day, of which there were a few.

It had only been two weeks. It was not always a bed of roses, and yet, so far, I had not one urge to leave. To summarize I will provide a list of pros and cons that had become apparent.

The Cons

Daniel was a total arse at times. If I got something wrong he would lose his shit.

It took up seventy-five percent of my time, which was the most I had ever let a job have.

Not being able to tell my friends whom I worked for was very hard, especially after my third glass of wine. I also barely got to see my friends, which reduces above problem, though still I missed them, drinking with Jasper had its limitations:

"Jaspy, fancy another glass of Prosecco?"
"Woof, woof."
"Okay, just me then. How about some takeaway?"
"Woof, Woof."
"Pedigree Chum for you, it is then."

The Pros

I could now look forward to Christmas, having announced to friends and family that I was working for a senior Parliament member and due to privacy laws I could not reveal his name.

Daniel was really nice when not being an arse.

My office was a super stylish mansion and I had twenty-four-hour access to a fridge full of amazing food.

I could probably retire in ten years.

It didn't feel like a proper job, even when Daniel was shouting at me.

I didn't have time to exercise (seeing as the ad was a joke, obviously I cancelled the yoga class.)

I had never met Daniel's family. Apparently, his dad lived in America and had very little to do with him. His mother, who had passed, was his idol and I strongly believe was responsible for making him a decent human being deep down inside. He had no siblings that he was aware of. His friends were his family, and he joked that included Jasper and me. The joke got a little close to home, if you pardon the pun. Upon hearing he was planning Christmas alone, I insisted he join mine. Highly inconvenient, considering he would have to pose as my boyfriend due to the fact I had already told my mum I worked for parliament. This in itself would open him up to a multitude of cringey moments every boyfriend of mine has had to endure when meeting my mum. (She had once actually farted on one's lap. Don't ask.)

We must inherit some of our mother's attitude towards men, right? Not that I go around farting on them, but I can definitely observe some similarities. As much as I love my dad, I would say she wasn't the best at picking them. Like, she doesn't deserve or believe she can get true happiness from a man. I have often worried it stems from deep-rooted rejection issues, having been adopted and told point-blank by her Jewish mother she wanted nothing to do with her. Nor does Jewish Gran want my mum to contact her brother or sister who she had later down the line when she was in a more suitable relationship. She had the decency to send a handwritten letter at least. I have not yet had the heart to tell Mum I read it. I accidentally found it in a living room drawer one afternoon while going through some family photos for an art project. One particular sentence has stuck with me:

"To reconnect now would be more trouble than it's worth."

I wish I could take away the pain that not knowing where she is from has caused inside her, and see what a difference it would make. She is already a wonderful human being. She will take in anyone who needs love and affection, including a selection of dogs that have become firm members of the family. Yet I can't help but notice a cloud that hangs over her, and I want to pop and burst it into a shower of love and see what affect that has on her ability to trust, love, and let go.

Daniel was delighted at the invitation and so was Jasper. Mum loved dogs. She has a way with them that has always fascinated me. Bobby, our latest addition, follows her command like military orders, yet ignores the rest of us. I have often wondered if she can talk dog. She has always been a great believer in the more the merrier.

Christmas was two days away, so I had zero time to talk myself out of this executive decision, not that there was anything executive-y about me. (I wish spell check realised that sometimes you know it is not a word but you are simply trying to express yourself in a way outside of its bossy little redlines.)

Dan's Christmas list was a brutal reminder I was the PA

in this relationship. So I whisked myself off to Selfridges to shop for my family, and also (on Dan's) behalf his three or four current girlfriends.

Nothing feels more like Christmas than being amongst the last-minute shoppers hustling and bustling though Oxford Street on a dark cold night. I was debating whether to go way over budget on a handbag for Mum that I knew she would adore, in the hopes it would spray a karmic effect on Christmas and she would not fart on Daniel. Oh, Christ, I was trying to buy karma. I headed for Gucci first to get the business bit over first, presents for Daniel's sweethearts, who, luckily for them, had a much higher budget. I suddenly heard a familiar voice.

"Hey hun, fancy seeing you here. What you doing looking in Gucci? Maybe I should get a job with Parliament!"

"Hey sis. Oh, I'm just browsing. 'Look, but don't touch,' as they say." I laughed.

"Okay, well, I would say let's get lunch but I have so much shopping to do, so best on. I will see you at Mum's though. You're coming, right?"

"Of course, wouldn't miss it. But don't buy her a handbag because I am getting her one, not from here, obviously."

"Mum wouldn't even notice it was Gucci." She called over her shoulder already wandering off in the direction of the perfume. "See you Christmas day."

That was a close call. I decided Bond Street would be far safer for discreet shopping and headed there. If my sister caught me with handfuls of Gucci bags my life would get even harder.

Daniel insisted we took a car to my mum's house, not that I was complaining. As I relaxed into the Bentley's soft cream seats, I was introduced to his driver, Richard.

"Are you not home for Christmas, Richard?" I asked.

"Home is Poland," he laughed. Richard's laugh made me feel all warm and hearty. He drove safely yet swiftly the entire way.

When Daniel occasionally demanded he step on it, Richard replied, "Not with the lady on board." I do not know what he was in such a rush for, Mum was always at least a few hours late with the turkey; still, at least we were all nice and merry by the time we sat down.

Mum answered the door dressed an elf. Of course she did. My brother announced his girlfriend was expecting and my sister was moving to Australia. This was all within the first half hour. It is a bit of a family tradition to turn up with a life changing event or decision. Normally there was a clear winner. I had only made it once having invited a member of The Rolling Stones to my dad's birthday. Mum had once come first at the annual garden festival, there wasn't much going on that year. With siblings busying themselves with making babies and planning to leave the country, my job announcement seemed a little less exciting. Nonetheless, it was better than nothing.

"So, what do you do, Richard?" Mum asked. Oh yes, I had asked Richard to join, he had planned on going to get a bed and breakfast and eat at a local pub but I was having none of it.

"Driver to the stars." Everyone laughed apart from Richard, Daniel, and I. Fortunately, my sister popped open a bottle of champagne and the cork landed on Mum's head, at which point the subject was changed. Drinks started flowing and we got into the swing of things.

The usual feast was laid out. Christmas was a day calories didn't get counted. Cauliflower cheese, slightly burnt around the edges, hot potatoes fluffy on the inside and crunchy on the out, lashings of stuffing, red cabbage, tender turkey, and parsnips that melted in your mouth. Mum had done us proud, and in between moments of topping myself up with cranberry sauce and gravy I noticed I had not once worried about Daniel. He was chatting away to my brothers and enjoying the fine cuisine. Richard and Mum seemed to be getting on great too, they even shared crackers and were the only ones wearing the silly gold hats. Mum had gone all out at M&S this year, an upgrade from Tesco's Finest which were so predictable and always full off shitty baubles and paper hats. M&S were cardboard hats making them all the sturdier, and you could get anything from a mirror, to a tape measure, to a lipstick holder in the cracker—

and I, for one, say Christmas is all about surprises.

We all knew to save sufficient room for round two, because after Mum had cleared the table (with the help of a very keen Richard) within the hour it was again covered with different kinds of delights. Cakes—one always homemade by Nan was this year a classic, Victoria sponge. How do nans always make the best cakes? She could put Mr Kipling out of business if she could be bothered. The reality was she would rather watch Coronation Street—cheese and biscuits, chocolate Yule, mince pies, and a big fat Christmas pudding with lashings of cream. Just what we all needed before a night of munching Quality Streets and more drinking, just in case we hadn't had our diabetes fix for the evening.

Mum pulled a face whilst taking a sip of her traditional Christmas brandy that made me think she was about to announce she had forgotten to take her medication. Not that she was on any that I was aware of; now, whether she needed any—that's a different story.

"So, darling, what are you doing now for work?"

Wishing she had asked before I had also decided to enjoy a brandy, though determined not to miss my moment, I took a sobering bite of delicious sponge.

"I am an assistant to a member of Parliament. Please don't ask me anymore as I have been sworn to secrecy and such matters should not be discussed after the amount of wine and brandy I have had."

Richard's confused look concerned me. Tensing my arse in the hope it would somehow keep his mouth shut, I barely noticed Mum's reaction to my news. Every time he looked like he was about to speak I would tense and jerk out of my seat and make a strange squeak. For once my sister offered a welcome diversion.

"So are you two an item?" My sister enquired halfway through munching on a potato. Daniel looked amused and I knew what ever came out of his mouth next would be mischief.

"Yes, we have grown incredibly fond of each other, haven't we, Anna?"

"Yes, Daniel. I mean, what girl could resist that face?" My mum and sister looked at Daniel's handsome, beaming complexion, looked after by regular facials and face creams that cost more than our whole Christmas dinner. They nodded in mutual agreement that he was undoubtedly gorgeous.

Mum seemed genuinely happy for me. The first fake boyfriend I get and she loves him, brilliant. Maybe I should just hire them all in the future. My fake life was giving me an adrenaline rush. Richard seemed to have clocked on by now, allowing my bum muscles to relax again. Still, guess that was my exercise for the day.

Dan insisted on whizzing back to London late that night, as he wasn't used to being offered the sofa as a place to rest his pretty little head, poor love. I had to do the usual and endure the next day.

Though, really. What is the point between Christmas and

New Year? If I could re-arrange the annual calendar New Year's Eve would be the day after. Wipe out Boxing Day. What does that even mean? I have been told a few times. The fact I still have no clue accurately reflects my thoughts on the day. The only logical explanation I can summon up is the following: it was a preparatory day envisioned by some physic angel for the modern family, such as ours. Where each year one parent gets Christmas Day and the other Boxing Day. Then the label makes sense, as far more boxing is likely to occur as the tension of being forced to spend so much time together and to maintain a festive bubbliness that is increasingly hard to maintain, having over-indulged. With January around the corner, laughing at you. The only thing to get you through is to carry on drinking and eating, further fuelling January's state of hysteria. Might as well give her something to really laugh at.

I entered the New Year as per usual. With a vague memory of the night before, my hand stuck to my left cheek as I slowly opened one eye and then the next to check I was home. Yes. I could hear the flatmates laughing downstairs, could smell toast, and would shortly join them to find out what had happened as we saw in the new year. Hopefully there was marmite to accompany the many rounds of toast it would require to bring me back to human. I was also in desperate need of a chat.

"Girls, how bad was I?"

"Noel had to carry you home and you were trying to dress him as a girl. Don't tell us you're thinking of becoming a personal stylist next?"

"Funny you should say that…" Tweedle Dee looked like she wished she could take back what she'd just said, immediately concerned she could be responsible for another career change.

"If you give up this job, I will personally write you off as insane. You are working for someone who pays you to eat and sleep at their house, look after their dog, and buy presents for his play mates. And pays you more than I get paid for working like a dog for someone who also wants me to be his play mate." Tweedle Dee ejaculated her dismay with a few crumbs of toast that I felt land on my nose and around my eyes. The reason I was joking about the pondering a new job wasn't entirely due to my usual job slutty reasons. I had a sense a change may be on the horizon not instigated by my bouncy approach to careers. I knew working for Daniel was as great as the Tweedle's often pointed out with a playful jealousy.

Daniel had asked me to meet him early afternoon, and there was something about the way he had said 'chat' and his tone, softer than usual almost sympathetic that gave me a feeling he was going to deliver something I wouldn't want to hear. I had always had a buried guilt about my position with Daniel. The job that had never really existed in the first place didn't really have to. Daniel had allocated me jobs he already had other people doing and, granted, he loved having me around, sometimes I felt he was just paying me to be a friend who answers his calls twenty-four/seven, and makes him feel better when he is hung-over, anxious, or feeling depressed with my remarkable sense of humour. Which was really a bit of a waste and he should just get a therapist. If I was going to capitalize on my sense of humour surely stand-up was the way to go. Or qualify as a therapist, maybe. But according to a friend, therapy is very 2015.

My guilt rose to the surface sometimes. I felt a bit like I was hiding in an easy life, as much as I shook off the comments about how good I had it. I felt a little like the girl that was getting everything handed to on a plate. With Daniel, I didn't have to try too hard, there was no risk of testing my true potential. I had a strong sense of what was coming in our chat.

I met him at his home. He answered the door, and I knew right away my instincts were right. His head was low and he was displaying all the mannerisms of someone who was about to break up with someone.

As I walked into the living room, I saw a bag of my things all packed into the corner.

"You're letting me go?" My question was rhetorical, but he nodded regardless.

"Come and sit down."

He made me a coffee. I acknowledged this was the first time he had ever done this. At least there was one perk to being fired. I might as well ride the sympathy wave as long as I could.

"Any biscuits to go with that?" I felt a sadness ride through me at the thought of not having access to the posh biscuits Daniel always insisted I stocked the cupboards with. I loved that kitchen, the house, Jasper.

As he returned with a coffee, far too strong and a pack of my favorite pistachio and chocolate cookies, I let him get on with what he had to say. I could tell he was finding this really hard.

"Anna, I was thinking about you a lot last night." For a moment I thought he was going to declare he was in love with me.

"This is crazy; I see you like my little sister. I can't keep you working for me, as I know it's a waste of your potential. For once in my life I am doing the right thing. You make me want to do the right thing. You know you need more than this, mopping up my messes. It's not enough for you and if you waste the best years of your life doing it, you'll regret it, trust me. You'll come to resent me and I never want that."

Daniel was right. Though I had tried my best to ignore her,

my intellectual side had been stamping her feet in anticipation of our next venture. She had been thoroughly underused for a while and was ready to kick some butt again. Still, leaving Daniel was like throwing away another security blanket, the best one I had found in a long time. It made me feel sad, scared and vulnerable.

He was saying out loud what I knew already. I was a bit like a Playboy bunny. Instead of sexual and social obligations to Hugh Hefner, I had canine duties to Jasper and general duties of care to Daniel.

Gorgeous as Daniel was, there was no sexual desire between us. Like he said, it was more like a sibling kind of love. Besides, it's not like he needed another girl to shower him with romantic affection. He had a long list of girls who would be willing to take care of that.

Despite Daniel and me severing ties professionally, he would always be my friend.

"I will always be here for you, Anna, and so will Jasper. We just want you to go do something great."

The one boss that finally got me was sacking me. The irony of it made the moment truly bitter sweet as I walked out of his mansion as his PA for the very last time.

Chapter 13
FREE TO TRIAL WHATEVER I PLEASE

I woke up to the bliss of being unattached, battling the fear of the unknown and feeling totally rejected.

"Daniel had set me free," I told myself loud enough to drown out the other voice that was not so nice. "He rejected you, as you're useless, Anna." Did he? I had a conversation in my head as I replayed Daniel's reasoning for letting me go.

"No," I told the voice, repeating Daniel's words. *You are destined for much bigger things than managing my love life and walking Jasper. You have got so much potential, I am forcing you to spread your wings and go and fly.*

"Fly where?" The other voice laughed. "To your next career suicide?"

My reserves of self-belief were not quite strong enough to shut the voice up. In my best attempt to feel more upbeat I reminded myself of the good things I had going right now. I was free to wake up in the mornings with commitments to no one other than myself. I could spend them sitting in coffee shops, as I often did, observing in amazement everyone else going about the daily grind. I was so curious about them. What they were all doing and where they were all going? Did they like it when they got there? Would they rather be doing something else and did they have the time to even think about it? I so wanted to sit one of them down, buy them a piece of cake and have a chat. Humans. So interesting, so perplexing, yet deep down, so simple. A good friend of mine never really got the whole job thing. She once told me in complete sincerity that not having a job was a full-time commitment. Fortunately, she married a trader.

Approaching humans whilst caught up in the rush of life was a risk. An abrupt, rude, potentially violent response could be expected. Would I take the risk to get my answers? Probably. Eventually. That would be a project in itself, "The Jobslut Interviews." I promise I will get around to it, I can even take requests should any of you have an intense curiosity about a particular profession, ping me an email. I will risk a "fuck off" or two in the name of research. It's just I really need to finish this first or it will never get done.

My next job came to me by happy accident. I was sitting there, minding my own beeswax, watching the humans, when I noticed one was shuffling around by my feet in a bit of a flurry.

"Sorry, Miss. I dropped my balls."

"Oh."

His expressionless face told me he saw no comedic value in his bold statement. Two tennis balls pressed softly against my right foot, the bright yellow and demanding attention.

"I love tennis." I gave him back his dropped balls, mildly amused by his serious character. "Are you a professional?"

"No. I own a hotel and we have a court there for guests. Are you?"

"Absolutely not," I told him with confidence. Though I had thought about becoming one around the age of eighteen. I ignored the thought bubble. I did not want to overload him with information as he didn't seem the type to appreciate it.

"What do you do? Write?" He was unexpectedly nosy, a pleasant surprise.

"No. Well, yes, actually, not as a job anymore. I just finished working as a PA, so nothing at the moment."

"I need a receptionist. Do you have a CV you could send me? Actually, just come for a trial Friday night if you want to?"

"Sure." I loved Blake's hotel. And what harm could a little trial do?

The Harm a Little Trial Can Do

Five-star hotels are one of my favourite things. They transport you away from the rushing world and wrap you in a blanket of comfort and luxury. The fabric woven from subtle attentions to detail you barely notice. The gentle treatment from the ever-pleasing staff, the carefully chosen décor, a relaxing bar and spa that emphasize the atmosphere in the most beautifully understated way. The rooms with little chocolates next to the bed, inviting bathtubs, and cozy robes. Voilà, an oasis of perfection to hide away.

The pressure on a receptionist in such an establishment is pretty immense. They have a number of things to do. Though, most importantly, it is to make the guest feel important. Not like a rude, pretentious fucktard, which they do unfortunately have to encounter. Those revolving doors are no filter for the above and thus the receptionist will find them thrust in their face with the most annoying attitudes, requests, and complaints which is where having some experience in dealing with such people comes very handy. Experience otherwise known as life.

This is where I step in with my twenty-eight buckets of the stuff, buckets as varied as a rainbow when fused, forming the colourful arc of my timeline. Another job, another shade. So, first things first, I got the important stuff out the way. Where were the free chocolates and pens kept? I had already had requests from the flatmates for a load and I always like to deliver. Check.

Next: who is nice and who is not? I knew the drill with places like this; you would get the authority grippers who filled their balloons of self-importance from making new staff feel totally inferior. Seriously, some work places are just like the school playground if you fast forward ten or twenty years, add a few inches in height, and exchange teachers for bosses.

Ever get that feeling you're back where you started? I had a feeling of nausea and déjà vu that I blotted out with my sense of humour. The nature of the job took me back to my waitressing days. Except I was no longer a teenager and no longer had Sarah to save me by purposely slipping on a banana. It was nice to be working around a variety of people again, though.

My first week I caught one of my naughtier coworkers (whilst innocently going about my business stealing pens and chocolates from the backroom) giving a manager a—ahem—*present* she shouldn't have been. Turns out I struck gold. Laura, a tenacious, hot, eastern European who looked like Mila Kunis and had an attitude to scare the tits of the meanest of mean girls, was the known badass of the office. Our first meeting was certainly one to be remembered. She whipped our manager's pants up quicker than I could identify if he was a briefs or boxer kind of guy, and she said she was willing to do anything to buy my silence on the matter. I just wanted her to be nice, so although a tad suspicious, she seemed okay with it.

The rest of the gang couldn't believe my luck. The gang included Bernie the doorman, Belle the barmaid, Jack the waiter, and Alice the maid. There were loads of other people working in the hotel, though those are the ones I become natural allies with. We interacted on a daily basis and all had at least one thing in common. Bernie and I were openly judgmental of all guests' attire. He was camp as hell and insisted on celebrating this with matching brightly coloured socks and briefs every day.

He liked to say, "I like to remind my sausage what is what and what is not." I tried not to over-analyse this statement, though whatever made him feel less heterosexual than his grey suit and buff body portrayed was fine by me. You know how they say never to judge a book by its cover? Well, this also applies to the sexuality by a bellboy's suit.

Belle and I loved fine wine, despite still accepting to drink shit ones just to be social. We had discussed this at length within the first hour of meeting. I knew we would become good friends. Anyone that knew which chardonnay to pick me from a menu is inevitably a keeper. Jack and I loved trying to find a way to laugh at everything and everyone. Which was pretty easy here. Alice was a fellow Aquarius. This gave her an instant green card to be my friend, as I had guessed she had a wild side and loved all things sweet. She promised to steal me some of the special chocolates from the kitchen when she had a chance—what a doll.

As I discovered the backdrop to this collection of interesting staff, and the rumours that seemed to keep the buzz of working backstage alive, it felt like I had walked into the modern-day *Downton Abbey*. Love, scandal, beauty, heartache, birth, death, marriage, financial woes, the fundamentals are all there. It was a perfect environment to breed insecurity made worse by a lack of gentlemen and the dating system that can be summed up as, "Fuck and go." Thank you, Tinder.

The fact that men can now sweep through galleries of girls of all shapes, sizes, nationalities, and professions to hook up with by a click doesn't exactly help those of us waiting for Prince Charming to come and find us offline. Someone once told me that eventually soul mates meet, as they share the same hiding place. Call me a hopeless romantic, but I hold on to this to be true.

Being a jobslut fills the void I may otherwise be filling with pointless sex and dating. I find this a comforting thought as a Mrs Tipping drums a handful of nails on my desk and places the rest on her tiny hip. Bernie threw me a this-one's-a-shithead glance, preparing me for the inhumane treatment the lizard-like creature before me was about to deliver.

Nowhere does one feel the wrath of disparity in a workplace than between the staff of luxury hotels and their guests. When your training says that no demand is too big or too small and that the discretion of guests is paramount, the deck is really stacked in their favor. Once, Alice had to spend three hours filling a bath of roses and orange peel. I thought of Dan. I empathized with the staff of his regular abodes receiving the ridiculous requests for Mr Big Balls. His redeeming factor, as I mentioned before, was he got so wasted the large tips justified their efforts. Some of the guests I had so far endured were far worse. It was a tip in itself when they just left.

Others were quite lovely, mind. One gentleman had been occupying the penthouse for so long he was practically a permanent resident. His kindness wiped out the disgraceful auras of others. Like that of Mrs Tipping, who came off her iPhone just to click her spindly fingers in air at me and demand I, take her "stuffs" to her room, in her thick Russian accent.

"Yes, Madam. Someone will be along shortly to assist you. May I get you a drink?"

"*Pfff.*" She returned to her phone.

Total charmer. British people have a knack for sounding sarcastic even when we don't mean to be. For example, when I told her to have a nice day, the singsong tone and stupid smile makes it understandable she probably heard *Go fuck yourself.* It is a knack that always proves unhelpful when dealing with people who are SE2PO (super easy to piss off.) Americans were blessed with a tone of jolly geniality so when they dish out, the gesture is happily received. Which is why I had decided to put my time in L.A. to good use and greet all new guests with my best attempt at a Californian accent.

I was planning to launch into my American accent as I heard a familiar voice."

Excuse me where do I check in?" I looked up. And there he was.

Tom, looking more gorgeous than I remembered him.

"Anna! No way. What are the chances? I can't believe this."

"Tom, what are you doing here? I asked, expecting to see Stacy hovering behind somewhere.

"I got cast for a series. *Pride and Prejudice*, can you believe it? I am finally going to play my favorite role!"

"That's insane!"

I felt slightly ashamed as I looked at him glowing, having achieved the dream he had been working so hard for when I had left him in L.A. And here I was, checking him into a five-star hotel in the same suit I had been wearing for four shifts, as I couldn't be bothered to wash it.

"Man, I have to be on set in an hour and have to take a shower. Let me take you for dinner tomorrow." He handed me a card with his head shot, number, and agency details.

"Sure. Check-in is that way." I pointed him over to reception.

"Okay. Great, it's a date, our first date! Anna, this has made my day." He held my gaze for a second or two that felt like a few minutes. It reminded me of holding a yoga pose waiting for the instructor to release you out of it. He had this look in his eye like he had just found exactly what he was looking for.

As I quickly stepped out to get some fresh air and to process what just happened, Alice appeared from somewhere behind me and poked me sharply in the back. "You're going on a date with Tom Dart? Are you fucking serious?" Alice exhaled with her cigarette smoke not wanting to waste a second of our fifteen-minute breaks, or "intervals" as the Americans say.

"You know him?" I was genuinely shocked. Had I missed something? I didn't watch much TV, though surely I would have noticed had Tom become famous.

"Yes, of course. He is the new star of *Pride and Prejudice*!"

"Oh. We studied together in L.A." I was trying to take everything in; it had all happened so quickly. And there was so sign of Stacy.

"Wow, Anna. He is so hot."

"Your observational skills are very commendable." That was one thing I could not argue with. Alice smiled with satisfaction at the compliment as we made it back inside to finish our shifts. All I could think about was dinner tomorrow, or as Tom had called it, our first date!

Chapter 14
THE DATE

First there was a little life admin to deal with in order to ensure my date could go ahead. A Friday night dinner would mean asking Alice to cover my evening shift or making up a sincere-with-a-touch-of-obscene excuse as to why I would not be available. Why has someone not made the app already, selling coded pardons for every occasion. After all, one must always be appropriate with their excuses; it is key to avoiding offence. You wouldn't excuse yourself from a wedding in the same manner as after work drinks, now, would you. Honesty is not always the best policy.

This date was something I had not engaged in properly for a long time. I had well and truly given up when the last one bored me so much I escaped from the window of the ladies's toilets between the starter and main course. I did send him a text to say I had terrible digestive trouble and I left my share towards the wine with the confused-looking waitress.

I am pretty sure I have been on a total of two dates since my get away disaster. I decided the only men I needed in life were Ben and Jerry. When I read books about finding love or even listened to my friends talk about it, I can't help feeling they are faking it. Maybe that's just how I deal with the fact I haven't found it, or maybe they are faking. The idea of love for me had lost its mojo. I didn't believe in it. But, this was Tom. It felt different with him. He made me feel a way no one ever had.

That feeling made everything else seem slightly less important.

It was closely approaching evening. Tom was meeting me outside my local pub for a pre-dinner drink. Where we were eating was still a mystery. He has insisted on taking me somewhere he had found. His tall frame moved towards me in a crisp white shirt, buttons open to reveal a little bit of chest. Being around him with no Stacy to intervene in our affection felt deliciously exciting.

As we sipped cold wine and exchanged updates on our respective days, Tom pointed to a guy that sat perched alone on the side of the bar. I knew him; we called him Pepsi Pete. He was about seventy, and he came to the pub every night to drink Pepsi. His wife had passed away and he had no children. My friends and I often sat with him and shouted him a Pepsi. He loved how silly we got the more wine we consumed.

"I will ask him to join us. Can't have him drinking alone," I said. Soon Pete was walking over with his Pepsi and a packet of McCoy's. His big cheesy grin lit up his face as he plonked himself down and filled up my wine glass with the bottle we had in the middle of the table. He loved playing bar man for us.

"How you doing, Pete?" I asked.

"I am good, thanks for having me. Is this your boyfriend?"

"No, he is my friend Tom. Tom, this is Pepsi Pete."

"Are you going to have babies soon?" he asked Tom with a full mouth of crisps spraying directly in my face, and blissfully unaware his question was at all inappropriate.

"Maybe one day, a boy and a girl." He played along with Pete, who was turning out to be the surprise addition to our date.

Tom's phone stole our attention as it performed a vibrating

dance over the table. All three of us looked at it blankly before Tom decided to pick up the thing and excused himself from the table. He returned a few minutes later beaming from ear to ear.

"My sister just had a baby. I am an uncle!" Tom fist punched the air. "Must have been all that talk of babies, Pete."

"Yes, see, I knew someone was having a baby." He proudly slurped up some Pepsi.

"Congratulations, Uncle Tom," I said as I gave him a hug and then went and went to get us another round and Pete another Pepsi.

He eventually bid us goodbye, retreating in his sugar coma home, leaving Tom and me alone at last.

"So, Miss Anna. What happened to acting? My Juliet?"

"Well, Romeo, I decided after a long round of auditions my heart just wasn't in it. I am still trying to find where my heart belongs, to be honest. In terms of career, that is. Though I am still happy to be your Juliet, should you want me to be."

I smiled as seductively as I could muster. He moved his hand onto mine, and he looked into my eyes. "My job choices have been this random collection of moments; They seemed a really good idea at the time."

"I can relate to that," he said. I realized there was a lot about Tom I didn't know, like why did he want to be an actor? What had he done before? I wanted to know everything. Tom signaled our cab had arrived and we left for the restaurant.

We arrived at dinner a little late. The place was a stunning little Italian tucked away in Covent Garden. As we made tipsy apologies for being late a little waitress rushed us to our corner table.

"Good choice, Romeo." Tom looked delighted. He held my gaze for a second as if to say something then decided against it.

The waitress appeared, eager to get our orders. Tom told her to bring some wine as we investigated the lacy menus.

"The gazpacho is insane and I would consider flying to London for the calzone," he gushed.

"So. Do you seduce all your dates with calzone? As I am not going to lie, it's working for me."

I tried to imagine Tom sitting here with another girl, but I couldn't. He laughed, dropping his head. Seeing him so relaxed and happy made me melt. It was infectious. I had always adored him, but since he had achieved some success in his career he had a gooey confidence oozing out of him.

I decided I needed to find out exactly what happened with Stacy. Subtly not being a strong point, I dived straight in.

"So, are you still in touch with Stacy?" The answer was better than expected.

"Hell no. I finally realized that girl was toxic and crazy."

"Hallelujah." I high-fived him. "When did the penny drop?"

"I always knew she was a little nuts." His eye contact drifted before he came back to the conversation. "I never told you this in L.A.—she kind of had a bit of a hold over me."

I knew it. I waited as he told me more.

"She knew something about my past and threatened to tell everyone if I ever left her. Let's leave it at that."

Of course I couldn't leave it at that.

He gave me a look that reminded me of one he often gave in L.A. Like he's on the verge of telling me something yet unsure if he will regret it.

"Tom, you can tell me anything you want. I always had the feeling there was something you were holding back."

"Really?" He looked genuinely surprised. "Ah okay, what

the heck? It's in my past. Before I found my love for acting, I was a bit fucked up."

He took a deep breath then expelled the next sentences like stale air that had been clogging his lungs. "To be clear, I was addicted to cocaine and various meds for like a year. I had no money and ended up dealing. I met Stacy through a buddy who knew my game. She was one of my biggest clients. I finally got my shit together and quit it all, taking drugs, dealing. I moved away from all the people I had been surrounding myself with. Stacy stuck around, though. We had a messy relationship I should have thrown away with the rest of that shit lifestyle, but she just wouldn't let me."

"Wow, I had no idea. Well done. That's amazing you found the strength to change your life around."

"Thanks." He looked like a weight had been lifted from his shoulders by telling me.

"You should be proud of yourself. Don't be scared of your past; own it. Look at you now, you're an inspiration to everyone."

"It took me a long time and a lot of work, though I finally found the strength to let go of my past and she was the final piece. It happened over a stack of pancakes in Mel's diner on Sunset. And you know what? I stayed and ate the lot and decided enough was enough. I remember thinking I can't wait to get this over with so I can eat those pancakes. Which is why pretty quickly, I told her there was someone else. I don't think her ego quite believed it. She threw mw a few insults and stormed off. And that was that."

His delivery was so deadpan and matter-of-fact it made me want to laugh at the thought of him sitting with s stack of pancakes, watching Stacy's dramatic exit down Sunset Boulevard.

"The someone else was you, Anna. When you left L.A. I realized how much you meant to me. I wanted so many times to call you and tell you. I guess I was scared you didn't feel the same way and I didn't want to ruin what we had and make myself look like a total idiot, which I hope I'm not right now."

"Far from it." I reached across and stroked Tom's hand. We held each other's gaze. There was a mutual look in our eyes telling each other how sorry we were for not being honest about our feelings sooner. Being honest about your feelings after holding them in so long made me feel lighter somehow. I didn't even realize how badly I needed to hear Tom say he wanted me as much I wanted him. I had buried my feelings away in one of those 'it doesn't bother me' boxes like I did a lot of things. Since we were both confessing, laying it all on the table, I thought now was a good time as ever to flood him with my career dilemmas since I had seen him. It was in a way an attempt to build a bridge and close the gap distance and time had caused. And one part a way of letting him know exactly what he had on his hands if this was to go any further. I didn't sugar coat how lost and confused and unfulfilled I felt as he listened to my self-sabotage I felt lighter and lighter.

"You must think I am a total wacko now."

"Anna, I don't think there is anything weird about the fact you haven't found the right place to direct your talent."

"Tom, I am a total jobslut?"

"And what's wrong with that? Life's a journey, not a destination. What's the rush? If it doesn't feel right, you move on and that takes balls. I am proud of you."

I took a sip of wine, I was a little lost for words, for once. I didn't want this night to end. Tom pulled out a little purple book.

"You know, we are a good match, you and me." He opened

the book and started to read me a passage in what was an excellent attempt at a British accent. "Love match for Aquarius and Libra. Both Aquarians and Libras love socializing, talking, and being around people. Their social life as a couple will be rich, full, and rewarding. They will also enjoy pursuing and sharing their individual ideas and pursuits with each other. Libras's natural diplomacy also helps to counteract Aquarians's natural stubborn streak, and together, these two will find it easy to reach a compromise when rough patches arise."

"Sounds promising." I made a toast. "To the stars being aligned."

"Fancy ice cream for dessert?" He smiled. I wondered if he was remembering our last night in L.A.

I knew exactly what I wanted and it wasn't on the menu. Tom looked at me like I was treasure.

"Come and stay with me tonight." I didn't need to reply. He squeezed my hand and we left the restaurant a whole lot closer than we'd been when we had arrived.

The next morning, I woke up with Tom wrapped around me. We were officially spooning. Even our feet were intertwined. I felt his baby-soft skin against mine and gentle kisses on my back as he pulled me closer. After another well-spent hour in bed, I had to peel myself away from Tom and the most comfy bed I had ever slept on.   "Don't go yet," he pleaded. "That night was worth waiting for."

"The best things often are." I kissed him on the nose then slipped away.

I had text Alice confessing my sins and asking her to bring me a spare uniform. We planned to meet in the staff toilets so I could quickly get changed and start my shift without anyone finding out about my secret overnight stay with a guest.

Alice was all the more curious as to how my night with Tom had gone. She was ever so observant, I thought, as she placed her chin on her hands and lent her elbows on the side of my counter next to the demanding morning phone.

"Did you get laid?"

"A lady never tells," I teased.

"A smile like that is only caused by food or sex," she pulled my cheeks apart as if testing they were real. I thanked her again for the uniform she had dutifully supplied. There was still with time to grab a needed coffee before my shift officially started. As if by magic, Tom appeared with a tray of three Starbucks cups.

"Who needs a latté?" He grinned from ear to ear. Alice took her drink and raised her eyebrow at me.

"You have got me hooked on these," he said raising his Venti-sized Starbucks cup and snuggled it into his chest, the sweet smell of hazelnut on his breath. "Anyway, I have to go. Will message you later. I have to be on set in thirty."

And off he went. I had the strangest feeling of déjà vu as he walked away. It reminded me of my waitressing days. I felt so much had happened since handing in my apron; at the same time, I had gotten nowhere. Here I was, back in hospitality. I had a massive wake-up call. An epiphany. I felt an emergency exit coming on. I needed to find my purpose, passion, and master the self-belief to get on with doing whatever it was that gave me the same glow that Tom had when he talked about acting.

What was it? It was out there. It had to be, but it certainly wasn't in this hotel.

I went straight to my boss and informed him I would have to leave for the rest of the day due to personal problems, and later sent an email that I would not be returning. Alice was disappointed. Still, she had no intention of leaving. She was quite happy shagging the boss, and unlike me, had not had enough of the hospitality industry.

Tom texted me that afternoon asking if I was working the following morning.

It was with great satisfaction I replied, "No, I quit."

"Come to L.A.?"

Wow, I had not been expecting that, still if there was anyone I would move half way around the world for it was Tom. I thought it best not to reply after three glasses of wine with the Tweedles. We were in the middle of my standard post job-break-up procedure, they were giving me the more-fish-in-the-sea speech while I kept topping up our wine. I wasn't sure L.A. was the answer to my problems right now. I wish I knew what was.

Waking up unemployed, as you know, was a familiar feeling. It was not accompanied with any doubt I had made the right decision; I finally had a feeling I was moving in the right direction. I re-read the text from Tom to ensure I had not dreamt it. L.A. Did I really want to go back to the States where I had no visa—thus zero career prospects—with a gorgeous actor where we could continue our romance in the sunshine? Maybe. Flip a coin? Feeling overwhelmed by the decision on the table, I needed coffee and to read my horoscope. The caffeine helped, the horoscope not so much. You win some, you lose some.

Tom seemed so together. He made me compare my meandering track to his focused career path. His passion for acting was so alive. He made me feel like a doughnut with no jam, I was missing my passion and was seriously ready to try and find it. Tom gave me a new motivation to figure out what career I wanted. Stop living in a daydream. As tempting as romancing in the sun in was, I knew I would not find it there. I needed to go on my own little journey of self-discovery somewhere closer to home. I booked a train ticket to Cornwall for the weekend.

Tom clearly had no idea where Cornwall was.

"Is that in Europe?," he texted. Bless.

"No, it is actually a few hours away by train." A small part of me wished he was with me. Should I have asked him to come? Or was that too much too soon?

"I will call you when I get back to L.A. and I'll be back in London next month. Missing you already x."

I loved how every time I saw his name my stomach had butterflies. It made me feel sixteen again. I couldn't stop smiling as my train pulled out of Paddington Station. The lady in the seat next to me was French, wrapped in a delicious aroma of Chanel No. 5. I thanked my travel angels for sending me such a pleasant train neighbour. I was armed with a bag full of snacks from Marks & Spencer and a healthy dose of determination to find my passion because, really, what good is a doughnut without its jam?

Halfway through my journey my French lady turned to me—she had been quietly reading a book up to that point—and her sudden interaction took me by surprise.

"Why is love never easy?" She looked at me, her delicate French accent echoing in my right ear. She shut her book and turned to me, "Are you in love?"

"Me? Love? No. Well, no…I am not sure." The answer surprised me as much as her. How could I even be contemplating being in love with Tom? We barely knew each other.

"Ah, your eyes say different." Her accent was dreamy. "If you are in love, enjoy, don't ruin with complications we create in our mind." She started to pack her book away as the train slowed into her stop.

"Au revoir, enjoy your journey." I watched her slim frame slide through the door and swiftly move away into the distance, leaving me with the remainder of my journey to contemplate her departing statement delivered in the most beautiful French accent I've ever heard.

My decision to come to Cornwall had been completely lastminute.com. (Funnily enough the same website I used to book myself a cheap bed and breakfast by the sea.) It was everything you could expect from a "family run," recently renovated, idyllic, peaceful retreat. Two butch lesbians greeted me. Pat and Mich, who insisted I did not call her Michelle, as it was only her mum that called her that and she was born with a homophobic stick up her ass. Fair enough. The recent renovations referred to the fresh paint job the four-bedroom property had received, the crumbly ceilings and weathered furniture could have done with a re-vamp, too. Though, hey ho, it was £29 per night, so I wasn't about to complain.

"We only offer half board, my love. This is the breakfast room." Pat showed me through to a lounge with a central dining table with two long wooden benches where I and other lodgers would be breakfasting.

"We offer a buffet service from seven to eleven in the morning."

Pat's breathing was getting a little fast. She had very large breasts to juggle and was mildly overweight which made moving uncomfortable. Mich continued the rest of the tour. My bedroom was on the first floor with a sea view. It was a single bed with one wardrobe painted orange complementing the skirting boards. It would do. It was comfortable and had a cosy feel that sometimes even the most elaborate of residences fail to capture. Smelt clean.

"I am starving. Where is a good place to get a bite?"

"There is a great little pub over the road, they have the fish and chips. Pat and I will join you if you like." What the heck. I have no better offer for company. Soon after, I sat in The Moon and Stars with Pat and Mich sharing a bottle of Pinot and waiting for my battered halibut.

"What brings you to us, my love?" Pat had a gentle voice you didn't expect from a woman of her sturdy structure. She smelt like flowers and dressed in a mixture of elegance and bohemian. I would say Mich definitely wore the trousers in the relationship. She was a lot slimmer, dressed in a little too much denim and had more fire in her than Pat.

"I just quit my job. And this guy I was seeing asked me to go to back to L.A. with him, so I came for some head space to make the decision. Do I stay in London and embark on the next stage of my career, or take a break in L.A.? It's a tough one."

"What is this guy like?" Mich asked, filling up my glass as if reading my mind, which is normally pretty straightforward when it comes to wine. Keep it flowing.

"An actor, hot, down to earth, Virgo."

Like me, Pat smiled. "So, what's stopping you?"

"I am always jumping around. I'm no stranger to getting on a plane and hoping for the best. I am just not in the mood for it right now. I feel like I want to find something closer to home. Call it intuition."

"Well, there's your answer. L.A. isn't going anywhere."

"You're probably right. Tell me, how did you guys meet?"

"We came from a tiny little village in Wales."

"Like *Gavin & Stacey* Wales?"

"Yes, that's it though not from Barry. Our village was full of judgmental morons. Pat and I had a thing going on for a year before we decided to tell anyone. We met at a cooking class. We finally got so pissed off with being scared to be our true selves we thought fuck it. So we applied to be on the couple's special of a TV favourite in both our households. *Come Dine with Me.* We won it, didn't we, babe?"

"Sure did," Pat's eyes widened in appreciation as our food arrived. Big plates full of cod, chunky chips, mushy peas, and sauces on silverware. Pub grub at its best. These two were cracking.

"Here's to winning *Come Dine with Me* and at giving the biggest middle finger to judgment all in one hour." We all raised a glass.

"Yeah, then we thought we should get out of here. We started looking at options. We loved hospitality and cooking, it was all we had ever known. We just picked Cornwall and found the cottage. It was such a great place, we thought why not turn it into a B&B? And the rest is history."

That night, I found myself back at the loyalty bar of the B&B where I met two other lodgers, Paul and Janet. They had both found their way here as I had by chance. They had only known each other as long as I had, though there was a familiarity between them. They had a way of finishing each other's sentences like an old couple, the hilarious part was there were completely oblivious. My assumption they were happily married was quashed immediately.

"Oh gosh no." They both exclaimed as if I had just accused them of a crime.   "We hardly know each other." I accepted their denial of romance and took in my surroundings.

It was a cozy little room out the back of the building where they only invited trustworthy guests.

"How do you know if a guest is trustworthy?" I asked Pat.

"A feeling. If you feel like you want to take them to the pub for fish and chips, for example."

Pat poured us all an aged whisky that would be wasted on me (not being an experienced spirit drinker; I would have been happy with Jack Daniel's.) Still, I happily accepted, as did Paul and Janet.

"A nightcap," Pat said. We all raised a glass and continued chatting, genuinely keen to know more about one another. Paul had been coming here regularly for years, when he needed it.

"I come here for some inspiration and good whisky," he told me when I asked what bought him to the delightful seaside town. He was a writer from Ireland.

"Where do you live in Ireland?" I feigned interest, not that I had the slightest clue about the geography. My knowledge of Dublin ended at four-leaf clovers, Guinness, and Gerard Butler's dreamy accent in *P.S. I Love You*.

"I am kind of homeless. I travel around Ireland living in hotels. So right now this is my home, as much as it is yours, Pat's, and Janet's." He pointed at each person he named as we all listened to his slow voice. He had the presence of teacher and we took the role of students like ducks to water.

"We all experience the same feeling of living under this roof, and then we move on. And that's all life is. A collection of experiences that are all your own. So if you learn to enjoy the benefits of the experience without seeking the desire of some other's idea of ownership, it is bliss."

Janet was a food critic, which surprised me. With all due respect, I had imagined her holing herself up in some classy city hotels where she could sample far more sophisticated cuisine than local pub grub and breakfast buffets.

"It's a relief to be away from the pompousness of fine

dining and just relax, without a face staring intensely at me as I chew, waiting for me to tell them if it's any good. It's just food, for fuck's sake; I don't see the need to take it so seriously." This is the last thing I remember before calling it a night—a good belly laugh at Janet's refreshing honesty.

After a long, drunken slumber, I awoke to sympathetic and gentle sunlight easing me out of my hangover. I enjoyed an orgasmic stretch from the tip of my fingers to the tip of my toes then relaxed back into the sleeping position before fumbling around for my phone, which started to vibrate under my left leg.

After failing to work the shower three times, I succumbed to a quick strip wash and made my way downstairs to find coffee. Janet, Paul, and Pat were already in the breakfast lounge with papers sprawled in front of them.

"Give me five minutes," said Pat, busying herself laying the table. Aromas of fresh croissants, sweet oranges, and coffee swirled around the room reminding me I was hungry. The atmosphere was so relaxed. Like waking up at home on a Sunday morning with your dad frying bacon in his underpants. Though everyone was dressed in relaxed attire. I slunk onto the couch next to Paul and started to read his paper over his shoulder. He opened up the tabloid for us both to devour the headlines. I love a scandal.

"Now that is a sight for sore eyes." Janet had the agility of a grasshopper springing past us to make her way to the breakfast buffet and attacked the piping hot eggs. An array of breads, jams, breakfast cereal, homemade scones, and clotted cream were all laid out. Crispy bacon and scrambled egg were covered in big silver pots.

"You know what my favorite food in the whole world

is?" Janet clasped her hands together and leaned forward in serious thought. "Jam on fucking toast." Her use of a swear word seemed to shock even her. She certainly convinced us all as we delved into fresh chunky toast, painting it strawberry red with jam. She had a point. Even I had forgotten how good it was.

"What's the weirdest thing you've had to try for breakfast by a wannabe chef, then?" I asked.

Janet paused her chewing, thoughtful for a moment.

"Duck's liver and poached egg with polenta."

I mentally crossed food critic off from my potential list of future careers. If for no other reason, this trip to Cornwall had been worth it to avoid being forced to try duck for breakfast. Gross.

"So how long are you stopping here, Janet?" Paul asked. Peering over his specs, he reminded me of an Olympic cyclist, long and thin. As Janet answered and they continued in small talk, I let my mind wander. Based on the physical, he and Janet would make an excellent couple. They could probably both fit in a single bed, unless Janet liked to starfish. Perhaps not appropriate subject of conversation for your first breakfast together. I put my matchmaking away.

Kind of.

"What star sign are you, Paul?" I said during the lull.

"Libra, and you?"

"I am also air," I reply. "And you, Janet?"

"Gemini."

I bit my lip to contain my excitement. My intuition about these two had been correct. A harmonious union guaranteed to last and last. Janet had told me she was divorced and Paul had not yet made it down the aisle. Neither had mentioned children nor partners. The runway was clear for love.

"Oh, wow. Three air signs? This is cause for a celebration. This being my last night in Cornwall, let's do drinks tonight. Say six? I fancy some frolicking by the sea today, finding a good bookstore, and doing a bit of soul searching."

"My soul searching will start at six with a cold Pinot," Paul laugh-huffed. Yes, this is a thing and, unfortunately, I cannot provide you with a sound demonstration. Try and talk, laugh, and huff at the same time, you will get the idea.

Superb response, I thought, as Janet poured tea and casually accepted the invitation. She smiled then returned to her signature resting face.

This would be fun. My plan was to get them both drunk and throw a few Cupid's arrows before leaving them alone to realise they should at least shag. And see how it goes.

My day of soul searching consisted of the following:
1) Naps: 2
2) Ice creams: 3
3) Talking to strangers: 5
4) Seagulls shitting one me: 1
5) Wines: 1
6) Bookstores browsed: 1
7) Books purchased: 0
8) Clothes shops browsed: 4
9) Items purchased: 8

Souls found: 0
Conclusion reached: there is nothing to find. I think I clung to the idea of finding myself as an excuse not to just accept myself the way I am. Don't judge yourself too harshly, as I bet my bottom dollar if you're reading this, you're not doing so bad. Give yourself a pat on the back.

My evening with Janet and Paul started as follows: they turned up one behind the other. Having bumped into each other just as they left the B&B, they embraced the awkwardness, and taken the fifteen-minute walk together. The conversation must have flowed well between the two of them, as their shoulders were relaxed and faces smiley as they entered the bar. Paul cheerfully offered the first round returning with a bottle of Chablis he promised was exquisite. During his absence, I assessed Janet's outfit. She had on a summery dress revealing shaved legs and a red lipstick. She was game.

"Good day?" I asked.

"Yes, I found this dress at a little shop in town." She checked no one else was in earshot and asked, "What do you think?"

"Love it," I replied. A navy-blue cotton number covered in little daisies, giving her a feminine air that did not suit her current body language. A little training might be in order.

Funny what a little approval from a fellow female can do. She sunk back in her chair and visibly relaxed. Over toddled Paul armed with wine and three glasses. After giving us all a generous pour he sat himself down next to Janet.

The wine was great. And so was the chat. We started with the subject of how Janet had managed to make it to forty-two with no children, divorces, or plastic surgery. Other than one long-term romance of two years (with a Taurus) which, by her own admittance, had been a relationship of convenience more than anything else, she had decided she would rather spend her nights at home in her PJs watching romance films than going through the headache of actually seeking romance. Her preference for releasing her inner Bridget was something I could understand.

"My friends are all babies and marriage, and I am just far too busy testing fine wines and truffles to be bothered with it all."

"Give me fine wine and truffles over babies any day." I raised a glass.

Paul raised an eyebrow and said, "Yes, though you never truly know what life's about till you have one." As I sat and watched Janet and Paul's flirting becoming less subtle with every glass of Chablis, I congratulated myself on being such a good little matchmaker. My work here was clearly done. I toddled back to the B&B, grabbing some well-deserved chips en route. Food for thought, literally.

I decided to journal my thoughts that night at the little desk overlooking the Cornish sea. I wrote about how I felt about having no job, whether leaving Daniel had been the best thing to do, how I felt about Tom, what made me happy. It hit me mid-paragraph—somewhere between Tom's gorgeousness and legging it to Cornwall—writing makes me happy.

I thought back to a conversation I had with Shan one of my post-job-breakup dates.

"Why don't you start writing again? You're good at that, mate. I don't blame you for stopping with the acting. Give yourself a break and do something you love doing. You always seem happy writing."

Shan had made sense. I had always been good at writing, from letters to short stories. In L.A. I had handwritten all of our scripts for the short pilot series we created. It's the one thing everyone was always telling me I was good at. Writing was therapeutic to me. With a blank paper and a pen you can make anything happen. Words can create any kind of action. Writing allows you to create characters that will do and say exactly what you want. It offers the opportunity to create situations to make people laugh, cry, and feel. It allows people to escape the confines of their own reality. I guess this is how I felt about acting. It was a way of escaping myself and becoming someone else. It takes the pressure off, well, being me.

I switched on my laptop, checked my bank balance. I had more than enough to do this. I found a journalism course via Google that looked promising, and clicked on the buy button. Even as I clicked a voice in my head said, "Anna, you are still a total job slut."

Chapter 15
JUST GIVE ME THE PEN

In hindsight, I should have done a little more research into what course would be right for me out of all the different ones to choose. Instead, I eagerly threw myself on my whimsically-selected course, enduring the fee and terribly inconvenient transport route. It was in a part of town in which even my caffeine-buzzed state failed to identify any saving graces. The local pub had fallen down, and all you could buy in way of food for about a five-mile radius were moldy bananas and dodgy looking vegetables. No, thanks.

Putting up with the sub-standard location would be a small price to pay for the fountain of knowledge I was about to receive, I thought. Wrong. What writer in their right mind really wants rules thrown in their face on what they can write about, how to write it, and deadlines to write to. This journalism course was like trying to date the wrong star sign. It made me want to run away before the second date. Was I becoming worse at picking careers? You would have thought I would be getting a little warmer by now.

I could not believe, as I looked around the room, that any of the other students were actually taking this seriously. Here we go again, that old familiar feeling of being perched on the edge of normality. As I listened to people introduce themselves and describe their various backgrounds I realised these people were professional human beings, and I felt a little disappointed as the enormity of my mistake dawned on me. I looked out the window at the trees blowing in the wind and wished we could swap places.

I made an executive decision. It was one of those emergency situations, like being on a date so bad you would consider telling them that you're going to the toilet and never returning. I knew it was only going to get worse.

I texted someone who could help, Tweedle Dee. She was very efficient in these kinds of situations. Tweedle Dum, on the other hand, would have tried to convince me to stay in hopes a few more hours, days, or weeks of this torture chamber would see me overcome a hurdle. No, if I was to become a journalist, there must be a back door.

"Please help—this course sucks balls. Please call and tell the receptionist there has been an emergency and I have to leave now. Must get out of here," I texted to Tweedle Dee. Thankfully, she fulfilled my request. I have no idea what she told the secretary, but she looked suitably alarmed and seemed sincere when she fetched me.

"I do hope your sister is okay." I thanked her, excused myself, and legged it all the way past the moldy bananas to the closest tube and endured the horrific journey home for the final time.

I missed Tom. He had left for L.A. before I returned from Cornwall and our relationship had been reduced to Skype calls and delayed text messaging. The time difference made communication a bit wonky, so we were never quite on an emotional par. My perky, caffeine-fueled morning mood sent out excited waffle texts, which would be replied to with a more tired pre-bedtime reflective response. I had seriously considered his suggestion to move to L.A. with him. A massive part of me wanted to jump in and take the risk without thinking and hope for the best. My intuition told me better, I did not want to apply my jobslut approach to a relationship I wanted to last. Tom had been a little disappointed though had come around.

"Well if we are going to go the distance we will have to endure a little distance." I had every confidence we would. I was unsure about a lot of my future was going to pan out. One thing was for sure I wanted Tom to be a part of it.

"How is the first day going, Bradshaw?" He knew Carrie Bradshaw was an idol and loved to tease me. I was in no rush to reply to tell him I had already bailed. Or that the non-refundable course fee could have paid for tickets to see him. My bank balance could certainly do with a boost. Since my job with Daniel my drop in income had not gone unnoticed and was proving very unhelpful with my wanting to jet off to L.A.

I had a date with my daddy dearest that evening, feeling particularly confused over my most recent shitty decision. Why, oh, why I keep turning to him for clarity and guidance is beyond me; still, he is more entertaining than most career advisors I know. Which is zero.

He seemed surprisingly proud of my decision to have bailed on the course. Especially considering he used to work at a newspaper. He had worked on the papers during his younger years on Fleet Street. As he guzzled beer and sprayed me with peanuts, he relayed the story. One particular evening he had been using a lift after a late shift when some guy sheathed in pages of the scantily-clad page three girls had told him he should not be using that particular elevator.

He repeated this to my dad once, twice, three times, upon which my dad, tired and annoyed, rightly replied, "Say that one more time and I will knock you the fuck out." Go Dad!

Turns out it was Rupert Murdoch. He didn't lose his job. A sign that trade unions were enjoying their heyday—not that he would have cared.

The course had sucked yet I still wanted to write. I just didn't want rules and regulations as to how do it, just give me the pen. Surely there was a quicker way around?

"Dad, do you not know anyone that could help me to get into writing in a different way? Any friends you're still in touch with?"

My dad shared my tendency to walk away. It suddenly became important to learn as much about him as possible. I knew he had a career as a footballer and after that I thought he had given up on pursuing anything else. His dream crushed, quite literally by a bus, that meant he would never play professionally again. I hoped he shared my logic not to burn bridges as I stared eagerly at him to come up with the goods.

"Well, I don't know anyone from work, but my friend's daughter works for a magazine. I will speak to her. Claire." He started to fish around his wallet for her card.

"Not now, Dad, call her tomorrow," I suggested. He was getting slurry.

"All I can do is try," he half-shouted at me as he went to get another beer.

So, it turns out Claire was in the magazine business which is one of my favourites. Dad had come up trumps and he was proud as punch. She had agreed to meet me, but had a very busy schedule so wanted to meet for an informal interview over coffee in Marble Arch next Wednesday morning. Hallelujah. I loved informal. She arrived ten minutes late but I was happy she turned up at all. After my first coffee, I had expected she had just forgotten, and that my Dad had made a drunken mistake, or had gotten the date wrong, or she was too busy doing other things to be meeting a nobody like me in the world of journalism.

"So sorry I'm late," she said after she located me in the coffee bar. Claire had that air of someone who runs around all day from meeting to meeting with an endless to-do list. Important, yet friendly, she offered a hand to shake.

"So, your dad tells me you want to get into journalism. What experience have you had?"

"Well, I er…" I didn't come prepared for this at all. I thought informal had meant a little chat about my latest ambition.

"I recently completed—started—a journalism course and it made me realise that a hands-on, more practical experience would be more beneficial. I have not yet actually worked for any specific company, though I have always been a keen writer."

"Oh, okay. Your dad gave me the idea you had some practical experience." And so it would seem my dad knew as little about my careers as I did about his.

"I am sorry, Anna. We have a million over-qualified candidates wanting jobs. Anyone we take on needs to hit the ground running."

"Okay, fair enough," I thought of saying something super clever to convince her she was making a big mistake not taking me on. All that came out my mouth was the truth. "I feel bad you coming all this way to meet me; let me get you a coffee at least."

"Sure. And I am happy to answer any questions, if that could be of help?"

I ordered us coffees and my gesture seemed genuinely appreciated which made me warm to Claire. Conversation moved to how she knew my dad. Her dad had owned a football club and so her dad and my dad were old buddies. It seemed she knew a lot about their antics. We moved onto childhood histories and she loved my no-nonsense summary of why my parents were not together and why Dad had had no girlfriends since. She loved my explanation of how it was all down to their astrological incompatibility.

"They were a total mismatch. Him a Cancer and her a Libra, chalk and cheese. Cancers are very emotionally draining for air signs."

"Oh, dear. I am dating a Cancer," she confessed.

"And, let me guess, you're a Capricorn?" She looked impressed. I gave her my forecast on how I saw her relationship, pinpointing a few good and bad points, and she described it as "stunningly accurate."

"I honestly think it would make for great reading. A regular column or something, called 'Dating by your star sign.'" I suggested. Claire laughed and clapped her hands.

"That's brilliant." Following our genius idea, we decided to go for a real drink. Claire promised she would see what she could do.

I wasn't expecting it to ever actually come to anything, given my total lack of experience. So when she called the next day, I fell of my chair. Well, actually, I accidentally sat on the floor, missing my chair entirely, but you get the idea.

"The magazine wants you to manage the horoscope section from now on, as well as our online dating blog. What do you think?"

"Hell, yes!"

I continued to write that article for…wait for it…three whole months. We had a total blast. Claire and I became good friends, despite our fifteen-year age gap. Her boyfriend was also a good ten years her junior and a wonderful cook.

Speaking of boyfriends, Tuesday was Valentine's Day and I had received some beautiful roses in the morning, which

already made it my most romantic to date. Around lunchtime, I got a text from the Tweedle's inviting me to dinner at a new tapas restaurant. I arrived suitably dressed for dinner, with the Tweedles dressing a little bit like lesbians in hope we may convince the waitress to give us some free champagne. I got to the bar where Tweedle Dee had said they were waiting, ready for a night of getting drunk while we played a stupid game we'd invented called "Guess how long," where we guessed how long surrounding couples had been together. Tweedle Dum was working on a backstory for a greying couple behind us.
"Third wife. Six-year marriage. Wishes he hadn't left the last one cause at least she cooked."

The hilarity was short-lived; I was greeted with a much better prize. Tom stood with a bottle of champagne. He was wearing a black jacket, white shirt, and his signature sexy smile. My whole body collapsed into his as he placed his hands firmly on my lower back. He raised my head and kissed me.

When we both finally came up for air he told me, "I have been waiting to do that since I last saw you."

He poured me a glass of champagne and insisted I answer something before we sat down. He slipped his hand into his right inside jacket pocket pulling out a small box. He replaced my glass with the pink silky package. I opened it as gently as its delicateness required. My breath was on hold as I pulled it open to reveal a tiny silver chain, a thumb-sized butterfly hung in the middle, understated and elegant.

"Anna, will you be my butterfly?" His eyes were warm, open, and hopeful.

"Yes, Tom," I giggled. "I will be your butterfly," I was utterly sure he was the one to stop fluttering my wings.

Said wings were even still on the work front, thanks to Claire. For the first time, I actually loved my job. Productive days followed by celebratory cosmopolitans and al fresco dinners, weather permitting. Coming to the office had become my favorite thing to do and I had not once wanted to think of an excuse to leave. My day basically consisted off typing away to my heart's content about stuff I actually wanted to write about. I liked the people I worked for. I had even managed to find someone in that limbo between weird and normal to enjoy it all with. Claire was a treasure chest of stories, information, and people. She had genuinely understood my need to put fun, sanity, and self-maintenance before job commitments; yet also the need to feed the exhausting pull to do something professional. The need to feel like you're progressing and find an outlet for all that intellectual energy that, if not sufficiently exerted, could eat you alive.

Claire's mother was still to this day one of the most interesting people I have ever met. Her views on life were so hilarious that it made her a joy to be around. She was very rarely without a glass of champagne and she always dressed immaculately. She taught me the importance of a good manicure and introduced me to a range of facial products I still use every day.

Claire's mother had been married four times and was still friends with all of her ex-husbands, including Claire's father.

When I asked her, respectfully, why she felt she had married so many times she told me, "My darling, men, to me, are like accessories. They should be changed often." She was a riot. She even came to me for dating advice once and asked me to email her daily horoscope.

I felt settled. Even the Tweedles had noticed it.

"You seem the calmest you have ever been since you moved in with us," Tweedle Dee declared one evening as I was stirring sugar into my tea. "Even your face looks relaxed," she said, prodding my cheek as if it was public property.

"I do feel calm," I acknowledged. "The face has had a helping hand from a little pot of miracles you can find in my bathroom drawer." As I exited the kitchen I called, "And keep it to yourself." Tweedle Dee could be trusted to take a small squeeze of my new skin cream, whereas Tweedle Dum would empty the modest pot in one application. She treated expensive perfumes and cosmetics like they had been purchased at the pound store. Still it made birthday and Christmas presents easy, anything to keep her greedy paws away from our beauty products was a worthwhile investment.

I had an uneasy feeling on Monday morning right from the moment I woke up. I felt like I had forgotten to do something. I pushed it aside and went about my usual morning, which had now settled into something of a routine. Monday did have a shock in store for me. I was called to head office to hear the announcement that would sever my commitment to my beloved column. The magazine had been bought out by an American company and was shutting down. I had to rationalize what had happened to accept it and move on. It brought back that horrible feeling in my stomach I had when Daniel let me go. I wanted to cry. Okay, I felt an actual tear trickle down my face as the news sunk in. I was being forced to say goodbye to my cool role as contributing talent, which allowed me to flit in and out of my cool office in Mayfair and indulge my inner Carrie Bradshaw. Was this job Karma? First Daniel, now the magazine; I get close to something I feel is a good fit and I am thrown out in the cold again. I let the tears flood down my face. Why couldn't I find my place to fit in this world?

After all, crying and feeling sorry for myself wasn't getting me anywhere, this was a massive wake-up call. I was ready to admit my needs had changed, or maybe they had always been the same, though now I could not run from them anymore. I had no post-job feeling of liberation and joy. Something was strangely different and I knew it from the moment I chose not to revert to Google in an excited rush to look for goodness knows what. Nor telephone some recruitment agent for an ego-boosting small talk.

Instead I looked in the mirror Tuesday morning and told myself firmly, "You, Anna, have got this." Soon after, I had one of those eureka moments. You know, where you think you have figured out what you should do with the rest of your life. These are the moments often occur in the shower, on the toilet, and when drunk; this time, though, it was when my back was pressed up against a wall.

I needed to set up a dating website based on astrological matches. Why hadn't I thought of it before? I was giving away all my talent to this magazine when I could have a much wider influence. There were clearly wandering souls like Janet and Paul from the Cornwall B&B sprinkled over the UK and beyond, just pining for hassle-free romance. The only true way to deliver this doesn't come with exclusive dating services or *The Millionaire Matchmaker*. No offence, Patti Stanger; I am an avid watcher, though how many long-lasting romances have you delivered, for all your efforts? And all they had to do was to check whether they are astrologically compatible. It is that simple. Now, I am not saying that dating your perfect match will lead to life-long commitment, but it at least guarantees a minimum level of enjoyment of the dating experience. Because time spent with a star sign you get on with always provides some level of fun, intellectual stimulation, good sex or, if you're lucky, all three. And so maybe I'd put in a provision for to guarantee a good time, or at least a money back guarantee clause.

Was matchmaking a natural skill? Was it my calling? I was so excited about the idea that I couldn't wait to tell someone. And then I realized the first person I wanted to tell was Tom.

Tom and I had somehow fallen into a pattern of calling each other every day. I had no idea how he would react, but thankfully he didn't think I was bonkers.

"You know what, babe? This is going to work. It's genius."

For whatever reason, his encouragement was all I needed to know it was the right thing to do.

Chapter 16
STAR-DATING

My idea was delivered in a series of job daydreams. The name Star-Dating was born like many of the world's greats—I am not too proud to admit—sitting on the toilet.

And what is the first thing you do when launching your debut as an entrepreneur? Get your best friend on board, of course. So, I called Shan.

"Mate, I have an awesome idea. What do we do best?"

"Erm..."

A long silence later, I continued. "If there's one thing you and I can do it's match star signs, right? So, let me introduce our new business doing just that: Star-Dating."

Her response was a simple, "Wow." I pictured her face looking fascinated into the air and contemplating how we hadn't thought of this sooner.

All that was needed now was to celebrate a long-overlooked simplification of the dating process; i.e. just shag the right star sign. Combine that with a few other appropriate life hallmarks such as age, mutually compatible occupations/age/etc., and what you have is a match made in heaven.

The idea had been born in Cornwall. Janet and Paul popped into my mind and as if to confirm my thought process, so I tapped Jan a little text.

"Hi, how was the rest of your trip in Cornwall. Hope to catch up sometime soon. Paul too? X"

An hour later my phone delivered a sign I was shooting an arrow in the right direction.

"Hi Anna, great thanks. As for Paul, he is with me now. He says hi and yes, we must. We owe you a drink x."

I realised I had my work cut out for me. I perched myself in my local Costa with my skinny latte which had taken three attempts by the new barista to get right. The first time, he had first accidentally put in vanilla syrup then made the next one with full-fat milk. The third time he had proudly produced the correct beverage and I had to admire his relentless enthusiasm, and forgave him instantly when he gave me some free biscuits. A bold move for a newbie, he would go far.

I made a rough business plan outlining costs:
Website: 500
Marketing: 500
Total: 1000
Allocated funds: 250

With £1,750 to raise, I planned a little dinner with Tweedle Dee and Tweedle Dum that night, as I was sure they would want a share in this brainchild. I served my pitch with plenty of fine cheese and wine and it went well. I left the Dragon's Den (our kitchen) fully invested, each of my tipsy tigers getting a ten percent share in return.

Vetting would be a simple process of video calls. Vetting was essential, due to the sheer volume of potential members and not wanting logistics to be a barrier to people finding their astrological dream match. Meeting clients face-to-face to check they looked like they promised wasn't realistic. A quick Skype call was set up after the application and would give substance to the claim that all members have been verified. It wasn't that membership was subject to attractiveness, simply that you had to look like you said you did, so if someone thought they were meeting up with tall, dark, and handsome, you don't find yourself face to face with a four-foot albino human. So, whether you are a crossdresser called Barbara or a tattoo enthusiast, all the application required was honesty.

A basic profile was as follows:
Name:
Star sign:
Birthday:
Location:
Occupation:
Sexual Orientation:
Photo:
Brief Bio:

For a fee of £19.99 per month, you received an initial email with dating advice on what star sign would be best suited for you and a link to three recommendations each month.

Fortunately, I knew someone who gave me a free injection of SEO on a promise I would give him VIP membership for a year. He was pleased with the deal, having had a particularly shit year in the dating department due to focusing on his IT business too much. Oh, the irony. Fortunately, his hard work paid off. Within a month he met Lucy, a Taurus, who was a nutritionist searching for her perfect geek. They nurtured each other's inner introvert and quickly progressed from dating to full-blown couple in no time.

Over dinner one night, where I had the pleasure of meeting her, it was amazing to see how much he had come out of his crusty shell. He was glowing. As I chewed on a tasteless vegetable that Lucy told me was full of vitamin C, I realised that the time that my little Virgo friend had spent on SEO for Star-Dating must have been the best investment he had ever made. I listened to them tell me their plans to take a year out and travel; I nearly choked on my broccoli. My friend had never even been to France, once refusing to even come on a boat ride to Calais to stock up on booze for Christmas because he'd recently watched *Titanic*. He suffered severe anxiety and often broke out in hives when challenging himself to leave his comfort zone. Which was his basement flat in Muswell Hill surrounded by computers, boxes of half-eaten pizza, and cereal boxes with spoons in. And now he was using cutlery like it ain't no thing, and ready to get on a plane—with not a hive in sight! The potential of Star-Dating was huge.

Knowing zilch about marketing tools, I shall not pretend I knew how my dear friend was waving his wand over the Internet and beyond. I was happy to let my IT godfather leave his cloak of mystery firmly on, the results told me all I needed to know. It was working. Within a week, I already had a hundred members subscribed and I was seriously considering recruiting a friend to London to help me with the increasing admin.

One particularly pleasant Thursday evening, I was cracking open a bottle of Malbec having just finished a Skype call with a new member named Josh. He had cute little Leo ambition coming out his arse like a noisy Ferrari engine. He made no apologies for his extreme nature saying he just wanted someone who could handle it. After the phone call I came up with a suitable bio brief:

A pocket-sized, driven, and handsome man. Only take on if ready for the ride of your life. In the fast lane. Romance is a given in portions as large as this lion's passion for life. They do say the best things come in small packages. A loyal heart and fun are part of this special delivery.

I emailed it to him, wishing him luck finding someone who could pipe him down.

My mobile phone/business phone/only phone I had owned since I left home danced across the kitchen counter to my wine glass.

"Am I speaking to the owner of Star-Dating?"

"This is she," I answered. The relaxed authority in this man's voice intrigued me. It made his following question sound less like the request of a stalker/serial killer than my usual suspicious self would assume.

"Can we meet?"

"It's possible. Who am I speaking to?"

"Tony Clarke. I am a friend of Daniel Brian's. He pointed me in the direction of your new venture and gave me your number. I funded the two most successful start-ups in the dating industry last year; yours clearly has potential I want to talk about doing a deal. Do you know The Ivy in Covent Garden?"

"Yes, I do."

"Meet me there Tuesday at sixteen hundred in the members lounge. Does that work for you?"

"Let me just check my diary..." I paused while I poured myself a large glass of wine. "Yep, I can do that. See you then."

I let the words "Daniel" and "successful start-ups" and the enormity of what had just happened sink in before calling my old boss/legend.

"Hey, trouble. I take it Tony has called?" Daniel said.

"Thank you, a million times over, Dan. I am still in shock."

"Let's just say he owes me a favor and I owe you one. Besides I do have my own self-interest to take care of: I want you to find me a hot Gemini. Long legs, blonde, you know the drill."

Yes, I did, and if anyone deserved a leggy Gemini it was Daniel.

The Ivy was her typical fabulous self. The iconic London club was renowned for hiding celebrities as they indulge in fine dining and drinking. Such places contribute significantly to London's charm.

A young chap cloaked in a full-length jacket took my cardigan-come-jacket and accompanied to find Mr Clarke. There were a few usual famous faces basking in the anonymity of the dark members lounge. Tables were dotted with champagne glasses and spiraled trays of delicate sandwiches and cakes. Tony was draining an espresso and raising his phone in line with his tiny coffee cup so as not to lose sight of whatever he was reading. He looked up, and took my outstretched hand and I experienced the strongest handshake of my life. No one had crushed my fingers so hard since my dad had nearly broken one squeezing my fragile bones with his giant paws in an over-excited drunken ramble one night.

A firm handshake, a love for espresso, and a strong sense of authority made Tony feel like a big security blanket. Like the uncle you always wanted. You could see him stealing the role in the latest *Terminator*. "Come with me if you want to live."

But that was not his opening line. It was actually:

"Do you like champagne?"

"I do."

A waiter nodded in his direction in response to a hand loaded with urgency held in the air for around three seconds. I had a feeling we were going to get on very well.

"Two minutes." He apologized as he finished whatever he was doing on his phone. The waiter returned with two glasses of bubbles.

"The usual, Sir?"

'Thanks, Simon." He visibly relaxed, shoulders dropped, phone went down. "Thanks for coming to meet me." We clinked glasses.

"Are you a Taurus?" I went straight in for the kill. The question amused him.

"Straight to business, is it?" He laughed. A hearty one that came from the belly. It reminded me of Christmas.

"Just a feeling I get. I can sense a Taurus a mile off."

"Guilty as charged."

"Knew it." I washed down my smugness with a sip of deliciously cold champagne.

"Were you born with astrological blessings, or is it something you have learnt?"

"It's certainly something life has taught me. Friendships. Relationships. Family. I have dated my fair selection of the astrological landscape and know I get on best with Geminis. My best friend is one, too. Leos are a no-no and, yes, I learnt the hard way. His name was Martin. To think there is a ten percent chance I could have married him had I let him have his way. You come to realise it is not a person's fault when they were born. Star signs are like a lottery of birth."

"And who are the winners?"

"Each has their strengths," I answered diplomatically. "Personally, I love air signs. It depends on what you are yourself. Geminis, Aquarians, and Libras I find I can spend a lot of time with. They have the same low tolerance for boredom and commitment, and a constant need for fun. Being bored actually makes me cry. I would jump out of a plane to make myself feel alive. Normality makes me feel very uncomfortable. The more normal a situation, the more tense I am."

I loved the way champagne gets honestly flowing.

"I see."

"Taureans love fun too. Just, a safer kind of fun. Organised fun. Making a plan doesn't terrify you, so that must be nice."

Tony smiled and nodded in agreement of my aforementioned aspects of his personality.

"You must have had children by now," I said with a challenge.

"Yes, two." He happily opened up some pictures on his phone and showed me two gorgeous girls. They were aged around ten and fourteen, had big smiles, ice creams, and were in some exotic location.

"I hope you think that's because I am a Taurus and not just because I look old."

"Of course. You don't look old; besides, age is just a number. Divorced?"

"Yes. Twice."

"Well, let's hope the third time's the charm. Bet neither of them were Cancers?"

"No. Aquarius and Aries."

"Oh yes. Of course you're divorced, Tony." Another good hearty belly laugh showed that clearly tickled him.

Before I knew it, several hours had passed. Two glasses and one bottle of champagne consumed along with two bowls of pretzels and one of pistachios. Evidence of which lay crumbled over my cramping legs.

We had browsed several topics of conversation from dating history to career, movies, and travel. If I had learnt one thing so far, it was I love Taureans. I had underestimated their fun rating and would certainly bump them up my social list going forward. It was just before I was going to relieve my patient bladder from a fair share of bubbles that Tony casually dropped the *raison d'être* of our meeting.

"I want in on Star-Dating. £100,000 and my full attention for a year—for a twenty-five percent share. Something to ponder while you pee."

Well, if I ever experienced a golden piss that was it. I made my decision before my bottom hit the seat.

I gleefully accepted Tony's offer. He insisted on one more glass of champagne to celebrate, and naturally, I could not refuse. We chatted briefly about marketing knowing serious conversation should be scheduled for sobriety. True to Taurean gentlemen form, he ensured I was safely placed in a taxi before he bid me goodbye. As he slammed the door of the black cab we both held a smile. I sped off into the warm London evening which was wrapped in the glorious dusky orange and reds of the September sky. A nostalgic feeling developed in my belly, reminding me of the pending change of season. Perfect for a new start, as any day can be, though this delivered the necessary dramatic full stop to a soul-searching autumn.

An intense two weeks followed. Meetings with Tony's marketing team, lawyer, friends, business partners, and brothers. He had two: Tim and Charles (Libra and Gemini, I could not believe my luck.) And his lawyer was also a Gemini. Yes, I did think about setting her up with Daniel, she was blonde and leggy, his favorite. The boys were handsome too, chips off the old block, so to speak. My agreement to a little cash injection had led to far more than I had anticipated. Radio shows, magazines, and member clubs. Star-Dating was going to be everywhere.

Membership had now been staged into three different options: Bronze, Silver, and Gold. Different prices reflected different levels of service. Gold membership gave you access to arranging date nights in private member clubs; basically, it was a five-star concierge for dating. You even had a number for your own therapist to discuss any problems. Applications were through the roof. Susie, Tony's PA, headed up a team to deal with the video call screenings for Bronze and Silver members, but Gold members had to be met in person.

I never really understood the expression, "Time flies," until that particular six-month period of my life. It does not fly in the same way as birds and planes, it's an intangible action you reflect on after its happened. Kind of like you have teleported and have a vague montage of the events that took place in your memory. Mine was a blur of late nights, airplanes, a lot of coffee, new faces, paperwork, early starts, and a bad diet. At the end of it, we had launched in five different cities: Paris, London, Amsterdam, Wales, and Munich. All cities in which I had an explicit interest in their diversity, from cuisine, people, and fashion, to views on the legality of weed.

There were a lot more on the hit list. Tony's team had applied marketing science to establish where we would take off the best and they had clearly done their homework. However, my skin looked terrible, I had gained some serious poundage, and I actually missed my mum. I needed to take control of this situation. I hired a personal trainer called Jamie and booked myself in for a month course of facials. I also booked my mum and me a spa weekend, much to her delight. But something was still missing. Having barely stopped for air since things got going, it was nice to pause and recharge my tank. As we sat, cucumbers on eyes in heavenly bathrobes, having been plucked, massaged, and deeply cleansed, I felt my mum's hand squeeze mine. Her skin felt unfamiliar. The touch was short yet deeply soothing.

"You know, I am so proud of you." The words sunk into me like into a dehydrated sponge. I peered under my right cucumber slice and gave her a smile.

Tom was patiently waiting for me to go visit him, having been the one putting the most air miles into our relationship so far. There were two reasons I was putting off L.A. Firstly, the amount of travel I had to do for work of late had put me off planes. And secondly, I was scared if I got to the sun-soaked city of angels, home to many of my favorite things—most importantly, my gorgeous boyfriend—I was not sure I could bring myself to leave.

Missing Tom created a space that needed to be filled with something. But what was it? I racked my brains, magazines, and even Google for the answer. Alas, it wasn't until one morning when I looked out of the window of the coffee shop in Munich that I found the answer. It was given by an immaculately-dressed lady who walked past wearing the exact type of happy I was after. As my gaze dropped to her feet I saw why. No, it wasn't just the Jimmy Choo loafers. Next to them waddled the most adorable little sausage dog.

"How can so much poop come out of such a little sausage?" I cried into the phone to Tom as I looked down at Cupcake, my new miniature dachshund.

She was adorable. A golden brown, bouncy, ball of perfection. That is, until I laid her in her soft, pink, plush bed fit for a princess and switched off the light…Have you ever heard a puppy cry? It's similar to a squealing, distressed bird. *Just keep quiet, it will stop*, you think. *Another five minutes*, you think. An hour later you will either 1) place puppy somewhere out of ear shot. 2) Take yourself somewhere out of ear shot. 3) Succumb and let puppy hop on your bed where puppy will snuggle up happily next to you and grant you your one wish: silence.

On waking, puppy will likely be licking your face and have left you a puddle of pee—or worse case, poop—somewhere on your bed. Delightful. Eventually you have to play tough and refuse bed sharing. You will feel a tad inhumane when you have to leave something so cute and small crying on its own downstairs whilst you sleep and admit to yourself as much as you love your pup, you also love an unsoiled bed to yourself.

Responsibility reduction has been a key strategy in my life. The fewer responsibilities, the easier one's life becomes, as I have reminded myself time and time again when giving them up all together. The strategy has been a strong deterrent against having children. When people tried to tell me having a puppy was like having a child, I laughed it off. Well, experience speaks volumes; to all those thinking about getting one, turn up the volume on this: THEY HAVE A POINT.

Optimism is admired, but I can confirm that all puppies shit and cry, so buying one pre-trained is highly recommended, especially if 1) Your life is already chronically busy. 2) You are extremely impatient. And 3) Basically, if you can afford it, just do it. I, however, one month in, felt far too invested. My currency? Emotions, time, and sleep. Ho-hum. Four months, numerous meltdowns, and a shitload of cleaning bills later, I pretty much had the perfect pooch. And just like giving birth, the pain is soon forgotten, though my four months of hardship seems far more appealing than nine months inflating my belly with a bowling ball then pushing it out of my vagina. Yeah, I guess puppy training isn't that bad.

Hiring. This felt very odd. You know when you try the opposite of what you're used to? Driving in the U.S. on the wrong side of the road, for example. Using your fork with the wrong hand. Well, something along those lines is how I felt as I sat perched at a desk in some office in Mayfair that was apparently now our headquarters about to interview a bunch of hopefuls for a management role in Star-Dating.

Jane was everything one hopes someone named Jane to be. A mouse-like pleasantness oozed out of her. Like jam from a doughnut, with Jane you knew where you stood and what to expect; she may not offer the excitement of the latest cake trend, though she would be consistent in her constitution. She was a safe bet when faced with an array of cakes you may or may not have not tried before. Any good cake selection needs a doughnut and so any good company needs a Jane. I decided to hire her immediately.

I put a big tick at the bottom of her CV as we went through a few questions. Her answers were considered and careful and coincided with all her credentials. She was very calming, her birthdate confirmed she was a Virgo.

Next up was Jules. Her arrogance jumped into the room before she did. A cake analogy did not spring to mind other than bad eggs. Her aura was noisy self-importance and not something I could deal with early mornings. I scribbled a little cross on the bottom of her CV. Tony asked a few questions.

"What makes you want this job, Jules?"

"It's Juuuules," she first informed him, he had not paid significant attention to the U apparently. "I am very good with people, and very successful at everything I do. Excuse me."

She took out her phone and, to our disbelief, answered it. She loudly started babbling into the receiver too quickly for me to have a clue what about. Tony and I gave each other "the look." With that, he raised his hand, clicked his fingers, gaining Juuuules's attention, and pointed to the door with a look on his face that I imagined he used when ordering his children to bed. She swiped her bag from the floor and scurried out still bellowing into her phone.

Two hours of recruiting later, we had hired Jane. Jules and everyone that followed had been incompatible in terms of ego, intellect, or general hygiene. A certain chap called Dean smelt like rotten baked beans. The silver lining being it reminded us to break for lunch.

Tony chowed down on a giant chicken sandwich. Between mouthfuls he enthusiastically stuffed it with cheese and onion crisps. I placed Jane's CV on our crumby table. Jane seemed like a good all-rounder. I am sure she could handle running Star-Dating. I have always been a massive fan of delegation. It really can streamline your life.

1) Cleaning—Hire a cleaner
2) Nails—See a manicurist
3) Cooking—Order in/ Boyfriend/ Flatmates
4) Life admin—PA/ Friends/ Co-operative family members
5) Finding Staff—Jane

You get the picture. Keep it simples.

Tony agreed with my genius. Jane was thrilled with the news of her recruitment asking, "Really?" five times before flooding us with gratitude and promises of dedication and the like.

"Well, that was easy," Tony clapped his hands to remove any crumbs from our rushed lunch.

"I wonder if she would be a love and type up her own contract..." Tony chuckled. (My suggestion had been sincere.)

"I will get Susie to do it." Regardless, there it was, delegation. I guess the art is to keep it appropriate.

Being appropriate is not my strong suit. In fact, it bores the absolute shit out of me.

At least there is a decent chunk of society that is willing to do it. I can manage a couple of hours a day in which I need to jam in as much as possible. But rest assured, for all the other important stuff I have become effective at appropriate delegation. Effective delegating and finding Jane have been the essential building blocks to my success and sanity. This should really be the motto of any business facing a crisis. Delegate and hire a Jane. The kind of crisis is irrelevant. Jane is the fairy godmother of the work place. She has left such an impression that I might even get Hire a Jane t-shirts printed.

Okay, guys, drum roll please. I think I may have actually finished something. The time has come for me to say goodbye to you lovely lot. It's amazing we have made it this far. Covering professions throughout the UK and beyond, this story has survived two broken laptops, several panic-attack-inducing moments when I have nearly deleted the whole thing, and now (unless I get my ass in gear,) the possibility of it remaining lazily on my laptop forever looms large.

So now to implement effective delegation, I have been luck enough to find a darn good editor. One who will scrub this up, ship-shape it, and shine it, to ensure you have as much fun reading it as I have writing.

I can promise you I am still a jobslut at heart, and you know what? I am okay with that. I have at least managed to muster up some much-needed self-belief during my job-hopping. I am happy to report, sticking to something, like Star-Dating has brought me all the happiness I was secretly afraid off.

I am always pondering my next potential career/business idea/invention. Who knows what could be next? At the same time, I'm not rushing into anything.

Some mornings I have to pinch myself to check I am this girl who has her own business and her own boyfriend. Tom is delighted I managed to book a ticket to go and see him. I am very excited. Equally excited is Cupcake. I managed to get my little sausage on the flight. I promise we will both be coming back.

There are still a few things on the to-do list. I wouldn't mind launching a fashion line, publishing a magazine, writing a movie, creating something awesome to leave as part of my legacy. You know, like a light bulb?

And with that in mind, goodbye for now folks!

Jobslut xxx

P.S. Obvs had to leave you a present. Attached is a glossary A–Z of loosely based research/interviews I conducted whilst writing. (Basically, being a nosy parker.)

Please browse at your leisure; though for goodness's sake, do not go handing any notices in on my behalf, especially if:
1) You have consumed wine
2) Handing notice in could cause dry period of unemployment in which no further wine can be purchased
3) The thought of cleaning toilets is not worse than current position.

Chapter 17
THE A-Z GUIDE TO CAREERS

A

Actress

Role: Holding the audio boom, reading scripts, singing, dancing, and anything else you have to do to make it. Dress up as a rabbit? Sure, why not. We all have to start somewhere—even Barack Obama started out serving Baskin-Robbins.

Best Parts:
- Variety of roles
- No nine-to-five
- You may become a fabulous film star

Worst Parts:
- Inevitable dry spells
- Lots of rejection
- Pleasing directors who can be arseholes

Qualifications:
- Drama School
- Sleep with a director
- Get lucky

Typical Day:
8:00—Alarm goes off
9:00—Affirmation in mirror. "You quit your job at Krispy Kreme, so you better nail this audition."
Run through monologue in mirror, playing middle-aged lesbian about to confront her mother. Consider not going to audition, remind self I have quit my job and rent due next week—will go.
10:30—Spilt coffee on trousers on the bus, consider going home to change. Director texts, "Anyone not on time will not be seen." Mine is 11:15—will go with coffee-stained trousers.
11:15 —Arrive just in time, wait another hour to be seen.
13:00—Debrief with a friend over doughnuts. He reminds me I am already five-pounds over than what is on my résumé and face is fatter than my head shots. Finish one more doughnut and pledge not to eat tomorrow.
15:00—Text my old boss and ask for job back.
16:00—Attend workshop with local theatre group, roll around on floor and spend an hour on breath control.
18:00—Go for drink with agent. Has news, callback for an audition I had two weeks ago. He has booked me a tour to Liverpool to play Little Red Riding Hood.
19:00—Old boss texts me back. "Yes, can you start tomorrow?" Had several large wines. Reply, "No, thanks anyway. Love Red x." Already getting into character.

B
Barmaid
Role: You got it! Serving drinks, food and banter to the drunk, sober, and everyone in between.

Best Parts:
- Free food
- Tips
- Flexible working hours

Worst Parts:
- Unsociable working hours
- Unsociable sleeping hours
- General feelings of wanting to be unsociable due to above

Qualifications:
- Life
- Various hospitality certificates

Typical Day:
11:30—Wake up after four hour's sleep. Agreed to work for a lock-in five minutes before clocking off at 10 PM. Got home at 4:00 AM.
12:30—Covering lunchtime shift. Chef was desperate and promised free hot pot.
15:00—I am offered a drink by "Budweiser Bill." Pretend to take a shot of vodka and just put £5 in my tip jar.
18:00—Help out in kitchen with start of dinner orders. I plate up food, deliver the food, serve pints and large wines to the after workers, engage in the usual banter. ("Go on make it a large, it is Monday.") Bar talk is my second language.
19:00—Irritable and hungry, swipe a free slice of garlic bread. Manager asks if will stay till 21:00. Brain says no, but my mouth says okay. Stay till 21:00.
21:00—Get in my car and thank fuck I can go home. Grab a takeaway en route and drink with a bottle of red I took as a "thank you" to my arse for working itself silly all week. Poor

manager too busy to even say goodbye. I refused the morning shift. Lay in—bliss.

C

Checkout Girl

Role: Scan groceries and charge customers

Best Parts:
- It is pretty easy
- Discounts
- Possibility of promotion

Worst Parts:
- Manager is an arse
- Bad for posture
- Counting change

Qualifications:
- Hands
- Communication skills
- Common sense

Typical Day:
8:00—Open till and take my pew for the day. Manage to sneak phone under desk and a bag of Haribo.
9:00—Morning rush results in spilt jam. Call for a clean-up on register two, allowing me sufficient time to munch a few sweets and check phone.
10:15—Coffee break with Helen from till number five. We discuss how our marketing campaign for biscuits has been a success and we definitely deserve to be promoted. Also, that new girl on till number two looks like a young Audrey Hepburn and will not last till end of week.

12:00—Audrey Hepburn makes a dramatic exit following an incident with baked beans.

14:00—Lunch in canteen is a sloppy cheese and tomato sandwich, washed down with a 7-Up and Mars bar.

16:30—ID a girl who is attempting to purchase a bottle of wine and looks about fourteen. She threatens to gas me—call out for help. She is escorted from the building without the wine.

18:00—Cash up. Tanya takes over. Tell her about half bag of Haribo under counter, she tells me I am a diamond.

D
Dentist

Role: Deal with people's dentistry issues from tooth decay to tooth replacement

Best Parts:
- Bringing peoples's smiles back tooth by tootH
- You get a receptionist
- With today's sugar consumption, unlikely to ever be out of a job

Worst Parts:
- Bad oral hygiene
- People trying to talk while you work—FYI, dentists do not understand what you are trying to mumble whilst they have opened your mouth with their tools
- Crying children

Qualifications:
- Undergraduate degree

- Four-year dental program
- Work experience

Typical Day:
7:00— I take my coffee through a straw with my morning porridge and paper while my wife tells me her friend wants teeth whitening at mate's rates and will be coming in to see me at 15:00. If she were not my wife, she would have made a great receptionist.

9:00—First client of the day is for a routine teeth cleaning. Likes to mumble away like most morning appointments clients. Energies tend to dip in the afternoon.

11:00—Tune in to a conference call from America about a new cosmetic procedure.

13:00—Lunch and another coffee through a straw attracts me a few confused looks from fellow diners. They are clearly not as invested in white teeth as I am.

15:00—Wife's friend arrives. I ask her how white she wants to go. She tells me, "As white as Simon Cowell's."

16:30—Interview for new dental nurse. Lovely girl, far too attractive. Have to decline for sake of marriage.

18:00—Home for bath and dinner with wife. Followed by decadent strawberries, which, I must add, are one of nature's best tooth whiteners.

E

Estate Agent
Role: Selling houses

Best Parts:
- Nosing around people's houses

- Free car
- Helping people find homes

Worst Parts
- Gazumpers
- Arseholes, arseholes everywhere
- Unrealistic demands

Qualifications:
Nowadays, a degree or a great sales pitch—ideally both

Typical Day:
8:30—Morning meeting. I inform the team about the amazing two-bed investment apartment I have taken on above a commercial premise. (It is above a fried chicken joint and tenant is council, two months in arrears.)
10:00—Call from buyer withdrawing from sale due to personal circumstances. Dug a little deeper to find out her cat had died.
10:15—Call back-up buyer and he agrees to sale. I check if he has any pets—not even a goldfish. Sigh of relief.
12:00—Tenant turns up at office with suitcase to move into property that colleague has not got keys for, and the landlord is abroad. Tenant speaks very little English but getting very upset. Fortunately, have viewing—leave colleague to deal with it.
14:00—Realise have no lunch. Grab a bag of peanuts. Steak tonight, worth the wait.
16:00—Client calls me to see there are if any higher offers for her property that is already under offer. Inform her no. She tells me if we get one, she will take it. I am sure she would.
17:00—Office breaks into round of applause for colleague

who has rented a stinky one-bed that's been on the market four months and is practically a health hazard.
18:00—All head to steak restaurant for "Wicked Wednesday's" half-price drinks and steak night. Manager's treat—tight ass.

F
Financial Advisor
Role: Telling people what to do with their money

Best Parts:
- Helping people grow their portfolios
- Gaining client's trust
- Very social

Worst Parts:
- Pressure of making a mistake
- Clients can be arseholes
- No summer holidays

Qualifications:
- Degree
- Work Experience
- Various licenses and certificates

Typical Day:
6:30—Gym. The endorphins to get you through the day.
7:00—Client breakfast at a Lebanese place for his benefit. I have a coffee and eggs. We discuss where I plan to put his £100,000 investment. Guy is a risk-taker and so am I.
　"Is this guaranteed to make me a decent return?"

"Definitely." I have no fucking clue, though nor did I with his last £500,000 which turned out okay, so fingers crossed.

9:00—Call from new client. Talk for an hour, mostly about golf. Never even picked up a golf club. Still, happy to chat about it for an hour if it gets the deal done. He agrees to release ten percent of his investment capital—will get myself up the local driving range.

13:00— Lunch with another advisor. After several martinis and a bottle of rosé he shows me pictures of recent female conquests. Do not know how he does it. Is four feet tall and eight feet wide. He pays for lunch.

15:00—Make a call to inform client we are behind in profits, but not to worry. Will pick back up next month. Tells me not to call till picks back up.

18:00—Hair cut.

19:00—Networking event. Mainly females and free bar. Happy Monday.

G
Golfer
Role: Hitting balls with a stick

Best Parts:
- You get to play golf everyday
- People thinking you're friends with Tiger Woods
- Women love a guy that can handle his balls

Worst Parts:
- Caddying for free for a long time
- Turning your hobby into a profession sucks some of the

enjoyment away
- Not quite knowing if you are ever going to make it till you do—and the ongoing horror that your career could be over if you lost your golfing arm

Qualifications:
- Natural ability
- Caddying/practice
- Expensive courses/good coach

Typical Day:
7:00—Travel to tour location—always travel a night before to avoid and delays. Besides, normally a nice hotel.
9:30—Arrive at tour location.
11:00—Two hours of practice.
13:00—Rest and lunch. More rest.
15:00—One more hour of practice.
17:00—Discuss strategy with caddy.
18:00—Get massaged. Swim in hotel.
19:30—Room service with my caddy—do not go getting any ideas, lovely chap. I like to keep my relationship with balls strictly professional.
21:00—Bed. Tour starts early and performance depends on a quality of rest, quantity of practice, and your relationship with your caddy. A shit one is the equivalent to a shit PA. But get that right and you're half way there.

H
Hairdresser
Role: Looking after the public's barnets

Best Parts:
- Amazing hair is a requirement of the job
- Making people look and feel great…because they are worth it
- Having a good old natter

Worst Parts:
- Finding hair in your bra
- Pressure of having someone's "hair life" in your hands
- Drinking on a school night is not advisable

Qualifications:
- Loves a good natter
- Good with scissors
- Good hair

Typical Day:
7:00—Walk my dog. She sometimes comes to the salon with me. Clients love her—we decorate her in pink bows and paw socks, so she loves it too.
8:30—Coffee. Careful not to overdo the caffeine. One shot too many can cause jittery hands which is not a good combo with scissors.
9:00—First client is a Kate Middleton-lookalike with very specific requests. Get my shampoo girl to prepare her for action.
11:00—Client leaves extremely happy (even if I say so myself.) I have done such a good job even Wills would give her a second look.
12:00—Quick blow dry with a regular who's been coming since the salon opened five years ago. We have a catch-up in between brushing. She thinks her husband is having an affair

with the nanny. She doesn't blame him. Apparently she's very attractive.
14:00—Quick lunch.
16:00—Another client.
18:00—Leave girls to sweep and clean the salon in preparation for another day of making people look fabulous.

I
Ice Cream Van Man

Role: Delivering people their favourite ice creams with a smile, and a jingle, at a wide range of venues

Best Parts:
- You are basically Father Christmas everyday
- No suit
- Nailing the lyrics to all-time classics such as "Twinkle, Twinkle Little Star"

Worst Parts:
- Running out of change
- On cold days with no sales you have moments when you will think *FML*
- Those that laugh when you tell them your profession. Deep down, they just want a Mr Whippy

Qualifications:
- A van
- And a dream

Typical Day:
7:00—Get the van ready. Always check the freezer and

whippy machine is working. Melted ice cream is impossible to sell.

7:30—Set for a busy day so need an extra pair of hands. Pick up Jack, the current, and only, employee. He has got potential in this business. That boy knows his crowd and can spot a knickerbocker glory-lover a mile off.

9:00—Pitch up at our location. Work fair in Hampstead. Weather not great, but irrelevant with the size of the crowd. Bound to sell out.

10:00—Send Jack to grab us bacon rolls and tea while I get the sound system up and running and our hand-picked collection of classics on repeat, starting with, "The Wheels on the Bus."

11:00—Trade picks up slowly.

14:00—Been selling steadily, no time for lunch, need all hands on deck. Nearly out of Calippos and Feasts.

16:00—Had a few requests for bars we don't sell. Get Jack to take a note see if worth stocking.

17:00—Crowd still rolling in. A few beers inside of some of them revs up the orders.

18:30—Bloody good day. Sold out and decide to leave. Fudge, the guy next door, looks glad we are leaving. Get Jack to buy a slab out of courtesy, now have something to munch on route home, as we have a sing-along to "Postman Pat"

J
Journalist
Role: Chasing stories, interviewing, delivering news as it breaks

Best Parts:
• Seeing a reader enjoy something you have written. Even if it is your boyfriend.
• Getting people to talk to you. Everyone has a story—from a homeless person to a CEO, all that differentiates them is choices and circumstance.
• Free stuff in exchange for a good review, from cocktails to cute socks.

Worst parts:
• Someone getting your story out before you. It's only news when it first breaks.
• Chasing people, quite literally. Who wants to be that stalker?
• The coffee bill and lack of sleep—and, no, they are not related.

Qualifications:
• Journalism degree
• Any degree + work experience—local papers

Typical Day:
8:30—No day is typical. One minute you are on the way to the office. One phone call later and you're chasing an MP, asking him as politely as possible if is it true he had sexual relations with male escorts.
9:00—If you do make it to office: log into a computer as we all hot desk. Drink coffee to contribute to the hectic buzz of productivity. Browse news. Attend morning meeting where we all shout around ideas suitable to generate a breakfast buzz.
13:00—Get asked to write a piece on the benefits of

chewing gum. Can't stand the stuff ever since someone put a strawberry Hubba Bubba in my already-short hair at age twelve, resulting in a shaved head and being mistaken for a boy for at least a year. Will not mention in the feature.

14:00—Grab salad from all-you-can-eat bar at Pizza Hut. Grab a few mozzarella dough balls—actually, ten. Call it a dozen.

16:00—Ping over my benefits on gum piece. Interviewing a very well-known actor in a half hour. Inspired by my own writing, I purchase some gum. Will give as a gift to break the ice.

16:30—Meet actor, give him the gum. Get chatting about my article. One of the benefits I found was "toned cheeks." On that note, he pops a piece and we get going with the interview. He is a very loud chewer.

18:00—Martini with my editor who is an avid fan of the actor I just interviewed. I pull out a napkin wrapped in a tight ball. Tell her to open when she gets home. Fresh from the bin where he had disposed of his gum (as had many others but pretty sure it was the right one.)

K
Karate Instructor
Role: Teaching people to kick ass

Best Parts:
- Looking twenty when you're nearly fifty-five
- You can kick anyone's ass
- Seeing kids get their first belt or students gaining strength

Worse Parts:
- A student quitting when making progress
- Being out from an injury
- Students not turning up

Qualifications:
- Coaching certificate
- Over eighteen
- Natural ability/good fitness

Typical Day:
5:00—Wake up and do solo practice for an hour
7:00—Breakfast with my recently-turned-vegan wife
8:30— Private session with regular client who tried to quit after first session and now close to getting black belt.
12:00—Meat-based lunch away from judgmental eyes of wife.
14:00–17:00—Kid's workshop for beginners. One young boy tells me he wants to beat up William.
　"Why?" I ask.
　"He stole my football." It is going to be a long afternoon.
18:00—Lesson prep while wife prepares a veggie-based dinner, during which I will look forward to tomorrow's lunch.

L
Lawyer

Role: Handling the legal aspect of business mergers and takeovers

Best Parts:
- Making a difference, as cliché as it sounds
- Entertaining clients
- The taste of champagne on closing a long deal

Worst Parts:
- The training contract is a total ball ache
- Being given the horrible clients, for example: one Scottish guy who sat down next to me on the first day of a big transaction and said, "So you are my lawyer. Now I have a face to the name so I know who to sue if this all goes wrong." I did not sleep for the entire deal.
- Chasing payments

Qualifications:
- Law Degree
- LPC or BVC
- Two-year training contract/six-month pupilage

Typical Day:
Whenever I wake up: Espresso and gym
9:00—Morning is spent on the phone or in meetings depending what country I am in.
13:00—Lunch is normally with clients, sometimes boozy, and this can take up most of the afternoon. Winning clients is the soul of the business.
16:00—Unavoidable admin and internal issues. This can involve setting up calls in a number of different time zones. Sometimes you get the short straw and end up on the phone at 2 in the morning.
19:00—More entertaining clients. If not, will chill with a

pizza, a good glass of red wine, and ice cream, and work on the million other things I have going on outside of my demanding career. Remembering, of course, that it does pay for the ice cream.

M
Model Booker
Role: Booking models onto editorials and runways, mentoring, and looking after the girls.

Best Parts:
- Attending some amazing shows
- Seeing one of your girls become a star
- Commissions

Worst Parts:
- Models not getting out of bed
- Models getting sick
- Models being a pain in the arse

Qualifications:
- Excellent communicator
- Sales ability
- Determination

Typical Day:
9:00—Office opens. Check on all your model appointments and call each one to make sure they know what they are doing. Some girls are very good, independent, and organized. Others won't answer the phone the morning they have a casting for Burberry.

10:00—Lots of coffee and cigarettes help in this business. One model has called me telling me she has a cold and cannot come to London for a casting with a top client. I want to cry.

12:00—After bombarding girl with texts, she agrees to come to the casting. This could make or break her career and it's important you make the girls realise the opportunity, as it goes in the blink of an eye. At the same time you do not want to push too hard. It's a delicate situation.

13:00—Meet one of my models at a casting to make sure she turns up. Then force her to eat a sandwich.

14:00—Meet a new girl and go through her résumé. Her breasts are far too big for the industry unless she does catalogue. She asks me if she should have a breast reduction and come back. Tell her to only make that choice based on personal choice, not to make it as model—as even at 5'9" with an A-cup, you never know.

17:00—Marc Jacobs books my newest face and wants her to fly to NYC that evening. I call and tell her. She screams, I scream. I order pizza.

22:00—Long day. Crash with phone in hand. Only ever half-sleep when I have girls travelling to shoots, as cannot rest fully in case they need me. Thank goodness for eye concealer.

N
Nurse
Role: Caring for patients by ensuring they are fed, watered, kept clean, and given medication. Looking after their emotional and physical needs as appropriate.

Best Parts:
- Seeing patients smile as you enter the ward
- Really close-knit team
- The gratitude you receive is so genuine and satisfying it makes it all worth it

Worst Parts:
- Long shifts
- Sore feet
- Emotional exhaustion

Qualifications:
- GCSEs
- A-levels
- Nursing degree/course
- Work experience

Typical Day:
5:30—Morning commutes to work starting a six. Working the twelve-hour shift. Morning is freezing and not even a coffee shop is open. Fortunately wrapped up warm.
6:00—The night staff fills me in on patient updates. Not paying attention makes your shift very difficult, which I learnt the hard way, so have had to learn to pay attention despite my start time.
7:00—Had a coffee and a banana and I am full of beans.

There is no room for a nugget of negativity on the ward as I start the breakfast rounds. Paying attention to the elderly patients is crucial. One was hiding her breakfast under her bed, which we found out after three days when the smell of rotting eggs became too much to bear.

9:00—Check on each patient to see how they are feeling. This can take a long time. One girl holds my hand and cries for around forty-five minutes as she opens up about the reasons behind her alcohol dependency. I push my long to-do list to the back of my mind. Listening is one of the most important parts of the job.

12:00—Do the lunch rounds.

14:00—Check a new patient into her bed. She has broken her leg and damaged her hip from a sports injury and is very distressed. I get her some magazines and bring her some chocolate and sit and chat with her. By the time I leave she has stopped crying and gives me my first thank you of the day.

16:00—Grab a snack from canteen. Start the meds: each patient has to be checked on to see how they are responding and feeling, and I have to take notes which must be handed over to the night staff.

17:00—Help an elderly patient with toilet assistance. She doesn't actually pee and admits she was bored and fancied a walk. Get her back to bed with a warm blanket, because her temperature has dropped. Tell her that her grandson is coming to see her tomorrow. Chat with her a while and leave her with a crossword puzzle.

18:00—Hand over all my notes and have a meeting with night staff before the handover.

19:00—Look forward to a hot bath, dinner, and a foot massage from my boyfriend before doing it all again tomorrow.

O
Oreo Producer
Role: Improving those little "Os" from production line to consumer

Best Parts:
• Seeing somebody enjoying an Oreo knowing you have helped in the process
• Reading ideas from our Product Idea box. "Oreo Pies" are a current WIP
• Our work jingle, "Do not be sad, eat an Oreo. That happy, that tasty, yummy little O."

Worst Parts:
• Media accusations such as, "Oreos are as addictive as crack cocaine.'" I bet they sure as hell taste a lot better and I am yet to have heard of an Oreo rehab.
• My doctor tells me my job is not good for my waist line. I tell him it's not the Oreos, it's the beer.
• A recurring dream of being chased by Oreos

Qualifications:
• Food management qualifications
• Work experience

Typical Day:
7:30—Visit factory where will be based for the day, meet line workers who are packing the Os.
9:00—Invite workers for a complimentary breakfast and motivational talk. We all sing the work jingle.
12:00—Look over production line and run quality checks that involve some obligatory tasting.

14:00—Announce I want everyone to submit an Oreo Idea during break time—Winner will receive a prize!
16:00—Read through idea box. "Oreo-filled doughnuts" wins hands-down.
17:00—Announce winner and prize to a stunned Janice. She gets a cash prize and week's holiday.
18:00—Discussions with head of marketing about important things.
20:00—Beer and debrief to regional director and celebrate what could go down in Oreo history. We sing "Do not be sad, eat an Oreo, that happy, yummy little O."

P
Pilot
Role: Flying planes

Best Parts:
- The office view
- Nothing can match the excitement of flying a plane
- Dynamic lifestyle and free upgrades for family

Worst Parts:
- Being away from family
- Insomnia
- Delays are just as annoying for us as you

Qualifications:
- Degree in aviation
- Two-months ground training
- 1500 hours of air-time

Typical Day:
Ha! Do not do this job for the love of a routine. Okay, let's do this...
5:00—Arrive at departing airport and go through security just like everyone else, hoping to have time to grab a Starbucks vanilla latte before boarding. If I have been on location, I make sure I have had as good a night's rest as possible. You do not always want to run out and explore every destination. You just want a hot shower, good food, and rest.
9:00—Take off from runway. Clearance is all on time. FAA guidelines state a maximum of eight hours flying time, though this does not include check-in delays and ground work. It can be a long day.
12:00—Flying from L.A. to Miami. I know the route. Once I am in the sky, I relax and enjoy the flight.
15:00—Throughout the flight there is a little turbulence so I have to turn on seatbelt sign. I have experienced very bad turbulence a few times and certainly have a few stories.
18:00—Constantly check the systems throughout the flight. From take-off I am preparing for landing. I am constantly updated with weather reports and conditions of the arrival airport.
21:00—Always clap a pilot for a good landing. It is a very hard job and sometimes done without help from control. I land smoothly.
22:00—Once everyone has left the plane, I head to the food court for some food, as I have a five-hour stopover before flying back to L.A.
There are also places in the airport for pilots to take a rest.

Q
Quality Assurance Analyst

Role: Evaluates software to ensure it meets consumer standards

Best parts:
- I never need technical assistance
- Solving a software problem
- Free upgrades

Worst Parts:
- Staring at computers for long periods of time
- Bad posture
- Pressure to fix problems faster than humanly possible

Qualifications:
- Degree
- Work experience

Typical Day:
8:30—I wake to the smell of coffee from my pre-timed coffee machine.
8:45—Over a bowl of oatmeal and chocolate sauce, I track my sleep on my sleep app. I have had the same pattern consistently since I started this.
10:00—Work on fixing technical areas for the software of a new start-up. Several abusive emails have been sent saying they can make no progress till done. I ask them if they would like to sort it themselves, and many other rhetorical questions in my head as I solve the issues.
12:00—Lunch is ham salad and boiled eggs. I stick to the same foods most days other than Fridays, "Surprise Fridays."

Last Friday I tried sushi. Strange food.

13:00—Back to work. I listen to several acoustic guitarist albums throughout my day, as am planning to start guitar lessons.

17:00—I resolve the problem for the start-up. They thank me profusely. I always welcome gratitude.

18:00—Watch a film at the cinema or in my 3D cinema room. I am an avid Star Trek fan.

19:30—Grab dinner of fish stew or pie and potatoes with my friend Buzz. He has recently started dating a girl and asks me questions. I have no idea how to answer. I find software queries far less challenging.

22:00—I read the latest science fiction novel. Currently it is 653 pages long. I am on page 73.

R
Roofer
Role: Putting roofs on homes and other buildings

Best Parts:
- Keeps you fit
- Extremely satisfying
- Work with good people

Worst Parts:
- Being at the mercy of rain
- Frustrating when things go wrong
- Dirt and dust up your nose

Qualifications:
- Physically in good shape
- A sense of humour

Typical Day:

6:00—The team meets at the boss's to review the plan for the day, then heads off to drive to our site.

7:30—Sit in the van and munch a bit of breakfast before we start. We all just bring snacks and lunch with us in case there are no decent places nearby.

8:00—Start precautions. We have to make sure we are all suited and booted before we start laying the house to protect it from any damage. Anything that looks like it will get broken, will—and stuff that doesn't probably will too.

14:00—By two we have tapped the entire roof and it looks like it's about to shower, so we take lunch. Sometimes we just crack straight on and finish earlier. Our schedule is very dependent on the weather. It is dangerous to be on the roof during heavy rain.

17:00—We have managed to complete laying shingles, so we call it a day and head back to the van to drive home. We all fit in one van and have a good old chat and laugh on the way back. Sometimes one of us is the victim of a prank. Last week one of the boys managed to put a sticker on my back that read "I LOVE GOATS."

18:00—Dinner and relaxing with the Missus.

S
School Teacher
Role: Teaching PE at a secondary school

Best Parts:
- Interaction with the kids
- School holidays
- Making a difference

Worst Parts:
- Having to be organised
- Girls who seem to be constantly on their periods
- OFSTED (Office for Standards in Education, Children's Services and Skills)

Qualifications
- Degree
- Work experience

Typical Day:
7:00—It's an early start. Why do you think teachers have coffee breath?
8:30—After a bit of banter with my colleagues, I head to my office to run through my lessons for the day. It is pretty full on from between nine and fifteen hundred today.
9:30—First lesson is hockey—never a favourite with the girls, and predictably, Emma is on her period for the fourth time in a month. This time I reply, "Yes, so am I. Let's get on with it." You have to draw a line.
11:00—Quick coffee break
12:00—Split student into two teams for netball. I used to let them pick teams but people always got left out or they'd form the same groups each time. You have a role as a teacher to prevent this kind of thing happening.
13:00—Lunch is a ham roll and more coffee. Catch up with a friend from science department. We share some funny stories. Yes, teachers do tell each other who they put in detention.
15:00—Last lesson finished, then on to my least favourite part of the day: paperwork. I have some government incentives I need to read and the dreaded OFSTED paperwork I need to compile. I also have progress reports for

each student to complete.

18:00—I am home early, which my girlfriend thinks is a valid reason to make me the house chef. I do not mind. I enjoy cooking, as I can switch off. The good thing about being a PE teacher is no homework to mark. I am also preparing myself for MasterChef. Watch this space.

T
Travel Agent
Role: Match people with holidays
Best Parts:
- Seeing people's pictures of fabulous holidays
- Turning the office into a different destination every week
- Discounts of flights and hotels

Worst Parts:
- Holiday envy
- Cancelled flights
- Customers making constant changes

Qualifications
- Communication skills
- Sales ability
- Travel experience

Typical Day:
9:00—Arrive at office. Today we are Hawaii. Reminder—I really need a holiday.
10:00—Elderly couple arrive, first clients of the day, wanting advice on where to visit in Asia. They insist they want to ride elephants and drink cocktails despite looking

about seventy-five. I advise Thailand.

11:30—A whole family arrive: two sons, mother, and father. Kids want to go to Disneyland, parents want Barbados. The kids win with my help and they leave with a ten-day trip to Orlando booked for September. Result.

13:00—Hawaiian lunch served. Basically, some ham and pineapple sandwiches.

15:00—Distressed phone call from a couple arriving in Mexico hotel who cannot find reservation. Spend an hour on the phone to a Mexican concierge and eventually get them checked in with a complimentary bottle of champagne and breakfast.

17:00—Meet with the PA of a big corporate company. She wants to use me to book her client's work trips, of which there are plenty. I buy the drinks in good faith.

23:00—Bed. Dreaming of my next holiday.

U
Unicorn Researcher
Role: Seeking proof unicorns exist

Best Parts:
- Following a childhood dream
- Working in unusual locations
- Making a discovery such as the *Elasmotherium* skull, which suggests that unicorns roamed the earth alongside human beings

Worse Parts
- Most people think you're joking when you tell them your jo

- The raising of funds can be challenging
- When a breakthrough turns out to be void

Typical Day:
7:00—I always wake early with butterflies in my stomach, excited to start the day.
8:00—On location where I have breakfast with my team. We set an agenda over poached eggs and coffee.
9:00—We spend hours using specialized equipment scouring patches of ground, which, research has led us to believe, may hold a discovery. We do not always know what we are looking for and can end up finding things that turn out to be nothing. Once, Andy found what we thought was part of a bone that turned out to be a part of an airplane.
13:00—It is hungry work. We break for lunch whenever someone suggests it. Often me. We refuel and discuss the morning.
14:00— If we find something, we start the research process. First, we send anything significant to a lab, then we write up our findings. This can take us well into the early evening.
 18:00—Again, on location we tend to call have dinner together. Sometimes wine if something is worth celebrating. We share jokes about our unusual careers.
For example, a recent cracker was: what is the difference between a unicorn and a carrot? One is a funny beast and the other is a bunny feast. Another favourite: my mum often tells me unicorns are real; they're just fat, grey, and called rhinos.
22:00—I go to sleep early. Bedtime is one of my favourite times of day. I like to daydream about tomorrow and what I may find.

V
Vet
Role: Looking after the well-being of animals

Best Parts:
- Being around animals everyday
- Relationships with animals
- Making people happy to see their pets get better

Worst Parts:
- When there is nothing you can do to help an animal
- It can be emotionally exhausting
- Seeing animals in distress

Qualifications:
- Veterinary degree
- Work experience

Typical Day:
6:00—A wet nose wakes me up. Pepper, my puppy, is the best alarm clock I have ever had.
7:45—I leave my house and drive to the surgery. Pepper comes with me, as we have a playroom where we can all bring our dogs while we work. She has more friends than me.
9:00—Emergency visits from Mrs. Green and her beloved cat Cherry. Cherry is constipated from breaking into the pantry and eating sardines and chocolate. Enema surgery required. My success results in Cherry's snacking all over my face. Well, at least she is no longer constipated.
12:00—Other than Cherry, the morning runs smoothly with standard vaccinations. I take a well-earned lunch break with Pepper in our local park.

14:00—Another emergency walk-in. A dog fight has resulted in Randy, a German Shepherd, having severe injuries. I advise antibiotics and lots of rest. Also tell the owner to keep him on a lead till he has fully recovered.

16:00—A visit from my favourite rabbit, Bundles, who has made a full recovery from a chest infection and come into say hello—with his owner, of course, who has bought me flowers to say thanks.

17:00—I leave the clinic on time, with a big smile and with a bigger bunch of flowers. Pepper is glad to be leaving, too. After a day of playing and lunching in the park we head home to unwind for the evening. It's a hard life. I will sleep well knowing I have helped some vulnerable animals today and look forward to what tomorrow brings.

***

W

Writer

Role: Weaving words together to create stories based on imagination, information or both.

Best Parts:
- [ ] Drinking coffee and producing greatness
- [ ] Being sent an idea
- [ ] Creating characters

Worse Parts:
- [ ] Self-discipline can be your best friend or worse enemy
- [ ] Distractions

☐ Writer's block

Qualifications:
　☐ Imagination
　☐ Self-discipline

Typical Day:

7:00—Get up. The only time I practice visualization. I visualize me drinking my first cup of coffee.

7:15—Get a workout done. Still visualizing the coffee.

8:30—Start writing in chosen venue, normally a cafe. I am a creature of habit so tend to stick to the same places even in different cities. I am blessed with an instinct for the best places for coffee and atmosphere. Maybe that was my writer's calling.

9:00—Write intermittently. When I start looking away from the screen I know it's time for a little break which, funnily enough, can provide the fuel I need to keep going.

12:00—This is the time my writer's brain tends to close for the day. Whether this is a habit I have created or an internal clock, I am still trying to figure out. When feeling brave I attempt to get my creative juices flowing at random times to see what comes up.

14:00—Get out and live a bit. How else am I supposed to find stuff to write about? My imagination gets a boost from seeing friends, hobbies, other forms of work that can contribute towards paying for stuff. It is where all the best material comes from, I find.

15:00—If I come back to do any writing, out comes the laptop. Often I just browse puppies for sale and think about what I'll do next. It is a work in progress.

17:00—Convince someone to join me for wine/dinner/both. If I have written more than five hundred words, and I do not feel like deleting them, for me, it has been a productive day. A great thing about being a writer is to turn everything into a positive. Even the bad stuff that happens, because people like to read about that and it happens to us all every single day.
22:00—Bed with a book. I read till I can no longer keep my eyes open. I tend to have paragraphs being written in my head in the night, and unfortunately when I wake up it is not all typed out so I try to remember some of the best stuff for the morning. Alas, my bestsellers could be all written in my head. Something I should probably work on.

X

X-ray Technician

Role: Use high-tech equipment to view inside the human body

Best Parts:
- Not sitting at a desk all day
- Using ultra-cool equipment
- Meeting unusual patients

Worst Parts:
- Making unpleasant discoveries
- Pressure and attention to detail
- Any kind of admin

Qualifications:
- GCSES
- A levels
- Work experience

Typical Day:

8:00—I arrive at my local clinic. I have worked here for two years where I met my wife Becky, the receptionist. We have no plans to leave.

9:00—I tend to start my first procedure at nine. Mostly this is a pre-arranged appointment. Today it was a young boy named James. He had injured his leg in football training and is hopeful nothing's broken.

11:00—James leaves with his leg in a cast and confirmation of very bad fracture. He is annoyed he cannot play football for six months, but I tell him he should be grateful he still has both legs. Not sure the message sunk in. His father, however, thanked me sincerely.

12:00—I take lunch with Becky, as she is on shift. We often nip out to a local pub which does my kind of fare: gourmet burgers and chips. Middle-class junk food.

15:00—Emergency surgery. Small kid fallen out of treehouse on his back. He is in a lot of pain. An x-ray reveals lower fracture. Parents are distressed. The nurse brings him a lollipop for being very brave and strong painkillers. Funny, he seems far more content with the lollipop.

17:00—Finish early today. I leave before Becky, much to her distaste. Promise to have dinner ready when she arrives home. I also have a ring. I decided today I will ask her to marry me. I ponder popping the question as I am driving home. How about:

"Will you, Becky Watson, let my x-ray vision look after your bones forever?"

19:00—She said "Yes."

Y
Yoga Instructor

Role: Helping people connect their bodies and minds to increase their well-being, freeing their minds and selves. Stretching muscles and toning bodies may be what brings people to the mat, but so much more keeps them there.

Best Parts:
- Doing what I love for a living
- My students, old and new
- Sharing the benefits of yoga

Worse Parts:
- Fitting everything in
- Getting tired
- Oh, the admin, for sure

Qualifications:
- A 200-hour teacher's training certificate from a recognized school
- A passion for yoga

Typical Day:
6:00—Wake up, make coffee, and do a light morning practice with my husband.
7:00—Light breakfast of fruits and cereals. He heads to his day job and I head to my studio.
8:00—First class of the day I normally have something energizing such as yoga flow or Vinyasa to get everyone's prana awoken. If it is cold, or I sense I have some super-tired students, I will adjust to the mood.
9:30—Have a coffee break and catch up with my receptionist.

She takes bookings for all classes and sets up my timetable for the week. She is superhuman.

11:00—I have a private session with one of my students who is pregnant for the first time. I go through hip opening and breathing techniques; she is not looking forward to giving birth, though her yoga practice has definitely calmed her down.

13:00—I take lunch by myself to recharge and read a little, have a coffee, and prepare myself for afternoon classes.

17:00—I hold gentle classes in the evening out of personal preference. This helps students and myself unwind. I once was doing more dynamic classes till late and got a little burnt out.

19:00—Have dinner with my husband, and we watch a movie and chill. If we are feeling really adventurous we go out for a nice bottle of wine somewhere quiet and talk about where we want to go on holiday next.

22:00—Bedtime for me after a relaxing bath. Cozy PJs and a good book till I drift off to sleep. One of my best-kept secrets to feeling your best is getting the right amount of zzzs.

Z

Zookeeper

Role: Assist in the running of a zoo

Best Parts:
- No day is ever the same—and I have done this for five years
- Building a relationship with the animals
- Meeting new animals

Worst Parts:
- Physically demanding

- Animals getting sick
- Early starts and late ends can be tiring

Qualifications:
- Good fitness
- Work experience
- Passion for working with animals

Typical Day:

7:00—Get to the office. Yes, even zookeepers have emails to check first thing in the morning. I relocated to Australia for this job, so fortunately my office is in the sunshine overlooking my colleagues—lots of animals.

8:00— I start my first task, which can take up most of the day. I am feeding and cleaning the tiger zone. Kerry is our newest member, a Siberian tiger who eats more meat than you can imagine. This job definitely makes you want to become a vegetarian.

14:00—I finish cleaning and feeding and playing with the tigers. Still in one piece. I have a big lunch as I have worked up quite an appetite. We have an on-site canteen where I eat every day and catch up with humans.

15:00—I assist in a show for the public. We have been working on encouraging natural behaviour from our monkeys. Which has been hilarious. Hilary, our favourite, is such a character and loves to play up to the crowds. We joke she should have gone to Hollywood.

19:00— I leave the zoo around nineteen hundred and head home. I share with three friends. We have a BBQ outside and have a few beers. They always want to see videos of the animals. And free tickets to the zoo—apparently, it's a great place to bring a date.

ASHLEY BROWN has experimented in every occupation from waitress to teacher, her inspiration for her first novel comes fresh from life itself.

When not writing or working as a realtor, she could be anywhere doing anything from downward dog in Bali to eating carrot cake in Norfolk. A true Londoner, her mornings always include an urgent rush, plenty of tea, and checking her horoscope if there is time.

Made in the USA
Columbia, SC
07 March 2018